Andrew wasn't surprised that she failed to recognize him. Three years of brutal warfare and eleven months in Andersonville had left their mark on him, as had the years of frontier service that followed. He wasn't the same man she'd teased and tempted six years ago, any more than she could be the same woman he'd once risked his life and his honor for.

Andrew halted a few paces from her and hooked his thumbs behind his belt buckle. Deliberately, he let his gaze drift from her face to her throat. To breasts mounted high and firm beneath the cherry-striped silk. To a waist he could still circle with his hands had he a mind to, and hips enticingly displayed by the drawn-back bustle of her skirt.

Color rushed into her cheeks at his blatant inspection. Her eyes flashed fire. "I expect better manners of an officer, sir. Even one who wears Union blue."

"Do you, Julia?"

The drawled reply drew her brows into a slashing frown. A look of confusion replaced the anger on her face. "Do I know you, sir?"

Sweeping off his hat, he bowed and smiled. Slowly. Savagely. "You did once."

The result was everything he'd anticipated. Her eyes widened. Every vestige of color drained from her face. She stared at him in shock, in disbelief, in dawning horror. Then, without so much as a whimper, she crumpled.

Watch for the next installment in the Wyoming Wind series
from
MERLINE LOVELACE
and MIRA Books

WILD INDIGO

Coming January 2002

Merline Lovelace

The Horse Soldier

MIRA

If you purchased this book without a cover you should be aware
that this book is stolen property. It was reported as "unsold and
destroyed" to the publisher, and neither the author nor the
publisher has received any payment for this "stripped book."

MIRA

ISBN 1-55166-784-3

THE HORSE SOLDIER

Copyright © 2001 by Merline Lovelace.

All rights reserved. Except for use in any review, the reproduction or
utilization of this work in whole or in part in any form by any electronic,
mechanical or other means, now known or hereafter invented, including
xerography, photocopying and recording, or in any information storage or
retrieval system, is forbidden without the written permission of the publisher,
MIRA Books, 225 Duncan Mill Road, Don Mills, Ontario, Canada M3B 3K9.

All characters in this book have no existence outside the imagination of the
author and have no relation whatsoever to anyone bearing the same name
or names. They are not even distantly inspired by any individual known or
unknown to the author, and all incidents are pure invention.

MIRA and the Star Colophon are trademarks used under license and registered
in Australia, New Zealand, Philippines, United States Patent and Trademark
Office and in other countries.

Visit us at www.mirabooks.com

Printed in U.S.A.

This book is dedicated to military personnel and their families down through the centuries who have served their country at windswept outposts, snowy bases, or desert sites far from home.

And to

The handsome young captain who swept me off my feet my second day on active duty! Thanks for thirty years of romance and adventure and exploring so many wonderful old historic sites with me, my darling.

Army map of Fort Laramie, 1867

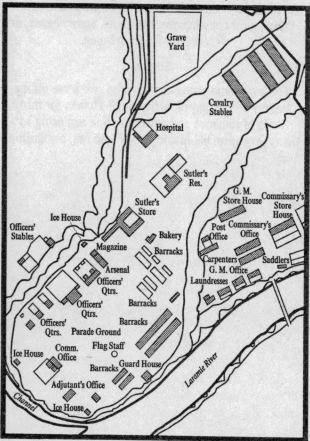

Grave Yard

Cavalry Stables

Hospital

Sutler's Res.

Sutler's Store

G. M. Store House

Commissary's Store House

Ice House

Bakery

Barracks

Post Office

Commissary's Office

Officers' Stables

Magazine

Carpenters

Saddlers

Arsenal

G. M. Office

Officers' Qtrs.

Laundresses

Officers' Qtrs.

Barracks

Officers' Qtrs.

Barracks

Parade Ground

Ice House

Comm. Office

Flag Staff

Barracks

Guard House

Adjutant's Office

Channel

Ice House

Laramie River

1

Fort Laramie, Dakota Territory
In the area known as Absaraka by the Sioux,
Wyoming by the soldiers posted there
June, 1867

"I won't have it!"

The shrill protest carried clearly to the officer guiding his mount up a sloping incline toward the wagons camped on the low bluffs.

"I won't have it, I tell you!"

Major Andrew Garrett glanced up at the circled wagons, lit by flickering campfires and the soft glow of the summer moon. From the sound of it, at least one member of the latest band of travelers to break their journey at Fort Laramie was feeling the strain of her weeks on the trail.

"Now, Augusta—"

"Don't 'Augusta' me, Hiram Hottenfelder!"

Like the caw of a crow, the angry reply cracked above the shuffle of oxen turned out to graze.

"That woman's not coming another mile with us. Not a single mile, until she pays for her share of the supplies you purchased at the sutler's store. And such supplies!"

Her voice rose to an outraged screech.

"How could you give a dollar...a dollar!...for a tin of peaches?"

Andrew shook his head in mingled sympathy and exasperation. The sutler's exorbitant prices produced a constant stream of complaints, not only from the travelers who stopped at Fort Laramie to resupply for the next leg of their journey across the plains, but from the personnel stationed at the post as well.

Aside from setting general guidelines of operation, the Army exercised little control over the sutler who operated the store at the fort. He was a civilian, a contractor whose connections in Washington had secured the lucrative license. He charged whatever he thought he could get for his goods. Since his store was located on post, however, the Army took the brunt of the complaints. Or, more correctly, the Army in the person of Major Andrew Garrett, commander, 2nd Cavalry Regiment, and currently the second ranking officer at Fort Laramie.

"You don't need to go on so about one tin of peaches, Augusta. You know how..."

"Don't go on so?" The indignant cry splintered into a shriek. "Don't go on so! I've held my tongue for weeks now, Hiram, but no more. All that...that French slut has to do is twitch her skirts, and you buy *peaches* instead of the flour and bacon we need! I'm telling you to your face, I won't have it.''

Hellfire and thunderation! For a craven moment, Andrew actually considered tugging on the bridle, turning Jupiter around, and heading back down the slope. He'd spent the past five days on patrol and returned only hours ago to find the post commander swimming in his usual laudanum-induced stupor. The surgeon, the chaplain and the infantry company commander were all lined up at the headquarters, waiting impatiently with matters that demanded Andrew's immediate attention. The last thing he needed or wanted right now was to mediate a dispute between a wagon master and his irate wife.

Particularly a wagon master who'd stated his intention of pushing on through to Montana Territory against the advice of Fort Laramie's adjutant and chief scout. Both had urged the major to talk some sense into the man's head before he pulled out tomorrow.

Andrew had agreed, although he knew talking would do little good. They were all so desperate, these travelers who swarmed across the Great Plains. So determined to follow their dreams. Thousands had been lured west by tales of rich farmland in Oregon, thousands more by the discovery of gold in California in '49. Five years later, followers of Joseph Smith had plodded behind handcarts piled high with their pos-

sessions, enduring blazing heat and bitter snowstorms
to reach the Zion founded by Brigham Young beside
the Great Salt Lake. And the Homestead Act signed
by President Lincoln in 1862 had reopened the flood-
gates.

For two decades now, immigrants had streamed
past Fort Laramie, leaving permanent wagon ruts in
the grass and increasingly hostile tribes of Sioux,
Cheyenne and Arapaho in their wake. With the discovery of gold in Montana Territory a few years ago,
another stampede had broken out. Eager argonauts led
by John Bozeman had carved a new road to the diggings at Bannack and Virginia City. The trail cut right
through the Powder River region—the very heart of
Sioux country and the last hunting grounds where the
Plains Indians still roamed free.

Settlers, miners and freighters supplying the Montana diggings thronged the new road. Incensed, the
Sioux and their allies had stepped up attacks on
wagon trains and on the forts along the trail. Last
December, an entire woodcutting party of eighty men
under the command of Captain Fetterman had been
massacred outside Fort Phil Kearny, some two hundred miles north of Fort Laramie. As a result, civilian
traffic along the trail was not only risky, it was down-
right foolhardy.

Which is what Andrew would inform the wagon
master...if the man could silence his wife long
enough for anyone else to slip in a word or two.

"She's bewitched you," the woman shrilled. "You

and half the men in this company. I've seen the way you look at her. I've watched you stumble over your own boots every time she smiles at you.''

Grimacing at the thought of intervening in what sounded very much like a private matter, Andrew guided Jupiter through a break in the circled wagons. The entire company must have gathered to lend support to the combatants. The men were dressed in the usual canvas pants and floppy hats favored by buffalo skinners, prospectors and homesteaders alike. Their sun-browned women wore sturdy boots, homespun skirts and bonnets.

Except for one. She stood alone, slender and ramrod straight. Her back was to Andrew, but he couldn't miss the stiff set to her shoulders and unyielding line of her neck beneath its heavy crown of hair. Thick and black under a light coating of trail dust, the entwined braids drew Andrew's startled gaze.

For a moment, only a moment, a long-forgotten ache speared into his gut. He'd once run his hands through a tumbled mass with the same blue-black sheen. Once buried his face in its fragrant silk.

Deliberately, he slammed the door on his thoughts. He'd spent too many months in hell to resurrect memories of the woman who'd put him there.

''I haven't bewitched anyone. I've merely tried to make the journey more pleasant with smiles instead of complaints.''

The ringing reply knifed into Andrew. He jerked on the reins, sending Jupiter dancing back a step or two. Even after all these years, he couldn't mistake that voice. Clear, proud, with a lilting note that betrayed her Creole origins.

"Smiles!" The wagon master's wife went purple in the face. "You've tried to make the journey more pleasant, but not with smiles, I'll wager!"

Andrew paid no attention to the tirade that spewed from her mouth. He sat frozen, his gloved fist clenching the reins, his attention riveted on the slender, stiff-backed figure in poppy-striped silk.

It was Julia. It could only be Julia. The certainty slashed through his chaotic thoughts like a saber. No one but the vain, spoiled Belle of New Orleans would attempt an arduous overland journey in striped silk.

And no one but the Belle of New Orleans could fan such passionate flames.

Those flames had once nearly consumed Andrew. Now, it appeared, they were about to consume the wagon master's furious wife.

"How many times have you crawled out of the wagon in the middle of the night?" she screeched. "How many times have you spread a blanket underneath? What decent woman would choose to sleep on the ground?"

"One who wished to get some rest!" the target of her venom snapped back. "You snore, Augusta. Most loudly."

With a shriek, the furious Augusta threw herself forward. Her husband caught her by one arm and planted both boots in the dirt to hold her back.

Andrew's mouth twisted. It was most certainly Julia. She could wreak havoc with a single toss of her blue-black hair. She'd certainly brought him to his knees easily enough. He was tempted to hang back and watch her play out the scene, but knew he'd better intervene or he'd have to call out the troops to quell a riot.

With a curt command to the men blocking his way to stand aside, he nudged Jupiter forward. The well-trained cavalry charger picked his way through the parting crowd with a jingle of bridle and plop of iron-shod hooves.

The wagon master greeted Andrew's approach with relief, his wife with a fulminating glance. The third player in the drama caught the direction of their gazes and spun slowly around to face the newcomer.

The years had been kind to her, Andrew saw at once; far kinder than they had to him, although there was little of the girl he'd known in the woman who now tipped her chin and met his gaze head-on. Her delicate features showed a taut edge, the creamy skin stretched tight across cheekbones more prominent than he remembered. A few faint lines etched the corners of her mouth. The slanting amethyst eyes that had laughed and teased and flirted so outrageously now held nothing but disgust and irritation.

Andrew wasn't surprised that she failed to recognize him. With summer twilight fast deepening into darkness, the flickering campfires threw only uneven light. Even if the sun were blazing directly overhead, he doubted she would know him. Three years of brutal warfare and eleven months in Andersonville had left their mark on him, as had the years of frontier service that followed. He wasn't the same man she'd teased and tempted six years ago, any more than she could be the same woman he'd once risked his life and his honor for.

His jaw tightened as a grim anticipation coiled in his belly. This was the moment he'd envisioned, the moment he'd played over and over in his mind during those black months in the hole, until thirst and hunger and gnawing rats had driven everything but survival out of his head. Now that the moment had come, he fully intended to savor it.

Dismounting, he passed Jupiter's reins to one of the men crowding beside him and limped forward. The gray felt slouch hat he'd worn on patrol shadowed his eyes. His saber rattled at his side. He'd splashed the trail dust off his face after he'd arrived back at the headquarters, but hadn't taken the time to change his uniform.

Salt caked his dark-blue blouse, an inevitable consequence of patrolling in the ninety-degree June heat. Dust dulled the gold braid on his shoulder epaulets and stole the sheen from his leather boots. He hadn't shaved, anticipating the ministrations of his orderly, and knew he looked far more like an outlaw than an officer.

The woman facing him evidently thought so, too. Her lip curled, although he suspected the disdain that flitted across her face probably stemmed as much from the residual hate of the defeated Southerner for Yankee blue as from his disreputable appearance. A scant two years had passed since the War of the Rebellion ended at Appomattox. The scars were healing, but slowly.

Andrew halted a few paces from her and hooked his thumbs behind his belt buckle. Deliberately, he let his gaze drift from her face to her throat. To breasts mounded high and firm beneath the cherry-striped silk. To a waist he could still circle with his hands had he a mind to, and hips enticingly displayed by the drawn-back bustle of her skirt.

Color rushed into her cheeks at his blatant inspection. Her eyes flashed fire. "I expect better manners of an officer, sir. Even one who wears Union blue."

"Do you, Julia?"

The drawled reply drew her brows into a slashing frown. A look of confusion replaced the anger on her face. "Do I know you, sir?"

Sweeping off his hat, he bowed and smiled. Slowly. Savagely. "You did once."

The result was everything he'd anticipated. Her eyes widened. Every vestige of color drained from her face. She stared at him in shock, in disbelief, in dawning horror. Then, without so much as a whimper, she crumpled.

Swearing, Andrew leaped forward. His thigh bone stabbed into his hip socket like a sword, but he caught her before she hit the ground. He barely had time to register the featherweight feel of her in his arms before a shrill cry split the night.

"She's sick! I told you, Hiram, the woman's sick!"

"Now, Gussie—"

"Yesterday I saw her leaning over a wheel, so dizzy she could scarcely stand. Now she's fainted dead away."

Whispers rumbled from the watching crowd. Augusta's raucous caw rose above them.

"She's sick, I tell you! We can all count ourselves lucky if she hasn't brought cholera or smallpox down on us," she ended on a wail.

Andrew swung around, an unconscious Julia in his arms. The alarmed wagon master and his wife were already backing away. Others followed their lead, almost tripping over their feet in their haste to skitter back. As Andrew knew all too well, the threat of disease could spread panic faster than a raging prairie fire or the scream of war whoops coming from just over the next hill.

A quick glance at the woman in his arms showed none of the cholera or smallpox symptoms he'd learned to recognize over the years, but her deep swoon had robbed her of all signs of life. She lay limp as a rag doll in Andrew's arms...and almost as weightless.

If he possessed an ounce of sense, he'd dump her on the ground and leave her to sort out her differences with the wagon master and his wife if and when she woke. That "if" put a kink in his gut.

With another vicious curse, he stalked across the dusty ground in his uneven stride. Tossing his burden over his charger's withers like a sack of grain, he thrust his foot in the stirrup and swung up. Once in the saddle, he pulled her upright and rolled her into his arms, furious with himself, with her, with the damnable twist of fate that had brought Julia Robichaud into his life a second time.

Like the god he was named for, Jupiter thundered down the path to the post spread across the flats below. The well-trained charger needed little guidance, knowing his way through the sprawling outpost as well as any of the cavalry mounts stabled there.

Set at the strategic juncture of the Platte and Laramie rivers, the army fort had been built on the site of an old fur-trading center. The trader's adobe-walled blockhouse had already crumbled into ruin when the government purchased it in '48 and renamed it Fort Laramie. Original army plans called for a wooden palisade around the barracks and headquarters building the troops hastily threw up during their first months of occupation. Tight budgets and the lack of an immediate threat had led to successive delays, then, finally, abandonment of any plans for outer defensive walls.

The jumble of buildings that now lay scattered along the flats defined by a bend in the river were a mix of concrete-lime, wood and adobe. In keeping with army tradition, most of the structures surrounded the rectangular parade ground. A few out-buildings had sprung up where nature best suited the need. The corral and stables were upwind of the main post, the latrine sinks downriver.

This late in the evening the bugler had already sounded first call for tattoo, when all personnel except the guards were expected to be in quarters and preparing for lights-out. Surgeon-Lieutenant Colonel Henry Schnell would already have left the post hospital and retired to his home. It was there Andrew now headed.

A two-story structure of wood and mud-brick, the surgeon's quarters reflected both his rank and his position as one of the cultural leaders of Fort Laramie's small community. The neat white picket fence and scraggly rosebush sending out more thorns than blossoms reflected his wife's determination to carve her own piece of civilization from the windswept wilderness of the Great Plains.

Schnell was a good man, a good soldier and a good surgeon. He'd arrived at Fort Laramie in the fall of '65, still haunted by the killing fields of Gettysburg and Antietam. Like Andrew and the rest of the regulars who'd breathed the suffocating smoke of cannon and rifle fire during the war years, Henry had found solace in the open skies and clean, biting winds of Wyoming.

Kicking free of the stirrups, Andrew threw a leg over the pommel and slid out of the saddle with the still-lifeless Julia in his arms. The jar when he hit the ground sent hot lances spearing into his hip. Ignoring the pain he'd long ago learned to live with, he carried his limp burden up the steps and hammered on the surgeon's door.

The brawny private who served as Henry's aide answered a moment later. The big, bluff Irishman's eyes popped when Fort Laramie's second ranking officer brushed past with a woman held against his chest.

"Is Colonel Schnell in quarters?"

"Yes, soor," Rafferty answered in his rolling brogue. "But he'n Mrs. Colonel Schnell have gone t'bed."

"Present my apologies for disturbing them so late, Rafferty, but I have someone who requires his immediate attention."

"Yes, soor."

While the private clattered up the stairs to relay the message, Andrew strode into the parlor at the front of the house. The high-ceilinged room contained the usual mix of stark furnishings provided by the Army and the personal memorabilia gathered over a long military career. Crossed swords hung above the mantel. Photographs and tintypes from past assignments decorated the walls. Lace covered a round, claw-footed table next to the humpbacked horsehair sofa.

Andrew had just bent to deposit his burden on the sofa when the post surgeon hurried into the parlor. Henry's snowy white hair stood out in puffs at either side of his head, almost as thick and bushy as his muttonchop sideburns and beard. He'd pulled on his uniform pants and stuffed in the tails of his un- bleached linen nightshirt. Needlepoint carpet slippers covered his bare feet.

"Rafferty said you'd brought a woman in. Not one of ours, I see."

With only a handful of officers' wives, a dozen or so laundresses and one as-yet unmarried housemaid in residence at the post, it didn't surprise Andrew that Henry would know at a glance his patient wasn't one of the army dependents.

"She's from the wagon train camped on the bluffs."

"What's wrong with her?"

"She fainted."

"Well move aside, man. Let me have a look at her."

Bending over the sofa, the surgeon lifted Julia's eyelids, tested her pulse, then bent to listen to the rhythm of her breathing. Finally, he laid the back of his hand against her cheeks.

"No fever or clammy skin. Pupils aren't glazed. Doesn't look to me like anything serious."

Andrew let out a slow breath. The tight knot in his chest eased. Annoyed that one had even formed, he crossed his arms and fought a frown while Henry con- tinued his examination.

The physician encountered layers of thick stiffen- ing and whalebone stays and chuffed in disgust. "Blasted corsets! If women would stop wearing those abominations, they might not faint so often. Won't let Mrs. Schnell bring one into the house, much less strap one around her middle.''

Muttering over the follies of female vanity, he shook his head. "What woman would wear a corset in the heat of summer, while traveling across the Plains?"

"This one would."

The caustic reply earned Andrew a sharp glance. "You know her?"

"Yes."

"Well, who is she, man?"

Andrew stared down at the face he'd loved and cursed with equal passion. A muscle ticked in the side of his jaw as he dragged the answer from the dark pit where he'd long ago buried all thoughts of Julia Robichaud.

"She's my wife."

2

Julia woke to find herself in a strange room on a strange bed. Someone had removed her outer dress and loosened her stays. They'd also freed her braids of the combs that anchored them to her scalp. She sat up quickly, gasping when her senses swam. Swallowing nausea and panic in big, fast gulps, she searched the shadowy darkness.

"Suzanne?"

"Are you sick, Mama?"

Her daughter's frightened question snapped Julia's head around. Suzanne huddled at the edge of the wide bed, her brown eyes huge. Her thumb hovered an inch from her lips, and she clutched the porcelain doll that was her prized possession hard against her chest.

Julia's choking panic receded. With a sob of relief, she opened her arms. "No, *ma petite papillon,* I was just a little tired. Come, let me hold you."

The five-year-old needed no further urging. Scrambling over the mattress, she cuddled against her mother under the goose-down comforter. Julia wrapped her arms around the child and tried to make sense of the confused thoughts swirling through her head.

The attempt started the pounding at the back of her skull that had plagued her for the past few days. Whirling black spots danced in front of her eyes. She squeezed her lids shut, buried her nose in her child's silky brown hair and gave herself up to the void.

She woke the second time to the piercing call of a bugle and the tantalizing aroma of bacon and coffee. Fresh ground coffee, made from real beans. And bread. Hot, baked bread! A mere whiff was enough to make Julia's stomach cramp.

Her mouth watering, she listened as the bugle's last note died away. Her first instinct was to turn on her side, curl into a tight ball and gnaw on her forefinger to keep from calling out and begging for a sip, just one sip, of that tantalizing coffee. Pride forced to her lay stiff and still and take stock of her surroundings.

Where was she? Whose bedroom was this? She recognized neither the oval portraits on the plaster wall nor the fringed shawl covering the table next to the bed. And where was Suzanne? The bed beside her was empty except for the flaxen-haired doll tucked neatly between the sheets.

The sound of footsteps outside the room brought Julia's head around. Fighting another wave of dizziness, she struggled to sit up in the bed.

"Good, you're awake."

A plump, cheerful matron dressed in a black bombazine bustled in, a tray held high in her hands.

"You've had a good sleep now, haven't you? I thought you might be hungry, so I brought you a bite to eat."

Eat! This stranger was inviting her to eat. Not just bacon, she saw when the woman bent to place the tray on the table beside the bed, but bread, too. Thick slices of white bread, slathered with lard and what looked like gooseberry jelly.

Julia's stomach spasmed again, so viciously her knees drew up under the downy feather bed. With an effort that put a sheen of perspiration on her brow, she ignored the cramping pains and politely refused the tray.

"I'm...I'm not hungry, thank you. But my daughter..."

"She's downstairs," the older woman assured her. "She finished her breakfast earlier, while you were still asleep. What a little trooper that girl is! She cleaned her plate twice, and still had room for the honey cakes the colonel's striker fried up for her."

Julia fell back on the pillows, at once confused, grateful and more than a little desperate. She had no idea how she'd come to sleep in a bed, much less how she would pay this woman for food or lodging. She'd sold every piece of jewelry she had left, even her wedding ring, to get Suzanne and herself as far as Omaha by train. What little had remained of her precious hoard went to secure places for them in the Hottenfelder's wagon and pay for their share of the supplies.

That share should have been enough, more than enough, to see them to Montana Territory. If summer storms hadn't swollen the rivers and delayed crossings for days on end... If lightning hadn't started a prairie fire and sent the wagons fleeing thirty or more miles back the way they'd come... If Julia hadn't passed her meager share of the remaining rations to Suzanne and become so dizzy and weak...

The "ifs" banged in her head like sticks on a tin drum.

If her father hadn't died and left Julia in the guardianship of her uncle.

If the Robichaud shipping line hadn't failed.

If her husband hadn't deserted her.

Sighing, she shoved aside the useless thoughts. She'd gotten herself and her daughter this far. She'd get them the rest of the way. Somehow.

"I'll leave this tray with you," the older woman said with her cheerful smile. "There's water in the jug on the washstand if you want to wash first."

Swallowing, Julia tore her gaze from the thick-slabbed bacon and bread. "Thank you, Mrs...?"

"Gracious, I should have introduced myself, shouldn't I? I'm Maria Schnell. My husband's the post surgeon here at Fort Laramie. He tended to you last night after you fainted."

"Thank you, Mrs. Schnell, but I'm—I'm not hungry."

"Hungry or not, you'd best eat every bite. We can't have you swooning again now, can we?"

Pride and shame waged a fierce battle. The only way to vanquish them, Julia had learned these past months, was to pin on a bright smile and admit the galling truth.

"You're very generous, but I'm afraid I'm temporarily out of funds. I can't pay for food or for the lodging you gave us last night. I'll have to write you a draft and send you the money when we—"

"Mercy, child, I'm not expecting payment for a bit of bread and bacon. Go on now, drink your coffee before it gets cold and call me if you want more. I'll go downstairs and see to Suzanne while you have your breakfast."

With another smile, she bustled out. Julia stared at the closed door for all of two seconds before she snatched up a slice of bread. Just enough of her tattered dignity remained for her to resist cramming it whole into her mouth. As it was, the first slice disappeared in four ravenous bites, the second slice almost as quickly. The bread's texture was coarse, the crust soft and soggy, but it constituted the first solid food she'd eaten in three days. No fresh baguette, no flaky brioche or cream-filled pastry from one of New Orleans's street vendors had ever tasted as wonderful.

She attacked the bacon as well, and had just lifted the china coffee cup when another piercing bugle call sounded, seemingly right outside her window. Startled, Julia sloshed dark liquid over the cup's sides and into the saucer. Fearful of staining her hostess's feather comforter, she quickly replaced the cup on the tray.

The sound of tramping boots and jingling bridles followed the bugle call, vivid reminders that she'd arrived at a military post yesterday. Or was it the day before?

Lifting a shaky hand, Julia pressed it against her temple. She remembered the wagons lumbering to a halt. Remembered feeling her stomach twist inside and out while she and the other women waited for the men to purchase fresh supplies at the trader's store. She remembered, too, praying fervently that she could convince Hiram Hottenfelder to take a promissory note for supplies to get her and Suzanne through the next stage of their journey.

Peaches!

She remembered Augusta shrieking something about peaches and calling her a slut. Julia had sent Suzanne to the wagon then, knowing the tensions that had been simmering for more than a week were about to burst. And burst they had, in front of the entire camp.

The entire camp…and a stranger.

Julia scrubbed the heel of her hand across her forehead, mortified all over again that an outsider had witnessed the humiliating scene. Not just an outsider. An officer. A Yankee officer.

Her hand dropped. She drew in a swift breath, remembering all too clearly now the major who'd stalked forward, stiff-legged and unsmiling.

A chill pumped through her veins and spread like winter frost into her chest. For a moment, when that savage smile had cut across the major's face, he'd looked like...

No! Hunger had played tricks with her mind. Cruel, vicious tricks. It was just a look about the eyes. The glint of chestnut in his hair. He bore a passing resemblance to another man, that was all. She hadn't let herself think about that despicable *bâtard* in years. She would not do so now.

Now, she'd best get dressed, collect Suzanne and go mend her fences with Augusta. The woman wasn't mean, not down deep, just waspish and absurdly jealous in all matters relating to her thick-necked, plodding husband.

Biting into the last of the bacon, Julia chewed thoughtfully while she straightened her stockings and petticoats, and struggled with the strings of her corset. A quick scrub with soap and a linen cloth made her wish with all her heart for a full bath. Unfortunately, she had neither the time nor the means for such a luxury. Smoothing the errant strands of the braid that reached almost to her waist, she wove it into a coronet atop her head and anchored it back in place. The bone pins dug into her scalp, but she was too used to the annoyance to notice.

Her sadly wrinkled walking dress lay over the foot

of the bed. She'd pulled the dress out of her trunk yesterday afternoon in the mistaken hope that a bright look might make it easier for her to swallow her pride and beg Hiram to take her and Suzanne on to Montana Territory with a promise of payment upon arrival. Instead, she'd succeeded only in fanning Augusta's jealousy into rage.

With a shake of her head at her own folly, Julia stepped into the skirt and tied the tapes of the bustle behind her thighs before buttoning on the blouse and silk half jacket. After straightening the bedcovers, she lifted the tray and opened the bedroom door.

A long hall greeted her, decorated with dark-framed hunting prints and family portraits. Rustling past the closed doors of the other rooms, she headed for the stairs. The narrow steps dropped at a steep angle, then cut a sharp right at a landing midway down. Catching her skirts with one hand, Julia balanced the tray with the other and started down. She'd managed only a few of the narrow treads when the sound of male voices slowed her descent.

"No, soor."

The accent was so thick Julia barely understood the words.

"She ain't be comin' down yet. Mrs. Colonel Schnell's in the kitchen, though."

"Please tell her I'm here, Rafferty."

The second voice halted Julia where she stood. Her heart slammed against her whalebone stays and the china on the tray began to shake. She recognized that deep, smooth voice. She'd heard it recently, at the wagons. And before, so many years before...

"Yes, soor. Will ye be havin' a seat in the parlor, then?"

"No, I'll wait in the hall."

Her pulse pounding, Julia took another step and reached the landing. In the hall below she saw the dark-blue crown of a cavalry officer's hat. The gold tassels crossed on the wide brim glinted in the sunlight streaming through the windows.

While she watched with wide, disbelieving eyes, he removed his hat and dusted it impatiently against the yellow stripe on his pants leg. As it had last night, the coppery glint hidden deep in his dark-brown hair drew her anguished gaze.

Julia couldn't breathe, could barely see for the spots that swam in front of her eyes. Her knees gave out. She sat down on the stairs with a thump and a rattle of china.

He looked up then, and her heart stopped in her chest.

For a stunned moment, the years rolled back. To New Orleans in the early weeks of the war, when women still wore wide hoops and lace, and danced gaily at balls given to raise funds for their gallant men in the field. To a mansion on LaFayette Street, its facade a masterpiece of iron grillwork, its tall windows thrown open to the steamy summer night. To the dashing rogue who wooed a silly, feather-headed girl with such consummate, cold-blooded skill.

His eyes, the same steel-blue eyes that had glinted at her in amusement the night they'd met, now looked up at her in cold contempt. Something else followed the contempt, something quickly come and just as quickly gone. Something so close to hate that Julia's blood chilled.

He had cause to hate her, she acknowledged bitterly.

Almost as much as she had to hate him.

He came up the stairs, taking each one slowly, his hard eyes never leaving her face. She wanted to scream at him. Wanted to throw the tray in his face. Wanted even more to scramble back and scuttle ignominiously away from this lean, dangerous stranger who planted a boot on the step below hers and pinned her to the tread with a glance of withering scorn. Instead, being Julia, she tipped her chin and fought to find her voice.

"I—I thought you were dead."

His mouth twisted in the same savage smile he'd shown her last night. "I came to wish I was. Many times."

He was so close, so overpoweringly close. She had to tilt her head back to view his face. The stair's edge cut into the small of her back.

"I saw you," she whispered. "That night you came back to New Orleans, I saw you lying in a pool of your own blood."

"Your uncle's aim was off. I took the bullet in the hip."

She could hardly believe the evidence of her own eyes! For so many years, she'd believed him dead. Now he was here, looming over her, a spectre from her past. She'd once loved him with all the passion of her young and foolish heart, and he'd betrayed her. All the pain, all the misery Julia had endured as a shattered sixteen-year-old came rushing back.

"*Trître!*" she spit. "I wish you had taken the bullet straight through your heart."

"I've no doubt you do. But just to set matters straight, I was no traitor. I was a soldier then, as I am now."

The flat assertion roused her fury. Her whole body shook with it. Fearful of breaking the china that rattled like old bones, she shoved the tray aside.

"You were a spy! A Yankee spy! You came to my uncle's house, you ate his food and drank his wine and you played your games with me, all to gain information about the Robichaud steamships and schedules!"

He leaned down, forcing her head back farther. She saw her own rage reflected in the taut line of his jaw.

"I came to your uncle's house and drank his wine to gain information. You, my so beautiful and so spoiled Julia, were an unexpected bonus."

Her rage burst forth in a spate of passionate Creole. Curving her fingers into talons, she launched herself at him, or tried to.

"*Cochon! Fils d'une cochonne!* I will strangle you with my own hands. I will— Oh!"

Pain shot up her arms as he caught her wrists and slammed them back against the stairs. Kicking, writhing, spitting epithets in French, in patois, in English, she tried to free herself.

"Before either one of us strangles the other," he snarled, "I want you to explain the girl."

She went still. Utterly, completely still.

"The girl?"

"The child the wagon master brought to this house last night, about an hour after I carried you in."

"Her—her name's Suzanne. She's my daughter."

"Your daughter?" he echoed, his voice low and so menacing Julia's heart hammered against her stays. "Or ours?"

"Mine!"

His grip tightened cruelly. "Were you carrying a child when I left you in New Orleans, Julia? Did you panic and tell your uncle? Is that why he was waiting for me with a loaded pistol the night I returned?"

"No," she whispered. "No!"

"He fired from the darkness, before I had even dismounted. Did you show him my note, tell him I was coming back for you that night?"

She stared up at his flinty eyes, hearing again the crack of her uncle's pistol, hearing as well the echo of her own moan when she'd rushed to the window and seen Andrew lying facedown in the cobbled street.

She'd learned the devastating truth about him only weeks before. The man she'd flirted and laughed and fallen hopelessly in love with, the man she'd married in a secret ceremony at St. Lucien's, the man who'd promised to return for her, was a Union agent.

Andrew Garrett would most certainly return, her uncle had jeered when he'd presented her with the incontrovertible proof. For more detail on the Robichaud line's shipping schedules. For more information about tonnage and cargo capacity. For more dalliance with the stupid little bitch who'd raised her skirts and tumbled so eagerly onto her back for him.

Julia hadn't believed her uncle, had *refused* to believe him...until he'd showed her the report he'd received, along with the daguerreotype of Andrew Garrett. *Lieutenant* Andrew Garrett, 2nd Dragoons, United States Cavalry. A graduate of West Point. A commissioned officer in the hated Union Army.

"Yes," she hissed, scored by the raw memories. "I told my uncle you were coming for me that night. But not because I carried a babe. Because you lied to me. Because you used me to gain information about our steamships. Because you were the enemy."

He opened his mouth, but Julia rushed on.

"No child of yours ever quickened in my belly, Andrew. Suzanne is not your daughter."

"Then whose—?"

He stopped, his breath hitching. For a moment, something that might have been compassion flickered in his eyes.

Julia guessed at once what he was thinking. Shame coursed through her, swift and all-consuming. The same shame she'd experienced the first time she'd realized that the uncle who'd assumed her guardianship along with management of her papa's steamships regarded her with far more than familial affection.

"No!" she spit. "I never let Justin touch me. Never!"

She owed this man nothing. No explanations. No justification of her personal conduct. Nothing! Only the need to protect her daughter forced a stiff admission.

"Suzanne is Philip's daughter."

The blue eyes just inches from her own narrowed dangerously. "Philip?"

"Philip Bonneaux. My husband."

His breath hissed in.

"I met him in Natchez," she said in a rush of hate and hurt. "That's where my uncle sent me to try to avoid the scandal of having my name connected with yours. We married and moved to his home in Mobile. Philip's in Montana Territory now, in the gold fields. We're traveling to join him, Suzanne and I."

Silence spun out between them, so heavy and thick Julia thought she might choke on it. Her neck ached from its awkward angle, her wrists from his unrelenting grip. She tried to wiggle up or down a step to ease the cut of the tread in her back, but he held her easily.

Finally, he broke the silence, his voice a cruel, deliberate drawl. "It appears, madam, you've collected a surfeit of husbands."

"No, I have only one!"

"We were wed, Julia, in the church you yourself chose, and your religion doesn't allow divorce. You might have thought me dead when you married this Philip of yours, but as you can see, I'm very much alive."

"You're not my husband now," she threw at him furiously. "Nor were you then. After we learned the truth about you, my uncle petitioned the bishop to set aside our marriage vows."

"On what grounds? We consummated the union… most thoroughly, as I recall."

The sardonic reminder sent heat spearing into her chest and cheeks. She refused to let her mind dwell on the brief hours she'd spent in this man's arms, refused to think for even a moment about the breathless passion he'd roused in her eager, untutored body.

"No banns had been called," she ground out. "And, my uncle took pains to inform me, you were not of the Catholic faith. The bishop declared the ceremony invalid, Andrew. We were never married! Never! Not in the eyes of the Church. Certainly not in my heart. Now let me go, you bastard, or I swear I'll—"

"Mama!"

The small, shocked exclamation halted her in mid-threat.

"Why are you lying on the stairs? With that man on top of you?"

Julia wrenched her head to the side. Heat flamed

up her neck and cheeks when she spotted not only
her daughter, but Mrs. Schnell, a bewhiskered officer
who had to be the surgeon, and a red-haired giant of
a trooper, all staring in stupefaction at the couple entwined so intimately on the stairs.

3

Mortified, Julia yanked her hands free of Andrew's loosened hold.

"Get *off* me!"

The furious whisper wasn't necessary. He was already disengaging. With an awkward maneuver of knee and sword, he levered upward. His face could have been carved from bedrock when he reached down to help her.

Swallowing the urge to bat away his hand, Julia crabbed up a step or two, yanked on her rucked-up skirts and scrambled to her feet unaided. Her eyes shot a fierce warning before she bent to pick up the tray and resume her descent. Her still-shattered nerves jumped with each thud of boots on the wooden treads behind her.

"I tripped coming down the stairs," she told her wide-eyed daughter with scrupulous truthfulness, if not precise accuracy. "When Major Garrett came up to, ah, assist me, we became a bit tangled."

The look Maria Schnell exchanged with her bearded husband told Julia the too facile explanation would require more detail later. At this point her only concern was addressing Suzanne's astonishment and harnessing her own.

Andrew's terse aside that he would speak to her later didn't help matters. Nor did the silence that once again settled over the hallway after the front door rattled shut behind him.

"It was nothing," Julia assured her bewildered daughter. "Just a silly accident."

"But he was on *top* of you, mama."

Another wave of heat seared her cheeks. "Yes, yes, I know." Brushing past Suzanne, she held out her hand to the surgeon. "Your wife told me you tended me last night. I'm very grateful."

"That's why I'm here." With a keen glance, he assessed her still shaky condition. "You should stay in bed for another day or so and regain your strength. Let Maria's dumpling soup put a spot of color back in your cheeks."

Her smile encompassed both the surgeon and his wife. "That's very kind of you, but Suzanne and I must get back to the wagon train. We're supposed to leave this morning and I'm afraid I may have delayed them."

"If you mean the train that was camped up on the bluffs, it's already left. They pulled out well before dawn."

Julia fought a wave of panic. She hadn't yet recovered from her confrontation with Andrew Garrett. She wasn't prepared for another blow so soon, or one so devastating.

"Are you sure?" she asked, her voice thin with desperation.

"Quite sure. I saw they were gone when I rode up to the hospital to make my morning rounds."

The weight of the Hottenfelders' desertion settled like a hundred-pound sack of feed on Julia's shoulders. They'd abandoned her and Suzanne. Left them hundreds of miles from their destination, with nothing more than the clothes on their backs!

In a more rational moment, Julia supposed she wouldn't blame them. Everyone must pay their way, in life as well as on a march across the plains. She had simply run out of the resources to pay hers.

"No doubt they wanted to travel as far as possible before the heat grew too intense," the surgeon explained gruffly.

She nodded, too numb to inform him that she'd grown quite familiar with the necessity of sparing the animals the heat of the day.

The red-haired private cleared his throat. "Beggin' your pardon, soor."

"Well, what is it?"

"Major Garrett brought something for the leddy when he come."

Stepping aside, the trooper waved a beefy paw toward a small, humpbacked chest.

Dully, Julia stared down at the trunk. Bound with

leather straps, it contained everything she and Suzanne now owned. Two dresses for her daughter, one for herself. The sturdy boots, heavy striped cotton skirts and shirtwaists they'd worn on the trail. Extra sets of linen drawers, chemises, a silk wrapper. The Bonneaux family Bible. The letters Philip had dispatched to her from St. Louis, from Omaha, from someplace called Adler's Gulch in Montana Territory.

Three letters. Only three, in almost two years.

Handsome, irresponsible Philip Bonneaux was no better at putting a pen to paper than he was at managing his financial affairs.

She had certainly chosen her husbands well, Julia thought on a wave of something perilously close to hysteria. The first had turned her silly head with his lies, the second had won her heart with his charm. And feckless charm, Julia had discovered to her chagrin, could prove every bit as heavy a burden as lies.

As if sensing how close her houseguest teetered on the brink of despair, Maria Schnell bustled forward and took charge. "Well, now that you have your trunk, what you both need is a hot bath and a fresh change of clothing."

Julia grasped at the offer. Surely, *surely,* she could think more clearly once she washed the trail dust from her hair and from her mind.

"That would be wonderful." Somehow, she managed a smile for her daughter. "What do you say, *ma petite?* Shall we see how many bubbles we can stir up?"

Dainty, fastidious Suzanne skipped eagerly down the hall.

As Andrew had anticipated, the news that Major Garrett's wife—who wasn't really his wife—spread through the post like a prairie fire fanned by the incessant winds.

Henry Schnell had issued strict orders to his spouse, his striker and his maid to hold their tongues. Both he and Andrew had recognized the futility of such an order, however. Gossip flowed faster than whiskey at these isolated outposts, where officers and troopers alike welcomed any diversion from the daily monotony of drill and fatigue duty.

No doubt Private Rafferty had told only his bunkmate, and then after swearing him to the strictest confidence. And the Schnell's maid had probably whispered only a word or two to her cousin, a laundress married to a private in the 4th Infantry's Company D. Either murmured confidence would have triggered a swift and inevitable reaction.

The cavalry troopers would have chewed the news over with their noon meal of beans and bacon. The laundresses would have telegraphed the delicious gossip with every slap of wet longjohns. From either of these sources, the rumors would have circled back to the officers and their wives with the speed and flash of summer lightning.

For that reason, Andrew wasn't surprised when the trooper detailed as orderly of the day rushed up across the parade ground just after the two o'clock call to boots and saddles.

"Colonel Cavanaugh's compliments, sir. He'd like to speak with you."

Returning the trooper's salute, the major acknowledged the order. "Tell the colonel I'll report to him shortly."

"Beggin' your pardon, sir. He said at once."

"All right."

With a word to the regiment's sergeant major to continue the drill, Andrew crossed the parade ground to a white-painted, two-story wooden building. Long verandas fronted each level and gave the structure a graceful facade. The largest building at Fort Laramie, it served as both the administrative and social center of the post. The working and living quarters of the commander took up one wing. Unmarried officers occupied the other. In between were the officers' mess, several storage rooms and a combination billiard and card room. The lively parties given by the building's bachelor residents had long since earned the building the nickname of Old Bedlam.

Andrew found Lieutenant Colonel Jonathan Cavanaugh in his office, hunched in the chair behind his desk. The much decorated veteran of the Cumberland Campaign peered at his subordinate through red-rimmed eyes.

"Well, G'rett, what have you to say for y'rself?"

The slurred words and carelessly buttoned uniform told Andrew that Cavanaugh was having another of his bad days. Unfortunately, the bad far outnumbered the good in recent months.

"Concerning what matter, sir?"

"You know what matter. Who's thz...?" Frowning, the colonel swiped his tongue along dry, cracked lips and began again. "Who is this woman I'm hearing rumors about?"

"I knew her as Julia Robichaud," Andrew answered stiffly.

"Well? Is she your wife or isn't she?"

"She was once."

"And now?"

"Now she's married to a man by the name of Philip Bonneaux."

Cavanaugh leaned back in his chair. A sly smile lifted the ends of his gray mustache. He was enjoying this, Andrew knew.

Personally and professionally, the colonel and the major were poles apart. Cavanaugh shared the infantry's traditional disdain for cavalry. In most cases the rivalry between foot sloggers and horse soldiers was a good-natured one, particularly at frontier outposts like Fort Laramie where mobility was as important as firepower.

In the colonel's case, however, the laudanum he poured down his throat to dull the ache left by the minié ball he'd taken at Chancerilorsville clouded both his judgment and his abilities. He resented the fact that Congress had recently created four new cavalry regiments to guard the frontier, while severely reducing the infantry. He resented even more the hostile Sioux and Cheyenne, whose demands for an end to the invasion of their lands had led to years of bloodshed on the plains. Like most of the men who served on the frontier, he'd taken as his personal credo the sentiment trumpeted by so many Eastern papers, that the only good red man was a dead one.

The old warhorse should have been invalided out years ago. Unfortunately, he had too many friends in Washington to go quietly into retirement, and too much pride to accept the fact that the rest of the post increasingly turned to Major Garrett as de facto commander. Andrew had borne the colonel's rancor for months. Only he knew that opium and frustration were fast turning rancor to hate.

"If you have no further questions, sir, I'll—"

A rap on the door cut off his retreat. At the colonel's growl, the orderly of the day presented himself.

"I'm sorry to disturb you, sir."

"Well, what is it?"

The corporal's glance darted from the commander to the major and back again. "Mrs. Bonneaux is here and wishes to speak with you."

A gleam of malicious delight shone through the haze in Cavanaugh's eyes. Andrew cursed under his breath.

"Show her in, Gottlieb."

"Yes, sir."

The corporal clicked his boot heels. With the precision of one who'd served five years in the Prussian army before emigrating to America, he did an about face.

"Right this way, ma'am."

Andrew braced himself, but the Julia who swept in on a rustle of silk skirts a moment later took him as much by surprise as she did Cavanaugh. She wore the same dress she had last night, the same shining coronet of braids. But her walk held a confident sway and her smile dazzled lieutenant colonel, major and corporal alike.

"Thank you," she told the gaping Gottlieb.

He recovered, clicked his heels once more and closed the door behind her. She glided forward, her stride checking for a moment when she spotted Andrew. Spots of color rose in her cheeks, but she looked pointedly away from him and nodded to the commander.

"It's kind of you to see me, sir. I know how busy you must be."

The malicious gleam in Cavanaugh's eyes deepened. "Your timing is quite perfect, ma'am. We were discussing you."

"Were you?"

Her little trill of laughter floated on the air. For a moment she sounded so much like the Belle of New Orleans that Andrew's gut knotted.

"How very fortunate that I came when I did, then. May I sit down?"

"Of course."

With a rustle of her skirts, she took the chair in

front of the desk. "I don't know what Major Garrett may have told you about me," she began.

"Nothing very much. I hope you will satisfy my curiosity."

Her color deepened, but she calmly removed her gloves and smoothed them in her lap before answering.

"There's really very little to tell. As you may have been informed, the major and I went through a marriage ceremony that was later declared invalid. I married another man soon afterward."

Andrew had to admire her poise. She recited the facts without a trace of emotion, as if the passion that had led them both into a disastrous union had never engulfed her.

"My daughter and I were on our way to join my husband—"

"Your present husband?" Cavanaugh inquired with a lift of his brows.

Her lips thinned at his baiting, but she continued in an unruffled manner.

"We were on our way to join my husband in Montana Territory when I fainted. I'm quite recovered now, and ready to continue my journey. Unfortunately, the company we were traveling with has already left the post."

"So I understand. They can't have gone more than ten or twelve miles."

"Yes, I know."

She smoothed her gloves again. Folding his arms,

Andrew waited to see how she'd explain to the colonel that the company had intentionally left her and her daughter behind, and that they wouldn't welcome her back. The wagon master's wife had made that abundantly clear last night.

Neatly, Julia avoided the awkward explanation. "Mrs. Schnell has very generously offered to let me stay with her for a few days. She also informs me a telegraph line was just completed to Virginia City. I thought, perhaps, you might be so kind as to send a telegraph to my husband."

"Certainly, ma'am."

Andrew entered the conversation for the first time. "The telegraph lines are down between Fort Reno and Fort Smith. They were cut yesterday."

Two faces swung around to his, one dismayed, one outraged.

"Why wasn't I informed?" Cavanaugh demanded.

"The report is on your desk."

The wooden reply raised a flush on the older man's face. "Is that why you came knocking on the door to my quarters earlier?"

"Yes, sir."

"You should have told me the contents of the report, major!"

Andrew refrained from pointing out that he *had* told him. Twice. With the onset of one of his swift rages, Cavanaugh's fist hit the desktop.

"It's that demmed Red Cloud. The savage massacres eighty of our men only six months ago, cuts our telegraph lines and harasses the railroad crews, and what do those pantywaists in Washington do? They pander to the heathen by trying to make peace with him!''

His vehemence startled Julia, who threw a quick glance at Andrew. He kept silent, unable to explain without enraging Cavanaugh further the complex, protracted negotiations to carve Sioux and Cheyenne reservations out of the vast territory that stretched from the Black Hills in the east to the Bighorn Mountains in the west. One of the old school, Andrew's superior considered negotiation and appeasement just one step above cowardice.

Making a valiant effort to hide her dismay, Julia swung back to the colonel. ''How long before the lines are repaired?''

''Fort Smith will have to send out a patrol to find the break,'' he grumbled. ''They've got less than half a company present right now. It could be weeks.''

''Weeks!''

''Or months. The Sioux and Cheyenne pull down the wires as soon as we string them up.''

Still heated with anger, the colonel pushed away from his desk. ''You'd best plan on an extended stay at Fort Laramie, Mrs. Bonneaux. I'm sure your husband—your former husband,'' he corrected with a sneer, ''—will do everything possible to make you comfortable.''

Color whipped back into his visitor's cheeks. Her

mouth tight, she pulled on her gloves, mumbled a polite thank you and left.

Cursing under his breath, Andrew requested permission to withdraw. "If there's nothing else, sir?"

The colonel let him wait for several ticks of the mantel clock before he nodded. "You're dismissed."

Old bugger. With a curl of disgust for the man's petty games, Andrew turned and strode out. Gottlieb and the company clerk jumped to attention as he passed.

He caught up with Julia on Old Bedlam's front porch. She was leaning forward, staring out at the dusty parade ground. Her hands gripped the porch rail as though its support was all that held her up.

"Julia..."

"Yes?"

The mask that dropped instantly over her face ate at his conscience. He'd loved this woman once, had hated her as well. Now he felt nothing but a nagging sense of obligation he couldn't seem to shake no matter how hard he tried.

"Maria Schnell told me something of your circumstances."

Her chin tipped. "Did she?"

Andrew hadn't needed Maria's worried confidence to confirm what the shrieking Gussie had already telegraphed to half the territory. Despite her silks, starched shirtfront and brave airs, Julia Bonneaux was as broke as any private the day after payday.

"We're sending a squad up to reinforce Fort Smith. It's just over the border in Montana Territory. Although it's against army regulations, I could include a letter from you in with the dispatches, and ask the commander there to forward it to your husband with the next wagons going through."

Surprise broke through her mask. "You would do that for me?"

"Yes."

"Why?"

"We were married once. I suppose I feel a certain obligation...."

"Don't!" she flung at him. "Don't *dare* speak to me of what we once were. I gave you my heart, Andrew Garrett, but every smile you gave me, every word you spoke to me was a lie."

"Not every word."

He'd scattered enough grains of truth among the lies to keep from tripping himself up. He'd even tried to warn her that he wasn't all he seemed.

"I told you there were things about me you didn't know."

"And I said I knew all about you that mattered." Disgust convulsed her delicate features. "What a fool I was! A silly, headstrong fool, as my uncle was so fond of telling me."

The mere mention of Justin Robichaud clenched Andrew's hands. Too well he remembered how avidly the man's gaze had followed his niece. Julia had been so young then, so damned vulnerable. Her mother had died at birth, her father a few weeks before her tenth birthday. Andrew certainly hadn't intended to feel first pity, then a growing lust for the nubile young female who teased and tantalized him. Nor had he anticipated the insane desire that grew within him to protect her from her uncle…and from himself.

He should have taken what she offered with every kiss, he thought angrily. He should have ravaged her mouth the way she ravaged his senses. Should have laid her back on a carriage seat or a sofa or the nearest bed. Lifted her skirts and plunged into her instead of giving her his name in a secret ceremony at a parish church, then risking everything to return for her weeks later.

"Don't try to convince me that your conscience bothers you at this late date," she said bitterly, breaking into his thoughts. "After all the lies you told me in New Orleans, you can't care two jackstraws what happens to me now."

"I don't," he replied with brutal candor. "But as long as you're on this post, you're the Army's responsibility."

"Army authority extends even to women?"

From the scorn in her voice, she had no idea the havoc an unattached female could wreak. Particularly a woman like Julia.

"*Especially* to women at isolated outposts like these."

She turned away again, her gloved fingers gripping the rail. Andrew saw her throat work as she fixed her gaze blankly on the flagpole on the opposite side of the parade ground.

"What are your plans?" he asked.

"I don't know," she murmured, more to herself

than to him. "I can't impose on Maria Schnell's hospitality indefinitely."

"No, you can't," he agreed. "Henry Schnell's one of the best men I've ever had the honor to serve with. He and Maria don't speak of it, but he spends more than half his pay to supplement the meager store of medicinal supplies the Army provides his hospital. They're as strapped as the most junior lieutenant on post."

She acknowledged his pronouncement with a single, stark nod. For an insane moment, Andrew was tempted to suggest she move into his quarters. The urge to protect her, to shield her and her daughter itched like a tick that burrowed into his skin. Damning himself as ten kinds of a fool for caring what happened to this woman, he offered the only other alternative he'd been able to come up with.

"One of our lieutenants is on detached duty with Custer's 7th Cavalry at Fort Riley," he said brusquely. "His wife gave birth a month or so ago and has no one here to help her. I could set you up in temporary quarters with her if you wish."

The grudging offer scored what little was left of Julia's pride. With all her heart, she longed to throw it back in Andrew's face. For her daughter's sake, she drew her tattered dignity around her and accepted with a stiff nod.

"Thank you."

4

Julia held Suzanne's hand firmly as they followed Private Rafferty along the dirt path that skirted the parade ground.

A blazing afternoon sun beat down on their heads and shoulders. The heat didn't seem to affect the burly striker, buttoned up to the neck in his blue wool uniform. With his flat-topped forage cap tipped jauntily over one brow, he carried their trunk on a muscular shoulder and pointed out the various sights along the way.

As Julia had already discovered, Fort Laramie was a jumble of old and new, of wood frame houses, adobe barracks and tents, all laid out on a flat tongue of land. The principle buildings surrounded the parade ground, a rectangle of hard-packed dirt with a wooden flagpole planted midway down one side. The Laramie River curled around the perimeter of the post, providing natural protection from attack. A wooden footbridge spanned the sparkling river and gave access to the buildings, tents and tipis on the far bank. Beyond the Laramie, rolling brown plains stretched as far as the eye could see.

There wasn't a single tree in sight. Not one, on either the post or the plains. Wood for cookfires and construction, Private Rafferty informed Julia in his lilting way, had to be hauled in from the pine-covered slopes of the Laramie Mountains forty miles away.

"Wood detail ain't what we jined up for, if you take my meaning, missus. Not at all the kind o'work suited for horse soldiers."

Horse soldiers, he explained good-naturedly, "being the ones what sported the yellow cavalry stripe on their pants legs," as distinguished from infantry red.

"The Sioux calls the infantry Walks-A-Heap," Rafferty chuckled. "'N walk them boyos do!"

Julia tried her best to digest his running commentary during the short trek from the surgeon's quarters to the row of frame houses huddled like hens on the edge of the windswept plain. There were three of them, constructed in a curious design Rafferty described as "Army duplex." Like the headquarters building, the houses had two separate sides, each with a private entrance.

"Mrs. Lieutenant McKinney has the far hoose."

"Do you always refer to the wives by their husband's rank?"

The striker looked surprised at the question. "And

how else would we be showin' them the proper respect?''

She had no answer for that. The Army, obviously, maintained a social structure even more rigid than that of the aristocratic Creole society she'd been born into.

At the thought of New Orleans, homesickness attacked her in a sharp, sudden rush. She could almost smell honeysuckle and jasmine spilling into air thick with humid heat. Almost taste the pecan-stuffed pralines that stuck to her teeth. Almost hear her father's teasing as he tossed her high in the air, much to her squealing delight.

She'd been so happy as a child, so secure in her father's love that she'd never missed the mother who'd succumbed to a fever just after her daughter's birth. So pampered and spoiled despite the determined efforts of the Carmelite nuns who'd tried their best to eradicate her frivolity. Then her father had died and Julia had gone to live with her aunt and uncle in their mansion on LaFayette Street.

In the blazing heat of the June afternoon, shivers danced along her spine. She gripped Suzanne's hand, fighting the memories, unable to stop them.

Her first few years at LaFayette Street she'd barely seen her uncle. He'd kept busy with his own sugarcane brokerage firm and the shipping lines Julia had inherited from her father. It wasn't until the niece had begun to fill out her gowns that the uncle noticed her. Really noticed her.

Naive and foolish, she'd laughed off the unease

that prickled her skin whenever Justin's dark eyes lingered too long on her face, her throat, her breasts. Then her gaze had collided with that of a handsome stranger across a crowded ballroom.

Julia's heart thumped against the bones of her stays as the remembered strains of a waltz buzzed in her ears. How young she'd been. How unforgivably stupid.

Andrew had swept her into the waltz, later partnered her in a lively reel. He'd asked to escort her into the midnight supper, but Julia had retained just enough sense to laugh and say she was promised to another. Andrew hadn't pushed...much to Julia's secret chagrin. But he'd appeared in LaFayette Street the very next afternoon driving a smart, high-seated gig and caught her just as she was stepping out for a walk.

She shouldn't have climbed into the gig and wheeled away with him for a stolen afternoon. Her maid had been scandalized. Her uncle, when she returned home, had been coldly furious. Even more so when Andrew called on her again the next day, and the next. Finally, her uncle had forbidden him to call at the house ever again, but by then it was too late. Fool that she was, Julia had already tumbled headlong into love.

Memories flooded into her, one after another. The stormy afternoon Andrew had told her he had to leave New Orleans. Her passionate avowal that she'd wait for him, forever if necessary, no matter what her uncle said or did. The grim cast to Andrew's jaw at the mention of Justin Robichaud. The hurried marriage at St. Lucien's. Her despondency the long weeks he was gone, and her joy when she received his note saying he was coming for her the next night.

Her devastation when she'd learned of his betrayal, and heard the crack of her uncle's pistol shatter the night.

"Mama!"

Blankly, Julia stared down at her daughter.

"You're hurting my fingers!"

With a jarring thump, she returned to the reality of a dusty outpost on the edge of a vast sea of emptiness.

"I'm sorry, *ma petite*."

She had herself once again in hand by the time they turned onto the board walkway leading to the front porch. Suzanne clutched her precious doll to her chest. Eyes wide under the brim of her bonnet, she took in the wraparound porch, tall shutters and tin roof.

"Are we going to stay here, Mama?"

"For a while."

The girl's footsteps dragged. A mulish expression her mother knew all too well settled on her face. "I don't want to."

"After weeks of traveling on that sooty train and then in the Hottenhelder's wagon, I should think you'd be happy to sleep in a bed that doesn't move for a little while."

Suzanne dug in her heels. "You said we were going to find Papa."

"I'm going to write to him, darling, and tell him where we are."

"You wrote to him before and he didn't answer." Her lower lip began to tremble. "You said we were going to find him."

Her heart wrenching, Julia drew back her skirts and dropped down on one knee. Suzanne adored Philip, and no wonder. He'd spoiled her atrociously from the first day he'd lifted her from her cradle. For all his other faults, Philip Bonneaux was a loving father.

"We'll find him, *ma petite*, or he'll find us. It just may take a little longer than we thought."

"I don't want to stay here." Tears welled in the child's chocolate-brown eyes. "I want to find Papa, like you said we would. I want to live in our own house in Mobile, like we used to."

Aching over the way her daughter's world had shifted under her dainty feet, Julia could only smile and try to rally her spirits. "We talked about this, remember? You know Mama had to sell the house to pay the bills. Now no more silliness, if you please. Let's go meet Mrs. McKinney."

Tears swimming in her wide, reproachful eyes, the girl tucked her hand in Julia's once again. She was still sniffling when they climbed the steps and waited while Private Rafferty rapped on the front door.

The woman who opened it a moment later stood a good six inches shorter than Julia. Wild tendrils of orangy hair sprang from the bun piled haphazardly atop her head. With a pat for the red-faced infant squirming against her shoulder, she smiled a relieved greeting.

"You'll be Mrs. Major Garrett. I heard you were comin'."

Embarrassment added to the flush of heat on Julia's face. "My name is Bonneaux," she corrected stiffly. "Julia Bonneaux."

The woman's carroty brows arched. "What's this? Do I have the story wrong aboot you and the major, then?"

"Yes, apparently you have." All too aware of the trooper and the five-year-old ranged on either side of her, Julia summoned a strained smile. "Perhaps we may take our conversation inside, where we can be more private?"

"Ooooch, I don't know where me head is! It must be this heat, and the baby frettin'...."

Thumping the infant gently on the back, the diminutive woman led the way inside. Julia saw at a glance the quarters were far more sparsely furnished than those of the Schnells. The parlor was empty except for a black, potbellied stove. The dining room beyond contained only an assortment of unmatched chairs and a low table made from a box with U.S. Army Carbines stenciled on the sides. Her stomach sinking at the stark emptiness, Julia reminded herself that a lieutenant couldn't aspire to live as well as a post surgeon.

"Are you sure we're not putting you out, Mrs. Mc-Kinney?"

"Ooooh, I should have introduced myself, now shouldn't I? I'm not Mrs. McKinney. I'm Mary Donovan. M'husband's the sergeant major o'Lootenant McKinney's company. I just came over to help his leddy by mindin' her baby for a bit. Now that you're here, Mrs. Major—er, Mrs. Bonneaux—I'd best be gettin' back to me laundry tubs."

With that, she passed the infant to Julia, adjured Rafferty "not to be standin' around like a lump o'stone," and swept out with a promise to return after first call for retreat to see how they all fared. The trooper deposited the humpbacked trunk and followed her out a few moments later.

Julia stood in the hallway, holding the red-faced baby in her arms. Sweat trickled between her breasts. Suffocating heat pounded at her temples. The enormity of being stranded so far from home, totally dependent on the kindness of strangers, threatened to overwhelm her.

She would have loved to indulge in a hearty bout of tears, but they were a luxury she could no longer afford. Cradling the infant in the crook of her arm, she tweaked one of her daughter's honey-brown curls.

"Let's go meet the baby's mother, shall we?"

Victoria McKinney fussed even more than her fretful infant and resented strangers living in her house. She didn't express her sentiments in so many words, but they became quite clear over the course of the next few days. Only too conscious of her own precarious situation, Julia swallowed her pride and held her tongue. But the holding became more and more difficult with each hour spent in the pallid, unhappy woman's company.

"I shouldn't have left New York," the young wife complained to her reluctant guests the third night of their stay. She sat at the box that served as a table, picking at the unappetizing fare on her plate. "My father owns a bank, you know."

"Yes," Julia replied, gritting her teeth, "you've told me."

Several times, in fact.

According to Victoria, most of the officers' wives came from wealthy, urban homes. Many, like the lieutenant's wife, found life without servants to wait on them and cooks to prepare their meals unendurable. A few hardy ones like Maria Schnell considered living on the frontier an adventure. Victoria McKinney, Julia had discovered, considered it a penance.

Adjuring Suzanne to eat her dinner and not tease the baby tucked in a cradle made from another crate, Julia sawed at her boiled beef. Although the monthly rations for married officers included two cans of peaches, one can each of oysters, tomatoes, peas and corn, and a half pound of dried mackerel, those treats were saved for precious occasions like birthdays and holidays. All other supplies had to be purchased from the sutler's store at exorbitant prices, when they could be had at all. As a consequence, the standard daily fare of the women and children at Fort Laramie mirrored that of the troops—bacon, beans and beef.

"Papa warned me not to marry William," the morose young mother confided. "He told me the smart uniforms and fancy dress balls at West Point were no measure of the life I'd lead on the frontier. I should have listened to him."

"Well, you're here now and you have a comfortable house," Julia replied with determined cheerfulness. "I'll help you make curtains, if you like, and perhaps put up some shelves for your books or pictures."

"There's no point to it." Disconsolately, her hostess stabbed at her beans. "William's the junior lieutenant on post. We'll get ranked out of these quarters when another officer senior to him arrives, just as we did at Fort Riley. We had to live in a tent then for almost six months."

Julia bit down on the impulse to tell this whining young woman that she wasn't the only one to lose a home. Her chest ached whenever she let herself think about the house she'd sold to pay Philip's gambling debts.

"Finish your beef," she said instead, in much the same bracing tone she would use with Suzanne. "Then I'll serve you a bit of custard."

"Custard!" Alarm brought Victoria straight up in her chair. "Never say the sutler got in some eggs! Surely you didn't charge them to our account?"

"No, of course not."

Julia had learned during her own travels the astronomical cost associated with transporting perishables like butter and eggs over hundreds of miles of prairie in a jolting wagon.

"I used Mary Donovan's recipe," she assured her worried hostess. "All it calls for is six tablespoons of cornstarch, boiled nice and thick and flavored with a bit of sugar and extract of lemon."

Thank goodness for the Irish laundress, Julia thought as she spooned the soupy mixture into bowls. True to her word, Mrs. Donovan had come by each day to check on Mrs. Lieutenant McKinney, as had Maria Schnell and several of the other officers' ladies. The officers' wives were polite enough, but Julia felt the weight of their curiosity and silent disapproval in every glance.

They didn't know what to make of her. Divorce was too scandalous a topic to discuss in polite company, and a marriage that wasn't really a marriage was outside their comprehension. They treated Julia with civility, but, except for Maria Schnell made no overtures of friendship.

Nor did Mary Donovan, if the truth be told. Invariably cheerful, the sergeant major's wife was careful not to cross the line between laundress and lady. Thankfully, she was also a wealth of information and practical tips, having lived on the frontier for almost a decade now. The custard, Julia thought, was one of her best.

Victoria wolfed down the treat, yet still managed to admonish her guest between greedy gulps. "You must be careful with the sugar. Even with the extra rations Major Garrett sent over for you and Suzanne, we have barely enough to get by."

Julia froze with her spoon halfway to her mouth. "Major Garrett sent over extra rations?"

"Of course. You don't think William and I could feed you and your daughter from our pitiful store, do you?

"No," she replied in a suffocated voice, laying her spoon aside with exaggerated care. "Of course not."

"Does that disturb you? Why should it? Everyone on post knows of your past... How shall I say it? Your past connection to the major. It's only fitting that your keep come out of his pocket."

"Is it?"

Dismissing the matter with a lift of her thin shoulders, Victoria eyed Julia's bowl avidly. "If you're not going to eat the rest of your custard, may I have it?"

"What?"

"Your custard? May I have it?" The all-too-familiar whine crept back into her voice. "I need to keep up my strength for nursing."

Wordlessly, Julia shoved the crockery bowl across the wooden tabletop.

She felt mortified beyond belief. And so very, very stupid. How naive of her to think that cooking and cleaning and caring for Victoria McKinney's baby would constitute fair exchange for a straw-filled mattress and the little she and Suzanne ate.

The idea of being dependent on Andrew Garrett's largess shredded the last remnants of her pride. The realization that everyone on the post apparently knew of it only added to the humiliation.

Even Mary Donovan, she discovered when the sergeant major's wife came by just after the buglers sounded evening assembly. Julia had brought one of the chairs out to the porch, as much to escape Victoria's petulance as to catch the hot breeze blowing down from the bluffs. Suzanne remained inside, rocking the baby she found as fascinating as her doll.

Mary huffed up the walk, her hair a blaze of orange in the last rays of the sun. A smile creased her face when she caught sight of Julia.

"Good evening to you, missus."

"Good evening."

The steps creaked as she joined Julia on the covered porch. "Ye're lookin' a bit peaked," she commented, leaning a hip against the wraparound railing. "Has the lootenant's leddy been treatin' you to a bit o'her melancholies?"

Victoria had treated Julia to more than just *a bit* of her melancholies. She was close to driving her mad with all her complaints. Unlike her hostess, however, Julia chose not to burden others with her problems.

"It's the heat," she said with a lift of one shoulder. "It's so draining."

"And don't I know it! It's a relief to get away from those washtubs, that I can tell you."

Although Julia guessed that Mary had changed before coming to call, sweat still sheened her ruddy face and left damp splotches on her dress. Hesitant to intrude in another's private affairs, she nevertheless couldn't help venturing a comment.

"Your husband's a sergeant major. Surely you don't have to bend over pots all day?"

"Oh, dearie, I don't *have* to. I want to. Sean's me third husband, don't y'know?"

"No, I didn't."

"It's a rough life out here, and that's the truth. I lost two husbands in seven years. Before I married Sean, I fought tooth 'n'nail to get me name put on the rolls."

"What rolls?"

"Army rolls."

"You're part of the Army?"

"That I am," Mary answered proudly. "Each company's allowed one laundress for every nineteen and a half men. Don't be askin' me where the half came from, now!"

Her hearty chuckles drew a smile from Julia.

"The Army pays us well," the laundress continued. "'Tis a dollar a month we draw for each trooper we wash for, four dollars from each officer. In addition, we get rations and the attentions o'the surgeon when we need him. Our own quarters, too, down t'Suds Row beside the river."

How odd, Julia thought. And how ironic! Victoria McKinney and most of the other officers' wives came from backgrounds of wealth and privilege, but held no status except that derived from their husbands. Yet Mary Donovan and her fellow laundresses, uneducated immigrants for the most part, were evidently considered an intrinsic part of the army establishment.

"I earn a bit more at the hospital," Mary confided, "washin' the bodies o'the sick and layin' out the dead. Some o'the girls pick up another dollar or two more maiding for the officers' leddies, but that's not my cup o'tea."

Flicking a look at the open windows behind them, she lowered her voice.

"There's some of the girls as earn a bit o'cash on their backs. It's not what I like to see, mind you, but a woman does what she must to survive."

"Yes, she does."

The flat reply took Mary aback. Her shrewd blue eyes turned thoughtful.

"You don't need to be worryin' yourself into a fret now, do you now? The major will see to yer needs while you're at Fort Laramie."

Julia's mouth clamped shut. Much as she longed to tell Mary and everyone else on this windswept post that she would rather starve than allow the major to "see to her needs," she must think of Suzanne. Thankfully, a long, piercing bugle call distracted her from her lowering thoughts and drew the women's attention to the flagpole at the edge of the parade ground.

"First call for retreat," Mary commented in delight. "Now you'll be seein' something proud. Major Garrett and the boyos from Company C are back from patrol."

"I didn't know they were gone."

"Three days now."

So that's why Julia hadn't seen Andrew about the post. Not that she'd been watching for him among the officers who assembled with the men for guard mount and retreat each day. He'd simply been conspicuous by his absence.

She couldn't miss him tonight, however. He rode at the head of a column of troops, back erect, seat easy on a massive chestnut charger. The last, slanting rays of the sun glinted on the sword hanging from his saddle and melted the gold piping on his uniform to shimmering gilt. A blue campaign hat shaded his eyes.

She was forced to admit that he and his men made a stirring sight. Bridles jingling, hooves raising puffs of dust on the earthen parade ground, they trotted four abreast until the platoon was centered on the flagpole. At a sharp command, the squad executed a right turn, then sat at attention in their saddles until the bugles rang out again. A few moments later, Colonel Cavanaugh and his officer of the day strode from the headquarters building to the parade ground and a long, stenorous command rolled across the field.

"Pre-sennnt arms!"

The air rang with the hiss of steel on steel as a hundred sabers came free of their scabbards.

The bugles sounded once more, signaling the lowering of the flag. Mary lumbered to her feet. Julia rose more slowly. The war was too recent and the scars still too deep to render courtesies to the Stars and Stripes without an inner wince.

She watched the flag come down, thinking of all the blood that had been spilled during the long years of war and all the lives that had been shattered, her own included. Looking back, she could barely remember the girl who'd danced and flirted and lost her head and her heart to a man who'd betrayed both.

She wanted to hate him. Seeing him tall and square-shouldered in the saddle, she tried to summon the fury that had ripped through her when he'd pinned her to the stairs in Maria Schnell's house. The hate tasted like ashes in her mouth. The fury wouldn't flame as hot and fast as it had three days ago.

Enough remained, however, to stiffen her back when the troop dispersed and the major turned his mount in the direction of the McKinney house.

Mary noted his approach, as well. Her gaze shifted to the woman beside her. She hesitated, then spoke her mind with the directness Julia had come to expect from her.

"He's a good man, don't y'know? M'husband says he'll go bail for his troopers, and that's the highest praise any officer can earn from Sean Donovan."

Julia folded her lips and said nothing. With another glance her way, Mary took her leave.

Andrew tipped his hat to her, then dismounted. He looped the reins over the hitching post in front of the house and walked up the boards. His uneven gait sent a little stab into Julia's chest. They'd hurt each other cruelly, she and Andrew.

He stopped a few paces away, his eyes shadowed under the brim of his hat. She couldn't help comparing him to the man she'd known in New Orleans. This Andrew's face was so lean, his mouth unsmiling. Despite herself, despite every intention to keep those long-ago days from creeping back into her mind, she remembered his rakish grin, remembered, too, the kisses those lips had pressed on hers. And his hands, his skilled hands...

Heat shot into Julia's belly, so swift and hot she almost gasped. Shocked by its intensity, she hid her clenched fists in the folds of her skirt. She'd lusted for this man once, with all the passion of a young and headstrong girl. She'd cut out her heart and broil it over an open flame before she let herself feel the slightest tenderness for him again!

Some of her revulsion must have shown in her face. The major greeted her with a curt nod.

"I just came by to tell you the reinforcements we sent to Fort Smith arrived safely. Your letter will go out with the next outfit that comes through heading for Adler's Gulch."

Julia tipped her head. "Thank you."

He hesitated, obviously no more willing than she to prolong the conversation.

"Are you and Mrs. McKinney getting on all right?"

"Yes."

"Do you need anything?"

"No."

Andrew bit back an oath. Her clipped responses irritated him every bit as much as her forbidding expression. Obviously, she still regarded him as something that had slithered out from under a rock.

Why did he care what she thought of him or how she fared, dammit? He owed this woman nothing. The mistaken passion they'd once felt for each other had burned out long ago. And, as she'd so acidly informed him the day of her arrival, their brief marriage had been wiped from the books. She was another man's wife now. Another man's responsibility.

So why had the blasted female crept into his thoughts during the long march these past few days? Why had tantalizing images of her ripe lips, slender waist and high, firm breasts danced on his closed lids when he'd bedded down at night? And why in thunderation did he ache to climb the steps, haul her into his arms and kiss that look of haughty disdain from her face?

Thoroughly disgusted with himself and the aching bulge behind the flap of his trousers, Andrew tipped two fingers to his hat brim and strode back to his mount.

Best to stay away from her, he decided savagely. Keep his distance. As he'd learned to his profound regret, Julia could destroy a man's peace with one flash of her violet eyes.

A talent, he discovered less than a week later, she'd more than perfected in the years since New Orleans.

5

"**B**ut you must come!"

Victoria McKinney's plaintiff whine grated on Julia's nerves like fingernails scraped across a washboard.

"It's Company A's annual hop. All the officers' ladies are expected to attend."

"I'm not an officers' lady."

"But I am. William says I must keep up appearances, and I do *so* need a bit of fun. If you don't come," Victoria sniffled, "who will mind the baby while I dance?"

"I'm sure Maria Schnell will be there. Mary Donovan, too. One of them would be happy to mind him."

The peevish look Julia had come to recognize all too well settled on the younger woman's face.

"I should think you'd show a little more gratitude. After all, I did open my home to you, despite your peculiar circumstances. I'm sure my mama and papa would be shocked to know a woman who's married to two men is living under my roof.''

Thankful that she'd sent Suzanne outside to play, Julia lowered the baby dress she was hemming and counted to ten before answering.

"I've told you several times, Victoria, my marriage to Major Garrett was set aside by the church. I have only one husband.''

"Well, I'm sure I don't care how many you've had,'' her hostess returned irritably. "But I do think it's odd that you put one husband aside, only to lose the other.''

"I haven't lost Philip. He's in Montana Territory.''

"How do you know?'' Spitefully, she preyed on Julia's own, secret fears. "The last letter you received from him is over a year old. Anything could have happened to him in a year.''

Heartily wishing she'd never shared that particular confidence, Julia tossed the baby dress on the wood crate that served as their table. She had to get out of Victoria McKinney's house, if only for a few hours, or she would scream.

"All right, I'll accompany you to…what did you call it? The hop?''

"That's what the troopers call it,'' her hostess said, brightening like an oil lamp just lit. "Probably because they jump around so energetically. You don't have to dance with all of them, you know. Some are so dreadfully coarse. But one of the privates in Company A used to be a dance master in the court of King Leopold of Belgium, if you can believe it.''

Julia could certainly believe it. In the short time she'd spent on post, she'd discovered that more than half of the troopers had been recruited just weeks or months after stepping off the boat from Europe. They came from all walks of life—hatters, blacksmiths, farmers and dancing instructors. Some had previous military experience and found a familiar home in the Army of their adopted country. Others had been driven to the recruiters by the lack of jobs and severe economic depression that had followed the War Between the States.

''Private Lowenstahl waltzes divinely,'' Victoria gushed, happy as a meadowlark now that she'd got her way. ''You must let him, at least, have a dance.''

Private Lowenstahl did more than waltz divinely, Julia discovered that evening. He could guide a woman around the pine plank floor in a polka, a german, or a two-step with sublime grace. Tall and slender and tanned by the sun, with blond mustaches that drooped splendidly, he'd joined the regiment only six months ago and was already something of a legend.

Mindful of her appointed duty as baby-tender, Julia hung back. She'd left Suzanne tucked in with the children of the captain who lived next door, but Victoria's baby would need feeding. He'd been carried in a wicker basket to the long, single-story barracks across the parade ground from the officers' quarters and now watched the proceeding with wide eyes.

Company A had done itself proud. The double-tiered wooden bunks had been pushed out of the way to form an empty space in the center of the barracks. A trestle table held lemonade for the ladies. The refreshing drink was chilled by the ice that had been cut from the river in winter and stored in straw in the icehouse for just such occasions as this. Evidently the men had pooled their resources and raided the sutler's store for tins of oysters, pickled pigs' feet and jellies.

Volunteer musicians playing the banjo, harmonica and violin augmented the company drummer and bugler. The makeshift orchestra pumped surprisingly melodious tunes into the air. If a distinct odor of earth, old leather and sweat permeated the barracks, no one seemed to take the least heed of it.

As Julia had discovered, a strict caste system regulated social life on army posts, just as it did civilian society. The officers and their ladies congregated at one end of the room. The enlisted men and their wives, the single laundresses and maids kept to the other. Given the paucity of women on the frontier, however, the lines blurred whenever the band struck up. Single troopers didn't hesitate to ask the officers' permission to partner their ladies in a dance.

Private Lowenstahl singled Julia out soon after her arrival. She declined his invitation to dance at first, but Maria Schnell took the baby's basket from her hands and shooed her out onto the floor with instructions to enjoy herself. Self-consciously, Julia placed her hand on the private's arm and let him lead her to the center of the room. They waited with several other couples for the first strains of the waltz. She hadn't danced in years, couldn't remember the last time Philip had taken her in his arms for a whirl about the floor. She'd so enjoyed it as a girl....

Her throat closing, she let her gaze drift to the officer standing beside the sergeant major of Company A. Both men wore their dress uniforms, the collars high and tight around their necks and the front facings piped with gold.

For a moment, the mud-chinked wooden walls and oil lamps hanging from the rafters faded from Julia's view. She could almost see the brilliance of crystal chandeliers, jewel-toned silks, pots of lush flowers. Could see, too, Andrew Garrett's lazy smile as he caught her eye across the ballroom floor.

He hadn't worn a uniform that night, Julia remembered. His shoulders had strained the seams of a cutaway frock coat. A snowy white cravat had circled his throat. She'd snapped open her fan and hidden her smile behind its lace and ivory ribs. Her girlish confidence had told her the handsome stranger would make his way to her side before the evening was out.

And he had, damn him.

He showed no such inclination to dance with her tonight. He met Julia's glance for the space of a heartbeat, then deliberately looked away. The slight stung. Quickly, she shrugged the little prickle of hurt aside.

She didn't want his attention any more than he wanted hers.

If the smile she subsequently turned on Private Lowenstahl was overly brilliant, she wasn't aware of it. He certainly was, however. Murmuring polite, effusive compliments, he swept her into the waltz.

It wasn't long before others in the room took note of the trooper's fascination with his partner. Slowly, the rest of the dancers cleared the floor. The entire room watched as Lowenstahl dipped and swirled Julia around the room with an artistry they'd never seen before.

"Just look at that!" a petulant voice behind Andrew complained. "I told her she should give him a waltz, but I didn't think she would make a spectacle of herself. The woman's as bold and brassy as you please."

Andrew didn't have to turn around to identify the source of the spite. Why William McKinney, who had all the makings of a fine officer, had married such a shrew baffled most of the men on post, his company commander included. Then again, Andrew thought grimly, Julia could tempt a saint to spiteful jealousy.

Or sin.

His own stomach had knotted the moment she'd walked through the barracks' door, and he certainly made no claims to sainthood.

Just look at her. Didn't the woman have enough sense not to deck herself in lavender silk trimmed with black lace? Or wear a gown with a bodice cut low enough to show the curves of her breasts? Half the troopers in the room were staring avidly at that swell of creamy flesh, the other half at the bustle that swayed so provocatively with each swirl.

Disgust, anger and desire all stirred in Andrew's chest. He didn't want to want her, dammit. Had tried to put her out of his thoughts. But by the time the music finally ended and Private Lowenstahl led a flushed, laughing Julia off the floor, Andrew's body had hardened and his collar felt so tight it threatened to choke him.

After that, officers and troopers lined up ten deep to dance with her. To give her credit, she tried to refuse gracefully after the third or fourth romp. The men's eager enthusiasm overcame her objections. Unfortunately, it also led to a near brawl.

No strong spirits were allowed at these company hops, but so many soldiers slipped outside for a nip of the coffin varnish that passed for whiskey in these parts that the stuffy air inside soon took on a flavor of its own. Usually, Andrew and the seasoned non-commissioned officers in attendance could judge to a nicety when to call a halt to the festivities and escort the ladies home. Tonight, matters reached flash point far sooner than Andrew could have anticipated. He should have expected Julia would provide the spark that set it off.

Laughing and begging for a rest, she retreated to the sidelines to fan herself after a lively reel with Private Rafferty. Her solicitous partner tried to help by snatching off his neckerchief and waving it energetically. In the process, he thumped the trooper waiting to claim the next dance square in the chest.

"Hey, watch yer bony elbows, man!"

"Watch 'em yerself, Hansen."

With a hearty shove, the second trooper tried to oust Rafferty from his position. Julia's kerchief-waving gallant refused to budge.

"Mind yer manners," the Schnell's brawny striker growled. "Can't you see the leddy's too hot and tired to dance with the likes of you?"

"She let you stomp all over her feet. A jackass would'a done less damage to her toes."

The private's jaw squared. The look of the Irish blazed in his eyes. "I told you t'mind yer manners, you rubber-jawed whiskey soak. Or are you wantin' me to pound some into you with me fists?"

"Gentlemen, please." With a placating smile, Julia intervened. "It's too hot to dance *or* exchange words like this. Would one of you be so kind as to fetch me a cup of lemonade?"

"I'll get it," the newcomer said, aiming a belligerent glare at his rival. "We'll take our turn about the floor after you've had a sip or two, ma'am."

Rafferty bristled. "The hell you will."

"Please," Julia pleaded, "I—"

"I'm ranking you both, gentlemen."

The deep voice behind her stilled the argument instantly.

"The next dance is mine...if the lady permits."

"Yes, sir!" the two men chorused, retreating.

Willing the smile not to slide right off her face, Julia made a slow turn. Every eye in the room was on them, she saw, from Victoria McKinney's pouting frown to Mary Donovan's keen glance. She pulled her gaze from the fascinated audience to Andrew standing square-shouldered in front of her. She could not— *would not*—walk into his arms. Not again.

"Thank you," she said, her voice as even as she could manage given the fact that she was the center of so many speculative gazes. "But I find I'm quite fatigued. I don't care to dance any more tonight."

"Then I'll escort you home."

Andrew held out his arm. Julia kept hers at her sides.

"Take my arm," he ordered softly. "You're leaving. I won't have you causing a brawl."

The unfairness of his remark raised a sting of heat in her cheeks. She came within a hair of turning on her heel and walking away. The cool, hard look in his eyes warned her not to embarrass either him or herself by such blatant rudeness.

Hiding her anger, she laid her fingers on his sleeve. Beneath the cloth, his muscles felt as hard as steel and every bit as unyielding. Head high, she allowed him to escort her out into the night.

As soon as they were outside, Julia snatched her fingers away. "You embarrass me and abuse your authority with such heavy-handed tactics, major."

"You brought the embarrassment upon yourself."

Anger flashed in her eyes. "By dancing?"

He reined in his own temper with a visible effort. "I suggest we discuss the matter at your quarters instead of in the middle of the parade ground."

Picking up her skirts, Julia stalked off. A full moon illuminated the way across the post to Officers' Row. The sentries' call as they marched their watch formed a counterpoint to the music floating on the night air.

Andrew matched his stride to hers. With every step, his charged mix of anger, disgust and desire multiplied. Just the sight of the damp tendrils that curled on the back of her neck stirred a lust that irritated him intensely. When his gaze shifted to the breasts rising and falling beneath the black lace, his muscles knotted even more. Swearing under his breath, he fought the memories that pulled at him like hot pincers.

Despite his determined effort, the vivid images filled his head. Julia laughing up at him from behind her fan. Julia whirling around a ballroom in his arms. Julia damp and flushed and panting the night they'd consummated their hurried, secret marriage.

His groin tightened as the memories of that night rose up to taunt him. He tried not to think of how she'd sprawled across the bed at his hotel. How he'd peeled away her underclothing slowly, feasting his eyes on the luscious flesh beneath. How she'd soon overcome her initial shyness and writhed slick and hot on the tangled sheets.

He'd forced himself to hold back, to prime her with his mouth and hands and a hard, rocking knee until she gushed wet and ready. Only then had Andrew parted her thighs and penetrated her virgin's shield with a single thrust.

She'd cried out in surprise, he remembered, sweating now beneath his uniform jacket. She'd tried to wiggle away. But he'd held her and kissed her and slipped into the rhythm that, far sooner than either of them expected, ripped another cry from her throat.

Andrew had never bedded a woman like Julia, before or since. The thought of another man, another husband, plunging into her hot, silken depths had him reaching up to hook a finger in his collar. Viciously, he tugged at the blasted thing. He couldn't breathe without drawing in her musky scent. Couldn't see for the image of her sleek, slick body under his.

Damn the woman!

He didn't realize he'd muttered the words aloud until she spun around, one foot on the first step of the porch fronting the McKinney's quarters. A quick step up brought her angry face level with his.

"Don't think I'm any happier about this situation than you, you arrogant bastard. As soon as we hear from Philip, Suzanne and I will be gone from here."

"*If* you hear from him at all."

"Why wouldn't I?" She sucked in a swift breath. "Have you received something back already? A telegram or dispatch?"

The anxiety that rushed in to replace her anger took the rough edge from Andrew's voice.

"No. I would have told you if I had."

Crossing her arms, she tucked her hands inside her elbows. The movement wasn't quite quick enough to hide the sudden tremble in her fingers.

"Why do you doubt my husband will contact me?"

"Word is you haven't heard from him in more than a year."

"I have Victoria McKinney to thank for that bit of gossip, I imagine."

"Is it true?"

She didn't want to answer. He could see pride warring with the inbred reserve she'd always hidden beneath her teasing smile.

"Yes, it's true," she admitted at last.

Despite the contradictory feelings she roused in him, Andrew didn't want to add to her burdens. Yet neither of them could deny the truth.

"A lot can happen in a year in the rough and tumble mining towns of Montana," he said quietly.

She turned away to stare across the treeless plains awash in silvery moonlight. He studied the profile she presented, searching again for the girl he'd once known in this woman's shadowed eyes and sculpted cheekbones. She didn't speak, but the desperation she tried so valiantly to mask ripped at his conscience.

He'd loved her once. Married her despite every dictate of common sense. Risked his life and his honor to slip back through enemy lines and return for her as he'd promised.

Curling a knuckle under her chin, he brought her face around and tipped it to the moonlight. "If he's alive, he'll move heaven and hell to come for you. God knows, I did."

She pulled in another breath, this one soft and fast. A rush of heat warmed the satiny skin under his finger. Without intending to, without even knowing that he did it, Andrew spread his hand and cupped her cheek.

Lord, she was beautiful. Her face was so delicate beneath the heavy coronet of braids. Aching for a touch of that silky hair, he slid his fingers from her cheek to her neck. The fine, damp curls at her nape lit a fire under his skin.

A pulse beat in the side of her neck, hard and fast against his palm. Wide-eyed and still as a startled deer, she stared up at him.

She felt it, too, Andrew realized with a shock. The same throbbing heat, the same remembered pull deep in her loins.

A fierce satisfaction stabbed through him, tempered by the knowledge that what he was about to do was sheer idiocy. He'd lost his head and almost lost his life once because of this woman. He'd be twenty kinds of a fool to fall under her spell again.

Even that stern admonishment didn't stop him. The need to taste her one more time, to see if her lips were as warm and ripe as he remembered spurred him on. Curling his fingers around her nape, he bent his head.

He was so intent on the brush of his lips against hers that Andrew could never afterward determine which came first, Julia's sudden jerk back or the voice that trilled out of the darkness behind him.

"Major Garrett? Is that—? Oh!"

Smothering a curse, he lifted his head. What a perfect time for Lieutenant McKinney's petulant wife to appear on the scene. Before he could take command of the situation, Julia shook free of his hand and stepped to one side.

"Are you back so soon, Victoria?" she inquired coolly.

"*Too* soon, it appears."

The arch reply locked Andrew's jaw. Turning, he pinned the young wife in place with a stern look.

"Perhaps you have something you wish to say to me, Mrs. McKinney?"

Faced with her husband's commander at his most forbidding, the woman clutched her baby's basket to her chest and quailed. "N-no, sir."

"Then may I ask you to be so good as to go inside while I finish my conversation with Mrs. Bonneaux?"

"Yes, of course."

Gathering her skirts, she scurried up the steps. Andrew waited until the door had banged behind her to face the woman who stood rigid as a flagpole on the steps.

"I'm sorry, Julia. I didn't intend—"

"Spare me your apologies," she said with icy disdain. "I don't want to know what you intended. Nor do I *ever* want to feel your hands on me again, Andrew Garrett."

6

The storm Julia expected broke over her head as soon as she'd fetched Suzanne from the next door neighbor's and carried the sleepy little girl up the stairs to the bedroom the two of them shared.

Victoria was waiting for her at the top of the stairs, having deposited her infant son in his cradle. One glance at the younger woman's angry, pinched face spoke volumes. It was obvious the cutting reproof Andrew had delivered outside still rankled. Badly.

Clutching her muslin wrapper around her night-dress with agitated hands, she followed Julia down the hall. "I never expected to be taken to task on the steps of my own home by anyone on this post."

"No?"

Still shaken from those inexplicable seconds on the porch, Julia was in no mood to pander to the woman's ill humor.

"Were I you, Victoria, I should have expected it

at any time. You would be wise to mind your tone and your tongue around your husband's superiors.''

Gasping, the younger woman gripped her wrapper even tighter across her thin chest. "How dare you question my behavior? You, of all people!''

Her outrage woke Suzanne. Stirring, the girl lifted her head from her mother's shoulder. "Mama?''

"Hush, sweetheart. Go back to sleep." Julia directed a warning glance at her hostess. "Mama and Mrs. McKinney are just talking.''

The fuming Victoria was forced to contain her ire while Julia tucked Suzanne into the wood frame bed Private Rafferty had procured from a source he'd declined to identify. The straw ticking rustled as she settled the girl and slowly drew up the sheet.

"Sleep well, *ma petite*.''

Murmuring sleepily, Suzanne curled into a tight ball. Julia stroked her hair, fighting a spurt of pure cowardice. With all her heart, she wished she could shed her clothes, crawl in beside her daughter and draw the sheet up over her head rather than face the angry woman in the hall. In truth, she had no defense against the accusations Victoria would undoubtedly sling at her.

Was she mad, to have stood still and unprotesting while Andrew put his hands on her? Was she the slut Augusta Hottenfelder had called her, to feel her pulse trip when his lips had brushed hers? She was married, for the love of all the saints! She'd sworn to honor Philip with her body and her heart.

Her fingers gripped the coarsely woven linen sheet. A feeling of panic rose in her chest. As much as she tried, she couldn't bring Philip's face into her mind. God help her, she couldn't summon a single one of his features! He'd been gone so long now, almost two years. And even before he left...

She closed her eyes, hating herself, hating the fact that she'd become more a mother than a wife to the charming riverboat gambler-turned-Confederate-naval-officer who'd soothed her aching heart during those long months in Natchez, where her uncle had sent her to stay to avoid the shame of having her name linked to that of a Union spy.

Philip had looked so dashing in his uniform, and loved her so tenderly. She'd come to love him, too. Not with the passion Andrew had stirred in her, perhaps, but with her whole, bruised heart. At least during those first years, when the demands of his war duties had kept him from the gaming tables that were his downfall.

And now...

Now, Julia had to struggle to recall his face. Another man, another set of lean, rugged features blocked her husband from her mind. Consigning Andrew Garrett to the hottest fires of hell, she loosed her grip on the sheet and smoothed it over her sleeping daughter.

Victoria was pacing the hall when she emerged from the bedroom and firmly shut the door behind her. The lieutenant's wife had used her few minutes alone to work herself into a righteous rage.

"I won't have you playing the harlot in my house, Mrs. Bonneaux. With Major Garrett or anyone else."

Julia folded her arms, saying nothing while Victoria vented her spleen.

"The major may outrank my husband in army matters, but not in matters of common decency. I won't have it, I tell you."

Her uncanny echo of Augusta Hottenfelder raised a bubble of hysterical laughter in Julia's throat. What was it about her that brought out the shrew in women like Victoria and Augusta? She was too proud, she acknowledged ruefully, and her chin had a tendency to lift too quickly, the way it now did.

"My conduct does not concern you, Victoria."

"It does while you reside in this house!"

The temper Julia had worked so hard to keep in check around Victoria finally slipped its leash. "Then perhaps it's best if my daughter and I don't reside here any longer."

"Perhaps it is!"

"I shall make other arrangements as soon possible."

"See that you do."

With a flip of her wrapper, the angry wife spun around and sailed down the hall to her own room.

Julia stared after her, trying to feel repentant, but the only emotion she could summon was anger. And disgust. She couldn't blame anyone but herself for those few moments on the porch that had brought her to this pass. Herself...and Andrew Garrett.

Damn him!

Dressed in her cherry-striped silk, Julia walked the short distance to the headquarters building after the buglers sounded stable call the next morning. She'd learned enough about life at a cavalry post by now to know Andrew would be at the stables, ensuring the junior officers and senior sergeants in his company set their men to work grooming their horses properly.

Lifting her skirts, she mounted the front stairs to Old Bedlam and made her way along the veranda to the commander's offices. With a brilliant smile for the orderly on duty, she asked if Colonel Cavanaugh was in.

"He's in, ma'am, but, well, uh..." The private looked for help to the corporal who'd jumped to his feet at her entrance.

"My regrets, Mrs. Bonneaux," Gottlieb offered in his heavy German accent. "The Colonel, he is ill."

Her heart sinking, Julia nodded. "Would you be so kind as to send me a note when he's well enough to see me? I would like to speak with him as soon as possible."

The corporal's heels clicked. "It would be my pleasure, ma'am."

"Thank you."

She'd turned to leave when the rattle of the inner door stayed her. The colonel slumped against the jamb, his uniform jacket buttoned all askew and his shirttail hanging down one side of his trousers. Peering at her through red-rimmed eyes, he essayed a crooked smile.

"I thought I h'rd you."

His speech was so slurred Julia barely understood him. Startled, she wondered if the man was drunk.

"Did y'wan to see me?"

"Yes, but—"

"C'm in, then, c'm in."

He lurched back into his office, tugging at the hem of his uniform jacket to straighten it. Hesitant, Julia glanced at the corporal.

"It's his medicine," the embarrassed trooper explained. "He feels the wound in his shoulder. He must take laudanum, you understand, to dull the pain."

The sticky-sweet odor that greeted Julia when she entered the colonel's office wasn't unfamiliar to her. Physicians prescribed the opium-based medicinal to men and women alike to ease everything from toothaches to the pains of childbirth. Julia herself had a bottle tucked in her trunk for emergencies.

Leaning crookedly against his desk, the colonel invited her to be seated. "Wha c'n—?" He licked his lips and started over again. "What can I do for you, Mrs. B'neaux?"

"I came to beg a favor, Colonel Cavanaugh."

Waving a limp-wristed hand, he signaled her to continue.

"I should like you to put me on the rolls."

"On the rolls?"

"As a laundress."

His jaw sagged. "A laundress? You?"

Julia rushed on before he could voice the denial she saw forming on his face.

"Last night at the hop Private Rafferty informed me that the husband of one of laundresses in his company recently finished his enlistment. He and his wife returned East, leaving a position open. I should like to apply for it."

"You can't be serious!"

"Indeed I am. I'm not unaccustomed to hard work, I assure you. After the war, I found myself in the same situation as many of my fellow Southerners."

Resolutely, she shoved aside the memories of the house in Mobile she'd closed off room by room. War had taken its toll on the Robichaud Steamship Lines. Philip's hopeless attempts at the gaming tables to recoup the fortune Julia had brought him had steadily stripped his family of all but a few, cherished possessions. Those she'd sold to pay for her journey west.

"I cooked and cleaned and scrubbed in those hard days after the war, colonel. I can certainly do so now."

"But—" He shook his head in a muddled attempt to take in her astounding request. "But you're a lady...."

"Ladies must eat, sir. As I'm temporarily without

means to provide for myself and my daughter, I would like a chance to earn some funds.''

"D'you mean to tell me Major Garrett's not providing for you? That demmed dog! I'll speak to him at once.''

"No!''

"Gottlieb!'' Roaring for the orderly, the colonel lurched toward the door. "Gottlieb, send a runner to—''

"No, please!''

Swiftly, Julia rose and stepped in front of him.

"Major Garrett has sent rations, but I don't— That is, I'm not—''

Thoroughly confused, the colonel blinked owlishly. "Not what?''

"Neither my daughter nor I have any claim on the major. Nor do we wish to be beholden to him.''

Particularly after last night. Julia cringed whenever she remembered how she'd stood there like a witless fool, her heart hammering in her chest, while her skin flamed under his fingers.

The past months may have stripped away her pride. She wouldn't strip away her honor. She had to be shed of Andrew Garrett, had to put him out of her mind and herself out of his reach.

"I'm willing to work for my keep, Colonel. Please, give me this chance.''

He stared at her with wide, dilated eyes. Slowly, the confusion gave way to a look Julia couldn't quite interpret. It was glee, perhaps, or enjoyment at some private joke only he was privy to.

"I wonder what Garrett will say to this," he muttered.

Her chin tipped. "I neither know nor care."

A malicious light crept into his eyes. His gaze lingered on her face for several moments, then dropped to her bosom. Julia didn't like the smile that drew back his cracked lips.

"There are other ways a woman can earn her keep, m'dear."

"So I understand," she said coldly. "Will you put me on the rolls or not, sir?"

"It's the company commander's right to appoint laundresses for his troop."

Julia's heart sank. The vacancy Rafferty had mentioned was in Company A, part of Andrew's regiment.

"In this instance," Cavanaugh said with a gleeful smile, "I might just pull rank."

The burly Private Rafferty was once again pressed into duty, this time to carry Julia's trunk to the laundresses' quarters. He spent the entire walk across the post regretting his artless confidence and earnestly urging Julia not to be so rash.

"I niver should have flapped me jaw about Dietrich and his wife a'goin' back to Pennsylvania," he moaned. "The major will have me head, and that's a fact."

Ignoring his wails, Julia clutched Suzanne's hand and picked her way along the bank of the Laramie to the quarters set aside for the laundresses and their families.

"Please, missus," Rafferty begged as they approached the squat, brick and plank buildings. "I wish you'd think about this again. Suds Row is no place for a lady."

Although her step didn't falter, Julia suffered a distinct qualm at her first close-up view of her quarters. Each building housed four apartments. These boasted only rough plank floors and a single room partitioned in half. A cast-iron stove served to heat both rooms in winter, but inhabitants shared a communal kitchen. It was set not far from the privies, which stank in the hot June sun.

The laundresses were already at their tubs, placed near the shallows of the river. Their lively chatter rose above the slap of wet uniforms against washboards and the general din surrounding them. Babies crawled, toddlers squalled and children shrieked and splashed in the river. Yipping dogs barked at their heels, while a lone cow mooed disconsolately from the yard.

Julia's arrival created a stir in their tight-knit community. One by one, the laundresses ceased their labors. Curious glances came her way. The chatter died. And when Private Rafferty hauled her trunk inside the empty set of quarters, fifteen or so pairs of eyes widened.

One of the laundresses detached herself from the rest. Frowning, Mary Donovan wove her way up the sloping bank. Her wet blouse clung to her generous bosom. Sweat and steam from the fires that heated the wash water had fizzed her strawberry hair.

"What's this? Why's that great gawk carryin' yer trunk into the Dietrichs' old place?"

"I'm moving in."

"Niver say so!"

"Yes, it's true. I'm joining your ranks."

"Glory be, you cannot! You're a leddy, right and proper."

"You said yourself a woman does what she must to survive."

"But—but Mrs. Lieutenant McKinney," Mary sputtered. "The major—"

"Mrs. McKinney and I decided it would be best if I moved out, and where I choose to work has nothing to do with the major."

"You're daft as two ducks if you think that," the older woman replied bluntly, planting her fists on her hips. "Major Garrett will be down here sure as thunder when he hears of this foolishness. He won't have you livin' with the likes of us."

Julia answered through gritted teeth. "The major has no say in the matter."

"Holy Mary, mither o'God, you can believe he does!"

When no answer to that was forthcoming, the laundress shoved her orangey hair off her forehead with an impatient hand.

"Listen to me, dearie. You don't belong here. The washin' and wringin' will break your back, don't y'know? You'll be so tired at nights you'll want to weep. You'll bake red as a brick under the summer sun and get chilblains on yer chilblains from hackin' through the ice on the river come winter...should you last so long."

"I'll last as long as I have to!"

Her vehemence took Mary aback. Deliberately, Julia changed the direction of the conversation.

"Will you be so kind as to direct me to the quartermaster's storehouse? Private Rafferty says I may obtain a tub and soap and other supplies on credit until I get paid."

"You're serious, then?"

"I am."

"I can't talk you out of this?"

"No."

Throwing up her hands, Mary conceded. "All right, then. Come with me and I'll show you about. But don't be too eager to run up a chit at the quartermaster's store. The major'll be wantin' a word or two with you first, I'm thinkin'."

The major wanted more than a word or two.

As Mary had predicted, he came galloping up to Suds Row less than an hour later. The dogs set up a din, echoed by the children who pranced along behind the massive chestnut charger.

Julia was sweeping out the dust that had accumulated on the planked flooring when she heard the tumult. Her heart knocking against her ribs, she lifted a hand to shade her eyes. She needed only a glance to identify the rider.

Hands suddenly clammy, she went indoors, put aside the broom and swiped her palms down the heavy cotton work skirt she'd donned to set her temporary home in order.

"Go outside and play, Suzanne."

"I don't want to, Mama." Her dainty, fastidious daughter wrinkled her nose. "I don't know any of those girls and—and they're not even wearing shoes."

"Then you should take yours off, too, and wiggle your toes in the water."

"Mama!"

A voice rang out above the rumble of hooves outside. "Where is she, Mrs. Donovan?"

"In number three, sir."

"Put your doll down and go outside, Suzanne."

"But—"

Julia caught the jingle of a bridle, followed by the hard stomp of boots.

"Now, if you please," she commanded.

Her lower lip protruding, Suzanne pushed off the bed Rafferty had set up for them and crossed to the door. A shadow fell across it, stopping her in her tracks. For a moment, the soldier and the youngster took each other's measure.

"You're the man who laid on top of my mama on the stairs," the girl announced in a clear, ringing voice that carried to everyone within listening distance.

"Suzanne!"

Ignoring Julia's anguished scold, the girl glared up at their visitor.

"I'm Major Garrett," he replied, returning her look calmly. "I once knew your mama very well."

"I don't like you."

"That's enough, Suzanne! Go outside at once."

The girl stomped out, leaving her mother prey to embarrassment and irritation.

"You're wise to send her out," Andrew commented coldly. "What I have to say to you is not for a child's ears."

"Say it, then, and get back to your troops. I have work to do."

"The only work you have right now is to pack your things and get back to the McKinney house."

"Victoria prefers that I reside elsewhere. So do I."

"Well, you're not residing here."

"That's not your decision to make."

"The hell it isn't."

"Colonel Cavanaugh has agreed to put me on the rolls as a laundress. I'm here on his authority."

"Then he's guzzled even more opium than usual." Stripping off his buff-colored gauntlets, Andrew slapped them against his thigh. "This is no place for you."

"At the risk of repeating myself, that's not your decision to make."

"The Belle of New Orleans won't last a day at the tubs."

The scathing prediction breathed fire into Julia's faltering determination. Her secret dismay at the sparseness of her new quarters went up in a puff of smoke.

"Perhaps I won't last a day," she snapped. "And perhaps you'll discover I'm not the same silly, simpering fool I was six years ago."

He stalked across the room, anger in every line of his long, lean body. "Dammit, Julia, I won't permit this."

"I don't need your permission. It's done. Now go away and leave me in peace."

He towered over her, so close she breathed in the scent of sun and horse and leather that came with him.

"Are you so desperate for money?" he growled. "There are other ways to earn it."

"So the colonel informed me. I won't whore for you, Andrew."

His eyes narrowed dangerously. "I don't recall asking you to."

"What was last night," she threw at him, "if not an invitation to sin?"

The gauntlets slapped against his thigh again, once, twice, each report cracking in the charged silence.

"It was a kiss," he ground out. "Nothing more."

But it could have been more. So much more.

Her stomach twisting, Julia knew he recognized that humiliating fact as well as she did. He must have sensed how close she'd come to lifting her mouth to his. How her traitorous body had tingled, and a desire she'd thought long dead had stirred to life. Only for an instant. A second, perhaps two.

She couldn't allow that spark to burst into flame again. She *wouldn't!* The last time she'd let it blaze through her, the resulting conflagration had consumed her illusions and destroyed her youth. This time, she sensed with every instinct she possessed, the fires would destroy her.

As if reading her mind, he backed away a step or two. He had no more desire to be burned again than she, Julia realized.

"When I mentioned earning money," he said gruffly, "I was speaking of the hospital. Henry Schnell could use another matron."

"I don't know anything of nursing. Although you don't choose to believe it of the *Belle of New Orleans,* I have learned how to scrub."

His gloves hit his trousers again. "Have you always possessed this stubborn streak, Julia?"

"Always." A little pain formed just under her breastbone. "You simply never knew me well enough to recognize it."

7

Life on Suds Row proved as arduous as Mary Donovan had predicted.

Julia soon learned that boiling batches of uniforms, long johns and socks in huge black kettles and lifting them out with a heavy wooden paddle required every bit of her strength. Bending over a washtub filled with cooler water to soap, scrub and wring the items out demanded even more.

Added to that was the chore of hauling buckets of water from the river to keep both the pot and the tubs full. Thankfully, prisoner details supplied precious wood from the fort's store to keep the fires burning, but the coarse lye soap stung Julia's eyes and burned her hands. Heat from the fires and the blazing sun drenched her in sweat, which seemed to attract the plague of mosquitoes that swarmed the riverbanks in early morning and late afternoon.

After the first day, she could barely drag herself back to her quarters at sundown, fix dinner for herself and Suzanne, and fall like a sack of loose bones into bed.

After the second, she seriously considered accepting Maria Schnell's repeated invitations for Julia and Suzanne to stay with the surgeon and his wife. Only Andrew's curt disclosure that the kindhearted Schnells almost beggared themselves to augment the Fort Laramie's medical supplies kept her from slinking back to Officers' Row.

That, and the grim news the major brought her the third day of her residence. He was riding a sleek bay instead of the chestnut this time, and wore what Julia now recognized as his informal dress uniform. The light-blue pants with the yellow cavalry stripe down the outside of the legs were reinforced with canvas at the thigh to protect him against long hours in the saddle. He'd unbuttoned the top few buttons of his darker-blue shirt to allow for the heat and knotted a yellow kerchief loosely around his neck. His slouch hat was a dull tan instead of the corded and tasseled dark-blue campaign hat. He looked, Julia thought with a thump in her chest, whipcord lean and leather tough.

Looping the bay's reins over the hitching post in front of the row quarters, he made his way down the bank to the tubs. The laundresses' ribald discussion of the dimensions of a certain private's prodigious member stilled. Julia, whose cheeks had already flushed with the heat and the women's frank commentary, warmed even more as a series of snickers and nudges circled the tubs.

"'Tis the major, coom t'see his lady."

"*Ja,* he's randy as a goat for her."

"They was sparkin' on the McKinney's front porch the night o'the hop."

The tittering comments carried to Julia's ears but not, she prayed, to Andrew's. Cheeks burning, she tossed the uniform she'd just ladled out of the kettle into her tub and laid aside the paddle.

"He near diddled her on the stairs, I heared."

"I wouldn't mind if a man like that tried to diddle *me.*"

"Will y'hush now!"

With a slap of a wet uniform against her washboard, Mary Donovan stilled the gossip. But she, like the rest of the women, fixed her gaze on the major as he made his way down to the bank and stopped before Julia.

"May I have a word with you?"

Scrubbing her hands down her skirt front, she nodded.

The circle of curious faces all around her prompted Andrew to suggest they walk along the riverbank. She hesitated before reluctantly acceding to his request.

"Mary, Suzanne's playing with the other girls in the yard. Would you keep an eye on her?"

"That I will, missus."

With Julia leading, they followed the bend of the river for fifty yards or so, until the flats gave way to a little eddy pool dotted by yellow crowfoot. Rooted deep in the mud, the aquatic buttercups poked their bright-yellow heads above the rippling water. Faint echoes of the busy post drifted along the river, but here in this nook of the bank they were cut off from curious eyes.

Andrew frowned at the buttercups while he tried to decide how best to break his news. Her appearance kept getting in the way of his decision. He'd never seen her in anything but silks and fine muslins before. This woman looked nothing like the Julia Bonneaux he'd come so close to kissing a few nights ago, even less like the Julia Robichaud he'd known in New Orleans.

Damp tendrils of black hair escaped her braid and straggled about her neck and face. Her heavy work skirt and the canvas apron wrapped around her waist seemed to weigh her down, but it was her calico short-gown that riveted Andrew's gaze. The blouse fit loosely over her waist and hips and tied modestly well above her bosom. It might even have disguised her slender curves completely if wash water hadn't drenched the damned thing.

The tantalizing sight of her breasts outlined in precise detail by sopping pink calico distracted Andrew so much he almost forgot what had brought him to Suds Row.

"You wanted to speak with me?" Julia prompted.

"The telegraph lines are back up."

She shoved her hands in her apron pockets. The

skin across her cheekbones stretched tight, as though she was afraid to hope for good news.

"Have you heard from the commander at Fort Smith?"

"I have. He sent your letter on to Adler's Gulch."

She searched his eyes. "You don't sound hopeful Philip will receive it any time soon."

"The odds aren't good, Julia. Especially now. Chief Red Cloud's called a meeting of the Ogalalla and Brulé bands of the northern Sioux."

The name meant nothing to her, he saw. She was too new to Wyoming to understand the hatreds that had piled up between the Sioux and the sweeping tide of white immigrants these past twenty years.

"Red Cloud has sworn to stop the wagons that keep pushing north to the gold and silver fields in Montana," Andrew explained. "He ambushed and massacred eighty troops in December. So far this spring, he's harassed every wagon and freight train that's tried to make it through."

He hesitated, searching for a way to soften what came next. There wasn't one.

"When the telegraph lines went back up, we received a report that a band of his men attacked the company you'd traveled with."

"Dear Lord!"

"The only casualties were two oxen," he assured her. "The train made it as far Fort Phil Kearny and has holed up there."

His calm assurance didn't lessen her shock any

more than it had lessened his own. Julia and Suzanne might well have been among the women and children who huddled in terror in the wagon beds. The idea of an arrow piercing her soft flesh had formed a pool of sweat at the base of Andrew's spine.

"I'm taking two companies out tomorrow morning to try to intercept Spotted Tail, chief of the Brulé band. General Sherman has empowered us to offer him and the rest of the northern Sioux certain concessions if they'd agree to come and negotiate for peace."

Of all the personnel at Fort Laramie, only Andrew and the angry Colonel Cavanaugh were privy to the contents of the dispatch they'd received from departmental headquarters that morning. Cavanaugh had ranted for almost half an hour, incensed by the preposterous notion that the Army would actually burn the forts it had established along the Bozeman Trail, as Red Cloud insisted. He couldn't believe the government would even contemplate withdrawing troops from the vast stretch of territory between Fort Laramie and the gold fields of Montana, leaving it to the Sioux.

Andrew grasped the politics of concession even if his superior didn't. Two significant events would soon eclipse the Bozeman Trail as the quickest route to the Montana mines. A new steamboat landing had just been constructed at Fort Benton, high up the Missouri River. From there, it was a relatively short trek south to the Montana mines.

Even more important, the Union Pacific was pushing relentlessly across the plains. The rail crews had reached Wyoming only two months ago. A whole new city called Cheyenne was now springing up at the railhead, a hundred miles south. When the railroad finally made it to Utah, where it would connect with the track being laid from California, stage and freight lines could then head directly north to Montana instead of trekking across the northern plains, right through the heart of Sioux country.

The completion of the transcontinental railroad could become a reality as soon as next year...if the angry Sioux would stop harassing the rail crews and tearing up the tracks as soon as they were laid.

In exchange for their agreement to cease hostilities, the United States government was prepared to cede all claims to the northern hunting lands they'd roamed for centuries. The task of getting the Sioux to come in and negotiate the specific terms now fell to the 2nd Cavalry.

Although she might not understand the intricacies of the proposed negotiations, Julia had picked up enough post gossip to identify at least one of the key players.

"I've heard this Chief Spotted Tail's name mentioned."

"I'm not surprised. He's visited Fort Laramie often. The last time was last spring, to bury his daughter."

"I've heard of her, too. Isn't her coffin the one set on a high scaffold in the post cemetery?"

"Yes," Andrew replied quietly, "that's Ah-ho-appa."

"Ah-ho-appa?"

"It translates loosely to Yellow Buckskin Girl."

"Did you know her?"

Thinking of the slender, bright-eyed maiden in supple buckskin who'd delighted in the fancy dress parades and parties at Old Bedlam, Andrew nodded.

"Yes, I knew her."

Julia eyed him curiously, as if sensing there was more to his reply than he wished to communicate.

"Do you think her father will listen to you?"

"I can only hope so. We'll be gone two, possibly three weeks. I've instructed Corporal Gottlieb to deliver any telegraphs that come in concerning you or your husband during my absence."

"Thank you."

He'd said what he'd come to say. He should leave. Andrew was damned if he knew what held him there. The way the sunlight sparkling off the Laramie brought out the blue-black glints in her hair, maybe. Or the tired shadows under her amethyst eyes.

"I wish you would reconsider and move back in with Victoria McKinney while I'm gone."

"I prefer the company of Mary Donovan."

"Julia, for pity's sake, think of your daughter if not yourself."

She turned away, hugging her arms tight around

her waist. Her gaze fastened on the buttercups stick-ing out of the water like tiny yellow totem poles.

"I *am* thinking of Suzanne," she said at last, her voice low and strained. "I must have some means of providing for her if Philip isn't... If he doesn't..."

Andrew bit back the answer that rose to his lips. Julia wouldn't have to worry about providing for Su-zanne if Philip Bonneaux was dead. Any of the two hundred men on post would jump at the chance to take such a young, beautiful widow as his wife.

The truth was, most of them wouldn't care whether she was widowed or not. Such matters tended to be-come blurred out here, where men and women formed the partnerships needed to survive. Andrew knew of more than one female who'd set up housekeeping with two or more troopers.

The idea that Julia might enter into such an ar-rangement sent a shaft of primitive possessiveness lancing though him. If she went to anyone's bed, he thought savagely, it would be his.

He took a step toward her, driven by an instinctive need to stake his claim. Just in time, he remembered her scathing comment that she never wanted to feel his hands on her again. He curled his fists inside the buff leather gauntlets. All he could do was offer the same comfort he had the night of the hop.

"If Bonneaux's alive, he'll come for you."

"If he's alive," she echoed hollowly.

Dammit, there were a hundred tasks and fifty men waiting for him. He needed to see that the troops had turned out to prepare their mounts and equipment for the march. He had to ready his own gear, and ensure his striker got Jupiter to the farrier to be reshod as well. Yet the thought of leaving Julia alone there beside the river carved a hole in his belly.

"I've tasked my striker to check on you while I'm gone," he said gruffly. "His name's O'Shea. Let him know if you need anything. Anything, do you understand?"

At her nod, he started back along the bank. "I'll see you in a few weeks."

"Andrew!"

"Yes?"

"Be—be careful."

"I will." He tipped two fingers to the brim of his hat. "Bring Suzanne to watch the troop leave tomorrow. It's a brave sight. A lot braver," he added with a quick, slashing grin, "than when we come back in, dusty and saddle sore."

Suzanne and Julia weren't the only ones who turned out to watch the platoon depart. The entire population of the fort gathered on the parade ground in front of the barracks, as well as most of the residents of the tents and tipis across the river. The event soon took on almost a festive air, as if to disguise the fact that some of the men preparing to ride away from Fort Laramie that morning might not ride back.

Mary Donovan came with six of her seven children to see her husband off. Huffing from her trek up from

Suds Row, she advised Julia that the post had seen a flurry of activity all night. In less than twenty-four hours, company farriers had reshod fifty or so mounts as well as the mules hauling the ambulance and supply wagons. The hospital steward had packed a chest of medical supplies. Quartermaster personnel had issued two weeks' rations and ammunition to each man. Sergeant majors had inspected their men's mess kits, field packs and equipment. Troopers had stashed their personal belongings in their footlockers, written hurried letters to their loved ones and oiled their saddles and tack a final time.

The sun was just beginning to raise trickles of sweat on the necks of those waiting when the bugles sounded boots and saddles. Almost immediately, a group of Indian wives dressed in calico and beautifully beaded jewelry began an answering chant. The watching crowd stirred in anticipation. Dogs barked and yipped. Children raced back and forth. Even the usually prissy Suzanne joined a group of barefoot excited youngsters that included the offspring of officers, troopers, civilians and the Sioux, Cheyenne and Arapaho families who made their homes across the river.

Another round of bugle calls brought the platoon from the stables behind the barracks. With bridles jingling and hooves thudding on the beaten earth, the squads assembled into a column of fours. First, the scouts in buckskin breeches, blue cavalry shirts and wide-brimmed hats decorated with feathers and snakeskin bands. Then the drummers and trumpeters, followed by fifty mounted troops led by their officers. The wagons rolled along behind the troops.

"They're going' out in light marchin' order," the knowledgeable Mary informed Julia. "They're only carryin' a little more'n a hundred pounds o'gear apiece. The major likes to move fast, he does."

To Julia's untrained eye, it didn't look as though these men were going out light. Each trooper had rolled spare clothes, an India rubber poncho, a blanket and a half tent at the front of his saddle. A forage sack with extra oats was lashed at the back. They rested atop bulging black leather saddlebags. Currycombs and horseshoe pouches hung from saddle straps, as did water canteens, mugs, coffeepots and skillets.

The troopers themselves presented a formidable appearance. Each was armed with a revolver, crossed ammunition belts and a long hunting knife, in addition to carbines in broad leather slings. Eyes shaded by broad-brimmed slouch hats, they rode erect and alert behind their officers and flag bearers.

The company pennants fluttered bravely in the breeze. Handkerchiefs waved in farewell. Wives called out to their husbands in a chorus of English, Gaelic, German, Norwegian and Sioux. Children and barking dogs raced alongside the column. As the troops trotted past, Andrew issued a command and the regimental band struck up a lively air.

"Oooch, it's me favorite," Mary exclaimed. Toes

tapping, hands clapping, she hummed along with the music.

> I'm lonesome since I crossed the hill,
> And o'er the moor and valley
> Such heavy thoughts my heart do fill,
> Since parting with m'Sally.

> I seek for one as fair and gay,
> But find none to remind me
> How sweet the hours I passed away,
> With the girl I left behind me.

One by one, the women picked up the chorus of the popular folk tune entitled, appropriately Julia thought, "The Girl I Left Behind Me." Suddenly, a clear, male tenor soared out above the tramping hooves and jingling bridles.

> Now I'm bound for Brighton camp
> Kind heav'n then pray guide me
> And send me safely back again,
> To the girl I left behind me.

Goose bumps raised on Julia's arms. Without quite knowing how it had happened, she found herself swept up in the emotion of the moment. Her heart thumping, she stood amid the other women, a good number of whom were now daubing at their eyes with their handkerchiefs. For a moment they were all sisters, each watching, each worrying, each wondering if the men riding out would come back to them. Julia sought out Andrew's erect figure. Without conscious thought, she murmured a brief, fervent prayer for his safe return.

No one moved until the column had climbed the sloping incline that led to the bluffs. The lilting strains faded on the morning air. Disturbed by the lump that had formed just under her breast, Julia lifted her skirts with one hand and looked around for her daughter. Her light brown ringlets were nowhere to be seen.

"Do you see Suzanne?" she asked Mary.

Rising up on tiptoe, the sergeant's wife peered around. "There she is."

Julia followed her pointing arm to the two girls standing in the shade of one of the barracks' buildings. A wary Suzanne held her precious doll close to her chest while a dark-haired sprite in a fringed buckskin shirt and calico skirt reached out a tentative finger to trace its porcelain features.

"Do you know that girl with her?"

"Oooch, everyone on post knows Little Hen. She's a sweetheart, don't y'know? She won't lead Suzanne into mischief."

"It's more likely to be the other way around," Julia drawled. "Does Little Hen live here in camp?"

"To be sure, she does. Her father's an Arapaho

scout in Company C. Her mither's a Brulé Sioux by the name of Walks In Moonlight.''

Although unfamiliar with the customs of the native tribes, Julia had somehow formed the impression that the Sioux, Cheyenne and Arapaho didn't intermarry.

"Not usually," Mary confirmed. "I think the story is Lone Eagle stole Walks In Moonlight from her band. She fell in love with him, and begged her father to let her to stay with him. I think she's a cousin or some such to Yellow Buckskin Girl."

"Chief Spotted Tail's daughter?"

"D'you know about her, then?"

"Andrew...Major Garrett...mentioned her name yesterday, when we walked by the river."

"Did he now?"

The odd note in Mary's voice drew a questioning look from Julia. "He said he knew her."

"To be sure he did."

Curious about the woman whose coffin rested on the raised scaffolding in the cemetery, Julia probed for a little more information.

"She was a beauty," Mary confided. "'N proud, too. Whenever her father came to treat with the commander, she'd ride about the post on one of her white ponies, all decked out in beadwork and feathers. Half the troopers were hot for her, me own Donovan included, but she had eyes only for one."

Her sideways glance told Julia exactly who that "one" was.

"She was sickly, though. It was the lung disease that took her, I'm told. Everyone was surprised to hear she wanted to be buried here, at the fort. Her father wrapped her body and put it on a travois. One o'the other of her ponies pulled the little cortege for fifteen days until Spotted Tail and his band reached Fort Laramie. The whole post turned out for the funeral, don't y'know?"

"No," Julia murmured. "I didn't."

"They wrapped her in a white buffalo skin 'n placed her in a pine coffin. The band played a funeral dirge that brought tears to me eyes, I can tell you, when they raised her on the scaffolding."

Her bosom heaving, Mary concluded her tale with a sigh.

"The post chaplain said the words, and her friends left gifts for her to take with her to the next world. Colonel Maynadier, the post commander at the time, presented a pair of leather gauntlets to keep her hands warm on the journey. The major..."

She paused, sending another quick glance toward her companion.

"The major?" Julia echoed.

"The major tucked something wrapped in oilcloth among the rest of the gifts. It disappeared soon after, along with most of the other presents. To this day, no one knows what it was."

An odd, prickly sensation formed in Julia's chest. It took a moment for her to recognize the feeling for what it was. When she did, disgust rippled through her.

She couldn't be jealous of a dead woman. She had no right to be jealous of *any* woman Andrew might have taken a special liking to over the years...even though he'd thought himself still married to Julia.

Still, she couldn't dismiss an irrational, illogical and quite ridiculous sense of pique as she called to Suzanne and made her way back to Suds Row.

8

As the days passed, Andrew occupied Julia's thoughts more than she wanted to admit—particularly at night.

With Suzanne tucked beside her on the rustling, straw-filled mattress, she lay awake, swatting at mosquitoes while her mind drifted from Andrew to Philip and back again with irritating inconstancy. They were so different, her two husbands, and yet alike in ways that caused Julia more than one twinge of acute discomfort.

Both were handsome rogues. Both had appeared in her life at a time she was particularly vulnerable. Both had deserted her, one to slip back through the Confederate lines to carry vital shipping information to his spymasters in Washington, the other to follow the tide of dreamers who thought to make their fortunes in Montana's gold fields.

Yet for all their seeming similarities, their differences ran bone deep. Philip would stake his fortune—

and the welfare of his wife and daughter—on the next
turn of the cards. Andrew, Julia was coming to grudg-
ingly admit, took his responsibilities very seriously.
He'd displayed more concern for her and Suzanne in
the short time they'd been at Fort Laramie than Philip
had in years. Wishing she could empty her thoughts
of both men, Julia tossed and turned and thumped the
straw-stuffed pillow in irritation.

Thankfully, her work kept her too busy during the
day to fret. She bent over the washtubs most mornings, but with half the company absent she found time
in the afternoons to add a few feminine touches to
her stark living quarters. Mary Donvan helped with
both advice and an extra pair of hands. Maria Schnell
came as well, bringing with her a length of cheerful,
green-checked gingham for curtains.

Much to Julia's surprise, Little Hen's mother also
appeared with a welcome gift late one summer evening. A tall, slender woman with the lustrous black
eyes and thick braids of her people, she wore an exquisitely beaded and fringed buckskin shirt belted
over her blue calico skirt. As reserved and quiet as
the daughter who tagged at her heels, Walks In Moonlight declined all offers of refreshments.

"I came only to bring you this." With a shy smile,
she passed Julia a thick bundle. "It is the same in
army quarters as in a tipi. A woman has few places
to store things."

Unfolded, the bundle proved to be a fringed calfskin pouch. Porcupine quills and thousands of the tiny

Italian glass beads carried to the plains by traders had been worked into a stunning pattern of red, white and green.

"I can't take this," Julia protested, awed by the artisanship. "It's far too fine."

"It is a gift," Walks In Moonlight replied with simple dignity. "One I have made with my own hands, to thank the mother of Suz-anne for inviting Little Hen into her home."

"Little Hen is welcome any time."

"Not all would say this."

No, Julia was forced to admit silently, they wouldn't. She'd resided at the fort long enough to know most of the whites shared Colonel Cavanaugh's dislike of the Indians. Too many troopers had lost friends, too many wives had worried and wept as husbands rode off to relieve garrisons under attack or to seek retribution for a raid.

Even those Indians considered nonhostile often were treated with contempt. Many of those who lived across the river had camped at the post so long they'd become known as the Laramie Loafers. Descendents or relatives of the scouts and interpreters employed by the Army, they made a precarious living by running errands for the troopers, hunting game, selling pelts to the sutler or, as Maria Schnell had explained to Julia, offering services no decent woman should talk about.

The Loafers were despised by their Sioux brethren on the plains, who'd rather war to the death than live on the white man's bounty. Likewise, they were scorned by the Crow and Arapaho scouts, traditional enemies of the Sioux. Julia could only imagine how difficult it must be for a proud Brulé Sioux like Walks In Moonlight to live among the dregs of her tribe and the enemies of her people.

She must love the warrior who stole her from her band very much, Julia thought, suppressing a twinge of envy for the calm serenity in the woman's face.

"Thank you for the gift. As you said, there's next to no storage in these quarters. I can certainly make good use of this pouch."

"You are welcome."

Julia was tempted to ask her about her cousin, Yellow Buckskin Girl, but Walks In Moonlight left before she could decide how to introduce the topic.

This one was different, the Sioux thought as she made her way along the row of houses. This Julia Bon-neaux looked out at the world with eyes as yet undimmed by the tears and grief that came to so many women—white and red—whose lives were inextricably bound with those of the horse soldiers.

And yet, if the rumors were true, Suz-anne's mother had once been the major's woman. Walks In Moonlight had heard the gossip. The residents of the tipis across the river enjoyed a juicy tale as much as the residents of the post. Although she knew each woman must find her own way, Walks In Moonlight couldn't imagine leaving the major's bed for another's. He had a brave heart, a true heart. Lone Eagle trusted him, as he did few others.

At the thought of her husband, so fierce, so proud, a smile feathered her heart. How she'd fought him! Those first weeks and months after he'd stolen her in a raid on her village, she'd clawed his face, left teeth marks on his neck and arms, called down every curse she knew on his head. Once, she'd snatched away his hunting knife and had come within an inch of disemboweling him.

He'd kept her, despite the urging of his band to let the wild one go. Despite the scratches and teeth marks. Despite the threat of savage retribution by her uncle, Spotted Tail. Lone Eagle had ridden out alone to meet Spotted Tail and returned bloodied and battered. But he'd paid the outrageous bride price Walks In Moonlight had insisted was her worth, and he'd kept her.

From that day on, she'd shared his bed. For him, she'd forsaken her own band. For him, she lived here, in the shadow of the white man's fort, and endured the small indignities that came her way every day. Like the stares and muttered comments that marked her progress.

Head high, face expressionless, she tucked her daughter's hand firmly in hers and made her way to her tipi.

Women weren't the only visitors Julia received during her first weeks on Suds Row.

Private Rafferty showed up at regular intervals, as did Andrew's striker, a short, wiry private with coal black hair and a pugnacious chin. Bowery-born and a New Yorker to the soles of his boots, Private O'Shea's bristling air made Suzanne nervous at first. He overcame her timidity by presenting her with a gift that almost displaced her precious doll in her affections—a squiggly little prairie dog pup. With Julia's reluctant permission, the striker hunkered down on his heels and held out the shoebox he'd lined with bits of wool from the scratchy army-issue blankets.

"One of the horses stomped on the mother during drill this morning," he told the wide-eyed five-year-old. "This little one was squeaking fit to beat the band. Mind you keep it away from the dogs outside. They'll make a treat of it."

"I will," the girl promised solemnly as she took the box he handed her. She poked a tentative finger at the furry creature, squealing when it wrapped its tiny paws around the tip.

"I'm going to call her Daisy," she announced.

"But we don't know it's a her, darling."

"It doesn't matter. She's the same color as the inside of a flower," Suzanne explained earnestly.

"Oh, well. In that case…"

"Can I go show Little Hen, Mama?"

"Yes, of course."

A delighted Suzanne scampered out. Between the pup, the relative freedom she enjoyed on the protected post and the fast friendship she'd formed with Little

Hen, the girl's dislike of her new surroundings was slowly subsiding.

Gradually Julia, too, became more and more absorbed in daily life at Fort Laramie. Since the officers' wives didn't quite know how to receive her, and the other laundresses had yet to fully accept the "lady" in their midst, she occupied a sort of social no-man's-land. Yet sufficient activities occurred on the post that crossed all lines and ranks to keep her busy.

An amateur theatrical group formed by talent drawn from all ranks put on melodramas and minstrel shows that thrilled their audiences. Company teams waged fierce battles on baseball and cricket fields during long summer evenings, cheered on by enthusiastic supporters. Church services were held on Sundays in the post administration building, and once a week a former college professor who'd succumbed to the lure of the West and enlisted as a trooper conducted lectures on botany and butterflies in the library. Hops, formal dress dances and even masked balls often filled the night with music. Julia received numerous invitations, but, remembering the near disaster of her first hop, refused most.

The Fourth of July came and went with a dress parade, a lively band concert, fireworks and a drunken brawl at Coffee's saloon that resulted in one dead trooper, a number of severely injured buffalo skinners and several soiled doves with cuts from flying bottles.

A mounted troop from the post had to be called out to quell riot.

The brawl provided the laundresses with considerable fodder for gossip. In their brutally frank way, they aired both their opinions of the women who serviced the troopers for a dollar a poke and their relief that the boyos found some outlet for their juices. Names like Fat Sarah, One-Eyed Sue and Calamity Jane were bandied back and forth across the washtubs.

Calamity Jane's exploits as Indian scout, buffalo hunter and enterprising prostitute astounded Julia, but she now realized the women on the frontier led lives that would astonish most Easterners. Even the women on the post enjoyed freedoms and responsibilities that were unheard of in the rigid societies they'd come from.

Wives of the businessmen and hoteliers streaming into Wyoming in the wake of the railroaders appeared to value their independence as well. Already there was talk of designating this area as a separate territory, with its capital in the new city of Cheyenne that had sprung up to the south. The delegation that had traveled back East to petition Congress for territorial designation had included among its articles of incorporation the shocking proposal that women in Wyoming be enfranchised with the vote.

Yet Julia didn't really appreciate the differences between the society she'd left and her life on the post until almost two weeks after Andrew had ridden out.

To the shrill delight of everyone on the post, the regimental paymaster arrived. Escorted by a heavily armed patrol, his armored wagon rattled down the hill just before noon.

"It's near on to two months since we were paid," an excited Mary Donovan exclaimed, shooing Julia inside to take off her apron and tidy her hair. "Hurry now, dearie. You'll need to be there when your squad steps up to the line."

"Can we come, Mama?" Suzanne danced at Julia's side, Little Hen trailing a step or two behind. "We can take Daisy, too. See, Little Hen and I made her a collar and a leash out of a scrap of calico."

Smiling at the sight of the pup wiggling at the end of a colorful string, Julia glanced from her daughter to her dark-eyed playmate. As Mary had indicated, Little Hen was a sweetheart. Her glossy black braids hung past her waist, and her shy smiles lit up her round, chubby face. Invariably neat in her beautifully beaded buckskin shirts and calico skirts, she made a perfect companion for Suzanne, who even her doting mama recognized possessed a tendency toward prissiness.

"Best leave them here," Mary advised with a shake of her head. "We'll be standin' in line for hours, waitin' for our pay."

"I'll take you to the sutler's store afterward," Julia promised instead. "You can pick out your own licorice twists or peppermint sticks."

"And a sugar cracker for Daisy?"

"I don't know if prairie dogs like sugar crackers, *ma petite*."

"This one does," Suzanne declared firmly.

"All right, a sugar cracker for Daisy."

With the promise of those delicious treats dancing before their eyes, the girls happily retreated inside the house.

Excitement crackled through the air like summer lightning as Julia hurried to the sun-baked parade ground with Mary. Trooper after trooper had already lined up behind their officers. Seated at a table flanked by guards, the paymaster doled out greenbacks as each man's name was called. The pay of those not present to collect it was either issued to his legal wife if she possessed a signed authorization or locked away in the post strongbox.

As Mary had warned, paying the garrison proved to be a long, time-consuming process. Each private received his basic thirteen dollars a month. To that was added any additional monies for special duties, like hospital steward or company bugler. Then the paymaster had to deduct amounts owed the quarter-master for lost or damaged equipment, new uniforms or extra stores. He also deducted a dollar from each troop's allotted share and four dollars from the offi-cers' to pay their laundress.

When her company had finally been processed, the paymaster called Julia forward and counted her pay into her hand. She moved slowly away from the table, staring down at the stack of bills in her palm.

"Oooch, I know it isn't as much as the others have drawn," Mary said consolingly, "but you've only been at it fer three weeks, don't y'know?"

"Yes, I know."

"Don't feel bad, dearie. That'll cover the supplies you've drawn from the quartermaster and leave a bit left over to buy Suzanne a nice treat at the sutler's."

"I don't feel bad, truly. It's just…well…I've never…"

Mary's shrewd blue eyes filled with understanding. "You've never earned a fistful o'cash by the sweat o'yer brow, is that it?"

"I've never earned *any* amount of cash," Julia admitted, closing her fist around the bills. "My father owned a shipping line and gave me all the pin money I could spend on fripperies and such. Even after he died and my uncle took over, I never lacked for funds."

"Your husband—not the major, your second husband—is he swimming in lard, too?"

Julia hesitated, reluctant to divulge the more embarrassing details of her private life, but Mary had been too kind to simply beg off the question.

"No," she admitted. "Philip isn't wealthy. He was a naval officer when I met him, but he'd made his living as a riverboat gambler before the war. The cards are in his blood, I'm afraid. Since we've been married, he's won and lost fortunes."

Mostly lost, she reflected wryly, and mostly *her* fortune. What little of her inheritance had survived the war and the collapse of the Robichaud Steamship Lines hadn't long survived Philip's runs of bad luck.

"Well, he can't gamble this bit o'cash away," Mary declared cheerfully. "Any more 'n my second husband, damn his soul, could drink it away. The bloody sod beat me black and blue, but I niver did tell him where I hid me stash. That handful of bills is yours, dearie, all yours."

All hers. Satisfaction shot through Julia, swift and surprisingly sweet. Her little roll of bills suddenly made the hours of bending over a washtub worth the backbreaking agony.

Hard on the heels of her satisfaction came a fierce resolve. She could make her way. Whatever happened, she could make her own way. It was a heady realization, and a welcome one after the months of worry, penny watching and, finally, being reduced to depending on the kindness of strangers.

Convent educated, Julia had never questioned that her inheritance, as much as her person, became the property of her husband upon marriage. Like most of the women of her class, she'd been brought up to believe that her primary purpose in life was to provide a gracious, well-run home and a succession of healthy children. The sudden thought that she didn't have to center her existence around an undependable husband was as shocking as it was exciting.

Mary's knowing smile suggested she, too, understood the incredible freedom the little roll of bills represented.

"It's yours," she repeated. "You worked hard for it, and the Army paid you for your labors. Now take your daughter to the sutler's store for her treat. Only do it quick," she warned with a glance at the slanting afternoon sun. "The troopers' pay will be burnin' holes in their pockets, don't y'know. The billiards parlor at the sutler's will be jam-packed, and the saloons and hog ranches will be jumpin'."

With a shake of her head, she issued a cheerful warning.

"You'd best stay home snug and safe tonight, missus. Wouldn't hurt to bar your door, either. The boyos tend to get a bit rowdy on payday. I'm not sayin' any man on this post would do you harm sober, but there's some that get a mite ugly when they've downed more'n a drop or two of the creature."

A little startled by the advice, Julia nevertheless took her at her word. Shoving her stash of bills into her skirt pocket, she hurried back to her quarters to collect Suzanne and Little Hen for the promised treat.

Mary's prediction proved all too true. The buglers had hardly sounded recall from afternoon fatigue duties before the sounds of revelry began to drift from the sprawling tent city across the river. Singing, shouts and the occasional crack of a bull whip carried clearly to Julia and Suzanne, tucked snug within their quarters.

A constant rattle of wagon wheels also announced the arrival of the faro dealers, whiskey peddlers,

bawdy shows and prostitutes who followed the paymaster from post to post. Hoots and whistles greeted
each new arrival, and more than one brawl erupted as
the night progressed. With each passing hour, Julia
understood Mary's dry observation that the guardhouse and hospital would both be filled come morning.

Given the presence of the sentries who marched the
watch on post and the many married men who resided
with their wives and families in Suds Row, the sound
of shuffling feet outside her door didn't unduly alarm
Julia at first.

Only when the footsteps turned and made a second
pass, then a third, did she push herself up on one
elbow. She peered through the darkness at the lighter
square of window behind the green gingham curtains.
Heart hammering, she watched a shadow pass by.

A sharp thud, followed by a muffled curse, brought
a lump to her throat. Whoever had made that noise
wasn't going away. Easing out from under the coarse
top sheet, she slid her legs over the side of the bed.
The rope supports creaked under her weight as she
grabbed her wrapper from the foot of the bed and
pulled it on over her nightdress. Feet bare, she tiptoed
across the plank floor.

Her pulse pounding, she lifted the gingham a mere
inch and peered out. The sight of a fully armed and
ferociously vigilant Private O'Shea marching guard
back and forth in front of her door widened her eyes.

Letting the curtain flutter back into place, Julia

leaned against the wall. When her racing pulse slowed enough for her to catch her breath, she dipped a cup of water from the bucket she'd hauled in earlier and made her way to the door.

Private O'Shea spun around at the sound of the latch lifting and treated her to his habitual fierce glower. "Begging your pardon, missus, I didn't mean to wake you by banging into the bench like that."

"You didn't wake me. Would you like some water?"

"I could use a sip or two," he said gratefully.

The soft July night spilled over Julia as she stood waiting while he downed the water. Laughter and the sound of voices raised in bawdy song almost drowned out the croaking bullfrogs along the riverbanks.

Smiling, Julia took the empty cup he handed her. "I appreciate your standing guard for me tonight, but wouldn't you rather be over across the river?"

"They'll still be peddling their poison tomorrow. I wouldn't feel right leaving you without anyone to watch over you tonight, you being the major's lady and all."

Although she knew by now it was hopeless, Julia made another attempt to explain her tangled relationship with Andrew Garrett.

"I'm not his lady, Private O'Shea. We were married once, but no longer."

His careless shrug told her the past didn't matter, but the major's orders to keep an eye on her most certainly did.

Idly, Julia fingered the dented tin cup. She should go inside. The woman she used to be would never have dreamed of standing outside in her wrapper and bare feet, carrying on a conversation to the sounds of drunken revelry. Strangely, she didn't miss that woman at all.

"Have you heard anything from him?"

"From the major? No, ma'am."

Biting down on her lower lip, Julia gazed at the vast, shadowed plains beyond the post. Bathed in moonlight, the land seemed to dip and swell like a dark ocean. Andrew was out there. Somewhere.

"You don't need to worry," O'Shea told her confidently. "Major Garrett's no shavetail. If anyone can bring his boys home right and tight, he can."

"You're very loyal," she murmured.

"Loyalty's got nothing to do with it. I've been with the major since Andersonville. I know him better than most."

Startled, Julia swung back to him. "You were in Andersonville? Both of you?"

"Yes, ma'am."

"I—I didn't know."

"It's not something a man generally likes to talk about. I can tell you this, though. I wouldn't have made it out of that hellhole if it weren't for the major. He wouldn't let me give up, wouldn't let none of us give up, though there were times we wanted to."

There was so much she didn't know about Andrew

Garrett, Julia realized with a shock. He'd cloaked his life before New Orleans in lies. Afterward...

Afterward, she'd hated as much as she'd grieved for the spy her uncle had shot down in the street outside the mansion on LaFayette Street.

So much had happened to him since. To both of them. With a prickly sense of unease, Julia acknowledged that the glimpses she was getting into the man Andrew had become were blurring her memories of the man he'd been.

"How long were you at Andersonville?"

"I was marched down with the first batch of prisoners in February of '64," O'Shea said quietly, leaning on his rifle. "The major was brought in that summer. Me and my mates were old, dried skeletons by then. Sergeant Danny Kennedy from the 9th Ohio Cavalry used to say it took seven of us sticks standing together to make a shadow. We'd thought we'd had it rough, but we none of us took the beatings the major did."

He reached up to scratch the back of his head. His forage cap tipped forward to shadow his eyes, but not before Julia caught a glimpse of the fierceness in their depths.

"Rumor went round the major was a spy who escaped the rebs down to New Orleans near the start of the war. Got shot in the hip in the process, they said. He claimed he'd taken a minié ball at Chickamauga. The guards never could break him of that story, though they slammed their rifle butts into him often enough trying.''

"Dear God!"

"Busted his leg twice, they did. Second time, they near shattered his hipbone in the process. Them butchers they called surgeons wanted to lop his leg off to prevent gangrene from setting in, but the major wouldn't let them.''

Julia lifted a trembling hand to her lips. Yesterday she'd felt the most ridiculous dart of jealousy at the thought that Andrew Garrett might have loved a Sioux princess. Tonight she wanted to weep at the knowledge of what he'd suffered. How in heaven's name had she become so quick to emotion where he was concerned?

"He's a good man," O'Shea said, unknowingly echoing Mary Donovan's words of a few days ago. "There isn't a man here on the post who wouldn't follow him straight into hell and back."

A burst of raucous laughter from down at the end of the Suds Row housing brought an end to the private's confidences. Straightening, he listened for a moment.

"Sounds like a few of the fellers might be coming to serenade Short-Legged Sal."

One of the few unmarried laundresses, the recent immigrant with a clubbed foot and an unpronounceable Polish name was the object of intense rivalry among the men.

"You'd better go inside now, missus. I'll just let

these boys know I'm here, so they don't go bothering you and your girl."

"I hate to think of you standing watch all night...."

"The major said to look out for you," O'Shea replied with a shrug of his shoulders. "I'll stand watch till he returns or hell freezes over, whichever comes first."

In the face of such single-minded dedication, Julia could only murmur her thanks.

"And don't be worrying about him," the private advised as she reached for the door latch. "If anyone can find old Spotted Tail, Major Garrett can. He'll deliver his message and bring his boys back all right and tight, you'll see."

Julia fell asleep praying that he was right.

9

"They's out there, major."

Arizona Joe Pardee shifted in his saddle. The former fur-trapper-turned-scout spit a stream of tobacco juice through the blackened stumps of his teeth and surveyed the terrain ahead. Andrew eased the ache in his back by rising up in the stirrups. Lone Eagle sat motionless on his other side, his black eyes narrowed against the glare of the sun that blazed low on the far horizon.

With only a few hours left in the day, suffocating heat still rose in waves from the waving grass. July on the plains was hot enough to broil the troopers in their wool uniforms. Several had already fallen out due to sunstroke and been carted back to the ambulance wagon. Their only relief had been the occasional thunderstorms that boomed across the plains like cannons.

The rumpled foothills of the Black Hills rose in the distance, their slopes covered with the thick pon-

derosa pine and blue spruce that gave them their
name. Close on to fifty miles of undulating terrain lay
between those hills and Andrew's weary column.
Somewhere among those fifty miles of dips and rises
was Spotted Tail's band of Brulé Sioux.

Shooting another stream of tobacco juice at a scur-
rying jackrabbit, Arizona Joe swiped the dribble from
his chin with a buckskin-covered forearm. "Ole Spotted Tail's led us a merry chase, but we'll catch up
with him tomorrow."

"Or he will catch us," Lone Eagle replied with a
twist of his lips.

Andrew swept another glance around the site the
two scouts had recommended for the night's camp.
The slight depression would provide the necessary
cover to keep the men and animals from being silhouetted against the sky. A dry, cracked streambed
meandered along the bottom of the depression. With
luck, they'd find at least a sluggish trickle of water
beneath the dried mud. Both men and mounts needed
water as much as they needed rest.

They'd covered more than twenty miles today. By
trudging along on foot every third hour to spare their
horses' backs and halting only during the worst heat
of the day to turn the weary animals out to graze, the
troopers had made the long, hot march with little
more than the usual grumbling. If they were to cover
that distance or more tomorrow, both men and mounts
would have to recoup their strength.

Turning to the officer waiting just behind him, Andrew issued the necessary instructions. "My compliments to the company commanders, Lieutenant Stanton-Smith. Tell them we'll camp here tonight."

The bewhiskered young lieutenant whipped up a salute and wheeled his charger. Within moments, the trumpeters sounded dismount. The piercing bugle calls echoed across the plains, as Andrew had intended them to. If Spotted Tail was within listening distance, he wanted the chief to know they weren't planning a stealthy attack.

The troops fell out wearily. After two weeks in the field, even the rawest recruit in the column knew the drill. The drivers brought the wagons up into the center of the column and picketed the mules around them. Under the company sergeants' watchful eyes, the troopers unbridled their horses and performed the preliminary grooming so necessary while in the field. Sponging the mounts' eyes and nostrils, the troopers whisped around their heads and down their necks to remove the sweat, picked their hooves and fed them a handful of hay.

Leaving the heated animals to cool off before unsaddling them, the troopers saw to their own needs. Some pitched the two-man tents. Others were detailed to dig sinks for latrines. Still others took canvas bags out to collect buffalo chips for cook fires.

As Andrew had hoped, bores dug in the cracked streambed yielded a trickle of muddy water. With the men's canteens refilled, he didn't have to order half water rations. Soon campfires crackled and the aroma of fresh coffee drifted through the camp. Refreshed by cups of the strong, black brew, the men set about soaking hardtack in water to soften it before frying up their day's rations of beans and salt pork.

Andrew and his officers messed outside the cone-shaped Sibley tent that served as his sleeping quarters. Although other commanders supplemented their mess with special rations or game brought down by the scouts, Andrew insisted his officers eat the same fare as the troopers while on the march. Otherwise, they couldn't gauge their men's strength or endurance.

"Pardee thinks we'll catch up with Spotted Tail tomorrow," he informed his subordinates.

One of his more seasoned captains stroked his bushy beard thoughtfully. "Shall we tell the sergeants to issue extra rounds of ammunition?"

"Twenty rounds per man," Andrew concurred, "although I'm hoping we won't need them. Remind your men this isn't a punitive expedition. Our orders are to intercept and parlay with the Brulé, not fire on them."

"Unless they fire first," the captain drawled.

"No one returns any shots unless and until I give the signal."

The officers eyed him speculatively. Most were aware of his friendship with Yellow Buckskin Girl, if not from firsthand observation during her many visits to Fort Laramie, then by word of mouth. At one point, the rumor around the post was that Spotted Tail might well become the major's father-in-law.

Andrew could have squelched the rumors easily
enough by revealing that he was already married, but
he'd kept his past to himself...until Julia's arrival.
Now his past was providing even more fodder for the
rumor mill than had his friendship with Yellow Buckskin Girl.

"Finish up," he instructed his officers. "It's time
for stable call."

With the horses cooled down and the men rested,
the serious business of the evening commenced. A
man's life could—and often did—depend on his
mount's condition. Any trooper whose horse went
lame or fell under him had to hitch a ride in the wagons, beg a buddy to take him up behind him, or walk.
None of those alternatives held much appeal when a
band of hostile Sioux were apt to come swooping
down from the hills at any moment.

Although Andrew could have detailed one of the
men to unsaddle and inspect his mount, he preferred
to do it himself. No true horse soldier would delegate
care of his horse to someone else.

The big chestnut nickered softly at Andrew's approach. They'd ridden a lot of miles together, he and
Jupiter. They knew each other's moods as well as any
old married couple. Better, he thought with a wry
grimace, considering that his wife had disappeared
from his life six years ago, only to reappear married
to another man.

"Let's take a look at your back, old fella, then
we'll get you watered and groomed."

Breathing in the rich scent of the charger's sweaty hide, he removed saddle and blanket and inspected his back for signs of galling. Only after a check of the pasterns, hooves, nose, ears and eyes did he go to work with currycomb and fresh straw.

With the sentries in place, he gave the order to extinguish lights at nine-thirty, after which the camp quieted down. Knowing reveille would sound at three-thirty, the men murmured among themselves for a while before the usual grunts, wheezes and whistling snores replaced their desultory talk.

Bone-tired but too edgy to sleep, Andrew kept his ear tuned to the familiar shuffle of horses on their picket lines and the snorts and sneezes of men settling into sleep. He should have been reviewing his plans for tomorrow's march, but couldn't seem to keep his mind on the familiar details. Folding his arms under his head, he stared through the tent flap.

Stars hung like crystals in an obsidian sky. For a fanciful moment, he compared them to the lights that glinted in Julia's dark hair. That, of course, was a mistake. The mere memory of their wedding night, when her silken mass of hair had spilled over her naked shoulders, got him tight and hard as any trooper with a dollar in his pocket, hightailing it to Coffee's Hog Ranch for a poke.

Dammit, how the devil had the woman slipped back into his head? And why in thunderation couldn't he get her out? She'd taken up far more of his waking thoughts than she should have.

He still found it hard to believe the Belle of New Orleans had chosen to live on Suds Row. He hated the thought of Julia struggling to lift the wooden ladles piled high with boiling hot uniforms. Hated even more the desire that tightened his balls whenever he remembered how her hair had curled on her nape and her damp blouse had stuck to the curves of her breasts.

As tired as he was, fantasies of laying her back on the riverbank, peeling off her wet blouse and baring those soft mounds to his hands and mouth raised a hard bulge under the flap of his trousers. He could almost taste the tang of salty sweat on her skin. Hear her little pants of shock, surprise, excitement. Almost feel the...

"War party approaching!"

The distant cry sent Andrew into a fast roll. In a single, fluid movement, he twisted onto his side, snatched his Colt from its holster and sprang to his feet. With the possibility of hostiles nearby, he'd chosen to sleep with his boots on, as had most of his troops. Like Andrew, they poured out of their tents, clutching rifles and pistols and slinging ammunition belts over their shoulders.

"Form the perimeter defense," he ordered the company commanders. "Set the men at ten yards apart and remind them to hold their fire unless and until I order otherwise."

With Arizona Joe and Lone Eagle running beside him, Andrew raced up the grassy incline. His whis-

kered young officer of the day panted along behind
him, ready to relay any orders his commander might
issue.

The sentry who'd sounded the alarm met them halfway. Skittering down the slope on his boot heels, he
panted out a quick report. "It ain't a war party, sir.
We thought it was at first, but it's only three braves.
One's a chief. He says he wants to parlay."

"Did the chief identify himself?"

"Yes, sir. It's Spotted Tail."

Lone Eagle grunted. As he'd predicted, the wily
old warrior had arranged the meeting on his own
terms.

Andrew aimed a grin at the scout as they climbed
to the crest of the slope. Lone Eagle's personal history
with his wife's uncle had left him decidedly wary of
the old man, but of all the northern Sioux chiefs,
Spotted Tail was the most willing to listen. If he carried the latest peace offer to Red Cloud, Crazy Horse
and Sitting Bull, maybe, just maybe, there was a
chance to avoid another bloody year on the plains.

His pulse racing, Andrew topped the rise. Spotted
Tail and the warriors who'd accompanied him sat on
their ponies, waiting patiently. A renowned orator
who'd frequented Fort Laramie as both child and
adult, the chief was also a great warrior. He'd counted
twenty-six coup in personal combat. In the Sioux culture, swooping in on horseback to touch a live enemy
with a hand or quirt counted for as much coup as

killing him. Each coup earned a warrior status and an eagle feather.

To Andrew's relief, Spotted Tail wasn't wearing his war bonnet, nor was his pony painted with honor marks or spiritual symbols. The old warrior was here, as the sentry had reported, to parlay.

"My greetings to you, Sin-te Ga-les-ka," Andrew said in fractured Sioux.

"And to you, Long-Knife-Who-Walks-With-A-Limp."

"I've been tracking you for two weeks."

A smile creased the old man's face. "So I have observed."

"Will you come into camp and talk?"

The smile faded. "The time for talk passed when the Great Father in Washington sent more long knives to reinforce the forts along the path you call the Bozeman Trail."

"I have a message from General Sherman about these forts."

"Unless his message promises their destruction, you bring nothing but wasted words."

Andrew couldn't lie. Nothing had been promised except more talk. "General Sherman will *discuss* the destruction of these forts if you and the other chiefs will meet with him. He's been named to head a peace commission that will come to Fort Laramie and talk with you. Will you carry that message to Red Cloud and the others?"

His head dipped. "I will carry it."

* * *

The cavalry troop that approached Fort Laramie five days later little resembled the one that had ridden out almost three weeks earlier. The riders slumped wearily in their saddles. Dust and mud covered their salt-caked uniforms. The wagons lumbering behind the column of fours carried a half-dozen sick and injured, one of whom had turned blue from snakebite.

In accordance with army procedures, Andrew sent Joe Pardee and Lone Eagle ahead to notify the post of their return. Even before the column of troops had crested the tawny slope above the fort, the bugles were announcing their imminent arrival.

By the time the column started down the incline that led to the flats, the regimental band had assembled and was filling the air with the lilting strains of "Fiddler's Green." One by one, the troopers sat up. Shoulders squared. Carbines were slung back. Troopers beat their hats against their legs, raising little clouds of dust all along the column.

Andrew shared the excitement that rippled through the ranks. Strange how this jumble of wood-and-adobe buildings tucked at the bend of the Laramie felt so much more like home to him than the townhouse in Philadelphia where he'd spent his youth. Strange, too, how the thought that Julia might be among the crowd gathering on the parade ground had him dusting his shirtfront and tugging his hat to square it on his brow.

He didn't see her at first among the women who

waved and called out greetings to their menfolk. Castigating himself for the keen disappointment that swept through him, he kept a light hand on the reins as he guided Jupiter toward the center of the parade ground. They were almost in position when a tumble of blue-black hair snagged his gaze. He glanced her way, his heart jumping at the smile of welcome on her face. Their eyes met above the heads of the crowd, and in that moment Andrew's sense of homecoming surged into something deeper, something urgent.

He couldn't deny the truth any longer. Whatever had happened in the past, whatever lies and half truths had shattered their lives, he still wanted this woman with an ache that almost doubled him over in the saddle.

Something of what he was feeling must have shown in his face. Julia's smile faltered. Her lips parted. For an instant, the girl that she'd once been gazed at him through the eyes of the woman she now was.

Andrew's breath caught. She still felt it, too. The same fascination that had drawn them across a ballroom on a hot, sultry Louisiana night. The same damned sexual pull that had grabbed them both and still hadn't let go. She might deny it. She might refuse to acknowledge it, even to herself. But she felt it.

He found himself hoping she'd received a telegraph or dispatch, hoping someone in Adler's Gulch had confirmed what they both secretly suspected...that

Philip Bonneaux's remains rested in a pine box buried under six feet of Montana mud. Claim jumpers and barroom brawls had ended the lives of so many of the dreamers who'd trudged north to make their fortunes. Scurvy, cholera and freezing winters had ended countless others. The odds were that Julia was already free of the bonds that tied her to another man.

The possibility tightened Andrew's gut and left him wondering just what difference it would make if she *were* free. He wanted her, yes. In his arms and in his bed. But he couldn't seem to think beyond the point of peeling off her clothes, pulling her slender body beneath his and parting her thighs. He didn't *want* to think beyond that point, dammit.

He was still wrestling with the lust that gripped him like a vise when he noticed the bandage wrapped around her left forearm. His stomach plunged to his boots. What had happened? Who'd hurt her? Why the hell hadn't O'Shea kept an eye on her, as he'd—

Suddenly, a child's shriek split the air.

"Mama! Daisy got away!"

Something trailing a length of colored cloth streaked across the parade ground and darted right in front of Jupiter. The startled charger danced back, neck arching, hooves pawing the ground.

One hoof caught the end of the cloth. Squealing, the creature tied to the string flipped on its back. Frenzied, it regained its feet and scurried back and forth under Jupiter's belly.

"Daisy, come back!"

Even a cavalry mount trained not to flinch at the sound of a pistol fired right beside its ear couldn't be expected to stand still while something that resembled a poisonous desert coral snake wrapped itself around his hooves. Particularly when a frantic child broke away from the watching crowd and ran straight at him, arms waving like windmills.

"Suzanne!" Julia screamed. "No!"

Ears flattened, Jupiter reared. His iron-shod hooves pawed the air above the girl's head. Yanking on the reins, Andrew wrenched the animal around and brought his forelegs down mere inches from the child, now frozen in fright.

Disaster might still have been averted if the critter at the end of the cloth rope hadn't been freed when Jupiter reared. Emitting a series of shrill pips, it darted straight between the charger's rear legs.

Bucking like a wild mustang, the chestnut flailed his hind legs and tried to dance away. By the time Andrew had him under control again, a white-faced Julia had snatched up her daughter and the shrill pips had been silenced.

Signaling the troops behind him to resume formation and continue past, Andrew swung out of the saddle. A shoulder to Jupiter's side shoved the charger out of the way. Heart pounding, he faced the shaken woman with her child pressed tight against her.

"Is she all right?"

"I—I think so."

His gaze whipped to the white bandage. "Are *you* all right?"

"Me? Yes, I'm fine."

"What happened to your arm?"

"It's a slight burn, nothing more."

"Has the surgeon looked at it?"

"Yes, of course. Really, there's no need—"

"Maaama!"

The heartbroken wail cut through their stilted conversation.

"He stomped Daisy!"

"Oh, no!"

Following the girl's tearful gaze, Andrew swung around. The mangled remains of a small, furry animal lay in a pool of blood on the dusty parade ground.

"Is that a prairie dog?" he asked Julia incredulously.

"Yes."

"On a leash?"

"It—it was a pet."

Shaken out of his customary control, Andrew swept off his hat and pounded it against his pants leg.

"Dammit, woman, don't you have any more sense than to let your daughter play with one of those little rats? They carry fleas and ticks and God alone knows what other kinds of vermin."

The harsh stricture brought Julia's head up. Eyes flashing, she'd just opened her mouth to reply when Private O'Shea stepped in front her.

"Begging your pardon, sir. I gave Suzanne the little critter."

"And Daisy didn't have fleas!" Tear-washed brown eyes lifted from Julia's shoulder and pinned Andrew with an accusing look. "Little Hen and I dunked her in mama's tub and scrubbed her good!"

Faced with a hostile child, an angry mother, a disapproving striker and the unabashed interest of dozens of bystanders, Andrew decided to do what any man in his situation would do—beat a hasty retreat. First, however, he offered his apologies to the sniffling little girl.

"I'm sorry Jupiter came down on your pet."

"You're a bad man," she answered, her brown eyes shooting daggers. "You yelled at my mama and now you mashed Daisy. I hate you!"

10

It took Andrew all of twenty-four hours to discover he was the object of considerable censure on the post, not only for inadvertently destroying Suzanne's pet, but also for allowing Julia to continue to work at the tubs.

Private O'Shea dropped several unsubtle remarks about the fact that the missus wasn't cut out for such work. So did Private Rafferty and Corporal Gottlieb when he reported that no information regarding Julia's husband had come in during Andrew's absence. Even Mary Donovan pressed her husband into service to relay the general consensus of the women on Suds Row that Julia didn't belong there.

The embarrassed sergeant major delivered his wife's message the day after Andrew's return. He and Donovan were observing mounted drill on the high grounds behind the stables. The sun beat down mercilessly. Swarms of flies buzzed around their horses' eyes and ears. Swiping the sweat from his ruddy face with his neckerchief, the grizzled sergeant cleared his throat several times before broaching the subject.

"Begging your pardon, sir, but the missus wanted you to know, uh…"

"Know what, Sergeant Major?"

"Well…"

"Well what, man? Out with it."

"It's the laundresses, sir."

Andrew glanced at the whiskered veteran. Given her husband's rank, Mary Donovan served as the unofficial commander of the laundresses. She'd proved invaluable at keeping Andrew informed of matters that needed his attention. She'd also quietly quashed some of the rivalries and jealousies that had led to serious confrontations on other posts. Thankfully, Andrew had never had to place a laundress under arrest for taking a meat ax to a rival for her husband's affections or drum one out of the regiment because she'd been disrespectful to an officer.

"What's the problem, Sergeant Major?"

"They feel a bit uncomfortable at havin' an officer's wife in their midst."

Knowing it would do no good to remind the sergeant that Julia wasn't an officer's wife, Andrew kept silent.

"Mrs. Donovan told them to keep their noses in their own tubs and never mind what others do, but even she agrees it's not proper, sir."

"Does Mrs. Donovan have a suggestion as to what I'm to do about it?" the major asked dryly.

He'd already decided in his own mind how he'd handle the situation, but he was curious to see what the red-haired laundress had come up with.

"Well, sir, she does," Donovan answered. "She's thinking you could put Mrs. Bonneaux to work at the hospital as a matron. It's hard labor, to be sure, but not so hard as the tubs."

"My compliments to your wife, Sergeant Major, but I've already suggested that and Mrs. Bonneaux refused."

"Did she now?" The sergeant pursed his lips and waggled his mustaches from side to side. "Mary'll not like hearin' that."

"I'm thinking of offering her an alternate position."

"May I inquire what, sir?"

"Instructress at the post school."

"Hmmm." The seasoned veteran chewed over the idea in his mind. "That might do, sir. It's a bit early, being only halfway through July, but what with Corporal Lassiter going down with the bloody flux this spring, the children didn't finish last year's work proper. They've a bit of catchin' up to do. Yes, sir, it will do."

In truth, Andrew wasn't sure whether the change in occupations would lessen or increase Julia's load. Although Fort Laramie had opened the first school in Wyoming Territory back in '59, the Army didn't officially authorize or fund frontier post schools until just last year. Even then, attendance was only mandatory for the children of enlisted personnel, since the more educated officers' wives generally preferred to teach their offspring at home.

The post chaplain had instructed Fort Laramie's students for years, followed by a succession of well-educated enlisted personnel. Private Lassiter was the most recent—and the most vocal about the little devils he taught. From the reports fed back to Andrew by the harried instructor, the students spent more time plotting tricks to play on their teacher than they'd ever spent on studies. Taking on that high-spirited, rambunctious lot could prove almost as much of a strain for Julia as bending over the tubs.

He'd leave it to her, Andrew decided. Not that he had much choice in the matter. She'd already demonstrated that she'd do just what she had a mind to.

The sergeant major cleared his throat. Embarrassment stained his cheeks above his bushy mustache. "She'd have to be kept on the rolls and be guaranteed her quarters and rations," he said apologetically. "Mrs. Donovan wouldn't advise her to accept anything less."

"Is that right?"

"Yes, sir."

"I wonder whatever gave us the notion that we run either this post or our companies?"

"Beats the hell out of me, sir. But while we're on the subject…"

"Yes?"

"Mrs. Donovan also suggested you might want to

be making your peace with the daughter, sir. Suzanne was a bit upset about her pet, she was.''

Some day, Andrew thought sardonically, he'd take off his uniform for the last time and go back to civilian life. Maybe then he'd discover what it was like to live without two hundred or more pairs of eyes watching his every step from reveille to retreat.

''You may assure Mrs. Donovan I have every intention of mending my bridges with the girl.''

''Yes, sir.''

It was, Julia decided as she settled her hips more comfortably on the split rail bench outside her quarters, the kind of evening poets rhapsodized about.

A violent thunderstorm had swept through only an hour ago, taking with it the worst of the heat. A balmy breeze had followed in its wake. The wind now frisked like a playful colt, kicking up the long johns and uniform shirts pegged on the lines to dry. Beyond the clotheslines, the Laramie sparkled clear, crystalline blue.

Even the mosquitoes that made the mornings and evenings such misery had taken French leave, as the troopers described their occasional unauthorized absences. Someone in one of the tents across the river was playing a haunting, unfamiliar tune on a harmonica. The notes floated on the breeze like small, perfect butterflies above the usual early-evening rattle of pots and pottery.

As the junior resident of Suds Row, Julia's turn in

the communal kitchens behind the quarters came last. She didn't mind the wait. It gave her the chance to take a break between the heat of the laundry fires and even fiercer heat of the cookstoves.

On an evening as fine as this one, the spare moments were doubly precious. Humming along with the harmonica, she rested her shoulders against the rough adobe wall and watched Suzanne weave bits of feathers and beads into her doll's hair under Little Hen's careful tutelage.

With something of a shock, Julia discovered that she felt more content at that particular moment than she had in months. She still hadn't received any word from Philip, but she and Suzanne had a roof over their heads and hearty, if somewhat monotonous, fare to eat. True, her hands were red and cracked and the burn on her arm she'd received from a splash of boiling water stung a bit. By and large, though, she felt too tired and lazy to worry about it.

But not too lazy to experience a sudden jolt when the clip-clop of hooves drew her gaze and she identified Andrew on his big chestnut. She hadn't seen or spoken to him since his return and Daisy's unfortunate demise two days ago.

She sat upright, lifting a hand in an instinctive and wholly feminine gesture to tuck her hair behind her ears. As flustered by her instinctive need to primp as by the sudden ribbon of heat that coiled in her belly, she dropped her hand. The contentment she'd enjoyed just seconds before shattered like a thin sheet of ice hit with a wooden mallet. Guilt flooded in, along with the bitter acknowledgment that Andrew Garrett could still make her pulse leap after all the years and all the lies.

Shamed by the heat spreading through her veins, Julia rose and smoothed her palms down her serge skirt. When she had her emotions firmly under control, she lifted her gaze to the officer silhouetted against the summer sky. Only then did she notice the pony Andrew led at the end of a long tether.

The two girls took note of his approach at that moment, as well. Snatching up her doll, Suzanne darted to her mother's side. Little Hen followed more slowly, her liquid brown eyes wide and curious. The three females stood together in a loose cluster while Andrew made his way toward them. He halted a few yards away and tipped his hat with a smile that included all three.

"Good evening, ladies."

All too conscious of the people milling about up and down the row, Julia inclined her head an inch or two. "Good evening, major."

Leather and wood creaked as he swung out of the saddle. "I came to see if I could make amends to Suzanne for, uh, mashing her pet."

Julia's glance swept past him to the pony at the end of the tether. She really couldn't afford to stable a horse, but one look at Suzanne's open mouth and awed eyes made her instantly recalculate how much it would cost to feed three instead of two.

"You brought a pony?" Distrust and childish wonder chased each other across the girl's face. "For
me?"

"For you." Gathering up the slack in the rope
tether, Andrew drew the dainty little pinto forward.
"Her name is Con-Ra-Wah-Ti."

"What does it mean?"

"Pretty Red One," Little Hen translated shyly.

"Because of her red spots," Andrew explained
gravely. "But you can name her anything you like."

Although the desire to reach out and touch the spotted hide blazed in Suzanne's face, she clutched her
doll to her chest and stubbornly held back.

"Mama says I shouldn't accept gifts from strangers."

"We're hardly strangers, but in any case Pretty Red
One's not a gift. You'll have to earn her."

Suspicion leaped into the girl's brown eyes.
"How?"

"She has to be groomed, watered and fed every
day, and taken out for exercise as often as possible.
When you've shown me you can take care of her,
we'll talk to your mother about whether or not you
can keep her."

Suzanne's lower lip trembled. "I don't know how
to groom a horse. Or ride one, either."

"I'll show you."

"And I will help," Little Hen volunteered with one
of her rare, sweet smiles. "I have a pony, too, which
my grandfather keeps for me."

Obviously torn between her longing for the little pinto and her dislike of the major, Suzanne looked to her mother for guidance.

"You'll have to take full responsibility for caring for her yourself," Julia warned. "I'll be too busy at the tubs to help you."

Andrew's glance met hers over the heads of the girls. "That's something you and I need to discuss."

"We've already discussed it," she replied, stiffening.

With a look that said the subject wasn't closed, he offered Suzanne the rope lead.

"Why don't you and Little Hen take Pretty Red One for a walk along the river and get to know her?"

Accepting the lead with a show of reluctance, Suzanne looked the pony over. Her glance darted to the man standing beside her mother.

"She's not as pretty as the doll my papa gave me."

"Suzanne!"

Blushing for her daughter's rudeness, Julia admonished her to show more appreciation. The unrepentant girl refused to give ground.

"If I keep her, I'll have to name her something else."

"If you keep her," Andrew replied with a nod, "that's certainly your choice."

Shooting the major a dark look, she tugged on the pony's halter. The pinto followed her and Little Hen with well-mannered docility.

"Please forgive her lack of graciousness," Julia

murmured, embarrassed for her daughter. "She's not usually so ill-mannered."

A smile crept into his eyes. "She's inherited some of her mother's stubbornness, I think."

"Unfortunately so. And since we speak of stubbornness, I hope you haven't come to tell me I should move back in with Victoria McKinney. You'd be wasting your breath."

"Would I?"

"Yes. I much prefer earning my own keep."

"There are other ways to earn your keep. And not," he said hastily, remembering their earlier, angry discussion, "on your back."

Heat flooded her face, but she lifted her chin and met his eyes squarely. "What, then?"

"The post school. It closed early this spring due to the lack of an instructor. If you feel you're up to it, you could take over teaching duties immediately."

She mulled over the offer, doubt and indecision creasing her forehead.

"It's honest work, Julia. We need an instructor."

"Would I remain on the rolls?"

"That was one of the conditions of employment Mary Donovan stipulated," Andrew replied dryly.

"Mary's behind this?"

"No, she told her husband to suggest the hospital, but when I offered this as an alternative, he seemed to think she'd support the idea."

A rush of affection for the Irish laundress filled Julia. Like a busy hen watching over the entire coop,

the warmhearted Mary Donovan looked after officers'
ladies and troopers' wives alike. Although Julia fit
neither category, she'd certainly reaped the bounty of
the woman's generous spirit.

"I'll have to thank her," she murmured.

"Does that mean you accept?"

"Yes, although," she added with a wry smile, rubbing a hand absently over her injured arm, "I don't
guarantee I'll make any better instructor than I have
laundress."

"Roll up your sleeve and let me see your burn."

Startled, she whipped her arm behind her back.
"It's nothing, merely a small scald."

"Henry Schnell told me it was more than a mere
scald and that it needs watching. Let me see it."

"Really, I don't think—"

"Burns can fester and kill as quickly as cholera or
smallpox out here. Let me see it, Julia."

With a glance at the neighbors loitering about, she
conceded with obvious reluctance. "All right, but
please come inside. I've given the post enough cause
for gossip without rolling up my sleeve and letting
you examine me in public."

Julia soon discovered that rolling up her sleeve and
letting Andrew examine her in *private* proved a far
greater mistake. Although both the door and the window shutters remained open to the balmy evening, the
walls seemed to crowd in on them when he followed
her inside.

He glanced around, his face expressionless as he

took in the austere quarters. The plank-and-rope bed Private Rafferty had scavenged for them filled the area behind the partition. Julia's trunk and a rickety crate upended to support the chipped pitcher and washbasin Mary Donovan had contributed took up the rest of the space.

Maria Schnell's gingham brightened up the front room considerably, as did the beaded and fringed buckskin storage pouch Walks In Moon Light had gifted her with. Julia had added another bright touch only that morning—a clump of primroses stuck in a tin cup and placed atop the cast-iron stove.

"We're very comfortable here," she said in defense of her temporary home. "Will I be allowed to stay on Suds Row if I take up duties at the post school?"

"It's not what I'd prefer, but unless you wish to move back in with Lieutenant McKinney's wife—"

"No, thank you!"

"The choice is yours," he conceded. Dropping his hat on the wooden crate that served as her dining table, he peeled off his gauntlets. "Roll up your sleeve."

He stood so close. Too close. Julia breathed in the rich scents of leather and wool and hot, sweaty male. Her fingers fumbled with the stubborn buttons of her cuff.

"Shall I help you?"

The hidden question behind the polite query brought her head up. She'd made it clear she never,

ever wanted to feel his hands on her again. The angry words came back to bite her now as she flushed and held out her wrist.

"If you would be so kind."

Her stilted politeness went up in a flash of heat the moment he grasped her wrist. It was just a loose hold, a mere brush of his fingers against her flesh, yet Julia's nerves seemed to jump under her skin. If he noticed her instinctive flinch, he gave no sign. His brow creased in a frown as he gently probed the blistered patch.

"Henry said he gave you a tincture of opium. Have you spread the ointment on today?"

"Yes, earlier this morning."

"Some of the blisters have cracked. You'd better let me put more on. Where is it?"

"There's no need for you to bother. Really, I—"

Impatience put a sharp bite in his tone. "For pity's sake, one glimpse of your naked arm isn't going to spur me to ravish you."

"I didn't think it would! You couldn't ravish me if you tried."

His head lifted. The look in his eyes stopped the breath in her throat.

"Do you think so?"

"I know so," she snapped to cover a sudden spurt of nervousness. "Whatever else you did in New Orleans, you never used my silly infatuation to seduce me into bed outside the bounds of marriage. Nor would you now seduce another man's wife."

"I wouldn't be so sure of that if I were you," he said slowly. Without taking his eyes from hers, he turned her arm and pressed his lips against the inside of her wrist.

Every instinct Julia possessed screamed at her to snatch her hand away. She was insane to stand there, insane to let her blood heat and her heart race while his touch ignited fires under her skin.

Afterward, she would never remember how she ended up in his arms, never know how her mouth came to fuse so urgently with his. One moment, she was staring as if transfixed at the dark head bent over her wrist. The next, she was swept up on a tide of need so hot and compelling she couldn't breathe.

She might have moaned. Might have swayed toward him. All she could recall later was the searing pleasure of his mouth crushing hers.

The sound of girlish chatter broke them apart. Stunned, Julia could only stare up at Andrew wordlessly. Whatever might have been said between them at that moment was lost when Suzanne called impatiently for her mother to come see how she and Little Hen had braided the pony's tail.

11

"Take the brush in your left hand and the curry-comb in your right."

Scrunching her nose in concentration, Suzanne picked up the implements. "Like this?"

Patiently, Andrew bent down to switch them. Her small fingers could barely grasp the flat-backed brush.

"Start at her head," he instructed. "Work down her forehead and over her face in smooth, even strokes. Slowly, now. Let the brush pick up the dust and dirt. When it gets full, clean it with the comb."

Stepping back to give the girl room to work in the narrow stall, he kept a close watch on her awkward movements. Andrew had spent countless hours in the stables watching while the senior sergeants drilled recruits, but this was the first time he'd put such a young one through her paces.

Dust motes danced in the sunbeams slanting in through the open stable doors. Swarms of flies buzzed around the stalls, their drone noisy in air redolent with

the familiar odor of leather, hay and horse droppings.
A few troopers lingered in the barnlike stables, giving
their mounts the extra measure of attention that
sprang less from duty and more from a true cavalry
man's love for the companion that shared his long
marches.

"Careful around her eye."

Andrew's warning came too late. The pony
flinched, jerking its head to avoid the bristles. With a
squeal of fright, Suzanne jumped sideways. The
squeal spiraled into a wail when her foot landed in a
patch of manure-filled straw.

"Ohhh! I stepped in horse poopy!"

Her face contorting in comical dismay, Suzanne
lifted her leg. The piece of canvas Andrew had
wrapped around her shoe to protect it came loose,
along with the shoe itself. She perched like a small,
unhappy stork on one foot while the other hovered
above the muck. Tears sprang to her eyes and might
have spilled down her cheeks if Little Hen hadn't
emitted a giggle from her seat on a handy wheelbar-
row.

Biting back his own smile, Andrew hunkered down
on his heels to retrieve the lost shoe. "You'll need a
pair of boots if you're going to groom her properly."

"Or moccasins with high leggings." With a hand
over her mouth to hide her merriment, Little Hen
averted the pending crisis. "I'll ask my mother to
make you a pair."

The sniffles halted. "With beadwork, like yours?"

Her friend nodded.

"Until they're finished, the sackcloth will have to do," Andrew said. Slipping her shoe back on Suzanne's dainty foot, he retied the strings of the canvas boot. "Ready to try again?"

Cautiously, the girl lowered her foot.

"Nice, easy strokes, now. When you finish with her face and head, throw her mane over to the other side and work your way down her neck to her shoulders."

Folding his arms, Andrew leaned against the stall support and watched the hesitant strokes. She'd pick up the rhythm with practice. The girl was sharp as a tack despite her overly fastidious airs. He had to admit, however, he wasn't looking forward to teaching her how to sponge out her pony's nostrils and anus.

"A good cavalryman grooms his horse twice a day," he told her sternly, laying the groundwork.

"I know. At morning and evening stable call."

"You'll be in school in the mornings, but I expect you to report to the stables every afternoon at five. If I'm not here, Private Rafferty or O'Shea will watch you work."

Frowning in concentration, Suzanne worked the brush down the pony's neck. The spotted hide rippled under her stroke. Once or twice, the animal swung its head around, as if to check their progress.

"When will I get to ride her?"

"When you've learned how to take care of her."

"When will that be?"

"A few weeks, perhaps. We'll see."

The brush stilled. Accusing brown eyes lifted to his.

"That's what Mama says when she doesn't want to do something. 'We'll see.' She thinks I'll forget, but I don't ever."

Her cherubic little face took on a decidedly stubborn set. A defiant note crept into her voice.

"Just like I haven't forgotten my papa. We're going to find him when we get 'nuff money."

"Maybe he'll find you first," Andrew answered calmly.

"I hope so! Then I'll get *him* to show me how to ride Daisy. That's what I'm going to call her," she announced with a toss of her curls. "'Cause you mashed my other Daisy."

He'd be a long time atoning for that heinous crime, Andrew realized ruefully. And a long time banishing this irritating sense of responsibility for Julia and her daughter. They'd crept into his thoughts these past weeks, become woven somehow into the pattern of his life. The idea of Philip Bonneaux teaching Suzanne to ride her pony rankled more than he was ready to admit.

Almost as much as the idea of Bonneaux putting his hands on Julia.

Andrew's annoying possessiveness toward his one-time wife had begun as a small canker, but now gnawed at his insides like a trapped beast. He couldn't forget that he'd been the first to claim her heart and body, the first to awaken her to passion. The passion was still there, even after all these years, simmering just below the surface.

Julia had pushed out of his arms and beat a swift retreat after their shattering kiss two nights ago, but Andrew was no fool, nor some green, johnny-raw fumbling with his first woman. He'd felt her response, tasted the desire that had flowed as hot and hungry in her veins as it did in his. She'd wanted him for those few, searing seconds. As much as he'd wanted her.

Every muscle in his body tightened at the thought of another man fanning the flames of that desire, another man running his hands and lips over her feverish skin. Fighting a scowl, he hunkered down to show Suzanne how to work the currycomb from the end of the pony's tail upward.

When Suzanne finished grooming and feeding her pony, Andrew escorted the two girls to the building that housed the offices of the post adjutant. Located at the western end of the parade ground, right on the bend of the river, the structure sat almost atop the site of the old fur-trading fort. It was a sprawling facility constructed in a mix of wood and adobe, with various additions designed by different architects.

Besides housing the post records and company rolls, the building also served as an unofficial social center. The library room contained over three hundred volumes in addition to subscriptions to various journals and newspapers, while the music room boasted an upright piano and a surprising selection of sheet music.

A large hall at the rear of the building served a multitude of purposes. It was here that the chaplain held services on Sundays and the Laramie Players performed their masks and minstrel shows. Here, too, Private Jacobs conducted his evening lectures on botany and butterflies. And it was here that Julia would conduct classes.

The hall's benches and tables were now lined up to form writing desks for the children who'd report for class the next morning. There would be twenty-three, a nervous Julia informed Andrew when he arrived with Suzanne and Little Hen. Most were offspring of enlisted personnel, although a few civilians and Sioux and Cheyenne were also sending their children.

"Where will Little Hen and I sit, Mama?"

"In the first row, by the window."

While the girls tested their seats, Andrew hitched a hip on the sturdy table that served as the teacher's desk.

"Do you have everything you need?"

A harried Julia tucked a pencil into her braided hair. "Yes, I think so. Ordnance Sergeant Schnyder has been most helpful."

If anyone could turn up whatever was necessary for the schoolroom, it was Leodegar Schnyder. The sergeant had arrived at Fort Laramie with the original contingent of infantry way back in '49. He'd lost his first wife to cholera and subsequently married a laundress named Cross-Eyed Julie. Currently, he served as post librarian and garrison postmaster among his many other duties.

"Let me know if there's anything Sergeant Schnyder can't scavenge for you."

She cast a quick look around the room. "All I can think of at this moment is a new set of maps for the geography lessons. That one is sadly dated."

Andrew spared a glance at the painted canvas map nailed to one wall. It depicted the boundaries of the United States prior to the war with Mexico that had brought Texas and California into the Union.

"The sutler said he could bring in a new set for us in his next shipment of goods," Julia explained, "but his prices are too dear."

"I can provide more current military maps as a temporary measure, but you might as well tell the sutler to go ahead and place the order. The officers' special welfare and morale fund can stand for the cost."

"I didn't know officers had a welfare and morale fund."

"It's, uh, unofficial."

"Unofficial?"

Grinning, Andrew confessed the truth. "We toss a dollar from each pot into a tobacco jar during our Saturday night poker games at Old Bedlam. That jar has funded everything from Lieutenant Stanton-

Smith's new reading spectacles to the recent delivery of two cases of Tennessee sippin' whiskey.''

Bemused by the grin that softened the hard angles of his face, Julia barely heard his explanation. For a fleeting moment he reminded her so much of the Andrew Garrett she'd once known that desire and despair gripped her in a brutal vise.

What was happening to her? Why was she so drawn to this man? She'd hated him for so long, then buried her memories of him so deep. How could he now stir her blood with a mere smile? Or quicken her pulse with just a whiff of the scent of leather and horse that clung to his uniform?

He'd rolled his sleeves up on his forearms and opened the neck of his uniform shirt in concession to the heat. If she reached out, she could trace a forefinger along the silvery path left by a trickle of sweat. If she bent forward just an inch or two, she could mold her lips to his as she had two nights ago.

Shaken by the intensity of her need to do just that, Julia turned away. Her heart skipped a beat when she found a pair of frowning brown eyes watching her from a front row desk.

''Do you like that seat?'' she asked, summoning a bright smile.

''No.'' Pursing her lips in a decided pout, Suzanne slipped off the bench and marched to the opposite end of the row. ''I'll sit here.''

Julia's heart sank as she realized even her daughter had sensed what everyone else on post already knew—that her past relationship with Major Andrew Garrett hadn't ended with the sharp crack of a pistol one dark night in New Orleans. They were still tied by old lies and new circumstances, none of which Julia felt up to explaining to a five-year-old.

None of which she *could* explain. For the life of her, Julia didn't understand how the cravings of her treacherous body could blunt the hurt she'd suffered at Andrew's hands. Or how each day she spent at Fort Laramie blurred even more the memory of her husband's face. Fighting a feeling of panic, she turned a determined smile on Andrew.

"If you're sure your fund can bear the cost, I'll place the order for new maps as soon as I've finished here."

He took the hint and rose to leave. Resolutely, Julia busied herself with the books Sergeant Schnyder had dug out of the library storeroom and refused to dwell on how empty the schoolroom suddenly seemed.

To Julia's amazement, she proved a rather competent teacher. Her secret relief at abandoning the drudgery of the tubs infused her with an enthusiasm that soon overcame even her most recalcitrant student's indignation at being sent back to school in the middle of summer.

Her unique status on the post also gave her an authority her immediate predecessor had lacked. Although not technically an officers' lady, she wasn't Suds Row, either. Her students had picked up enough from their parents to know she carried a certain cachet that stemmed directly from Major Garrett.

She spent the first week simply getting to know her pupils and classifying them as to age and ability. The second, in adjusting her hastily contrived lessons to accommodate their wide range of interests. Julia's own convent education had emphasized prayer, literature and setting exquisite little stitches in priests' robes and altar cloths. She soon discovered that the popular works of Washington Irving and James Fenimore Cooper held far more appeal to children raised on the frontier than Shakespeare or Jane Austen, and that sewing held as little interest for her students as it had for her.

She also discovered a wealth of knowledge scattered among the troopers at the post. Private Lowenstahl of the magnificent blond mustaches and superb dancing ability offered to teach an hour of music each week, aided by one of the company buglers who also proved extraordinarily proficient on the piano, banjo and harmonica. Private Jacobs expanded his lectures on botany to include nature walks that took the youngsters out of the classroom and gave Julia an hour or two of blessed quiet to set the room to rights again. Even the colonel's orderly, Corporal Gottlieb, volunteered his services. Taking to heart Julia's casual comment that she would like to capitalize on the diversity of the post's population to supplement history and geography lessons, the corporal drew up a duty roster. Soldiers of Russian, French, German,

Irish, Norwegian and other extraction reported to her on designated days, red faced and sweating in their best dress uniforms.

Mindful that at least a fourth of her students were of mixed white and Indian blood, Julia also planned a series of visits to her classroom by representatives of the Cheyenne, Sioux and Arapaho tribes. In this, she met unexpected resistance.

The first warning came from Mary Donovan, who invited Julia to take tea with her one Sunday afternoon shortly after July rolled into August. Although Julia had visited Mary's home on several occasions, this was the first time she'd been issued a formal invitation. Consequently, she dressed herself and Suzanne in their best frocks and tipped a parasol to shade them from the low-hanging sun while they made the short walk to Mary's quarters.

Like the other apartments on Suds Row, Sergeant Major Donovan's consisted of just two rooms. To accommodate their seven children from this and previous marriages, the sergeant had received permission to knock out a portion of the rear wall and add a lean-to. He and Mary had also collected sufficient furnishings over the years to make their quarters as comfortable as most on Officers' Row. A black-and-pink cabbage-rose carpet covered the floor of the front room, which contained a humpbacked settee and easy chair in addition to a hand-carved walnut hutch and sturdy dining table. What could be seen of the rear room beyond the partition showed a chest of drawers and a tester bed draped with mosquito netting.

Graciously, Mary invited Julia into her parlor. After plying Suzanne and her own brood with cookies made of hardtack softened in water, then baked with a honey glaze and sprinkled with coarse brown sugar, she suggested the youngsters go to the lean-to to play.

"What I have to say is not for their ears," she explained calmly when they'd dutifully filed out. Pouring a fresh stream of tea into a rose-painted china cup, she added milk and sugar and handed it back to her guest. Wondering what in the world the laundress wanted to talk to her about that occasioned such formality, Julia sipped the sweetened brew.

"M'second boy, Patrick, told me of your plan to bring the Sioux into the classroom," the older woman said when she'd refreshed her own tea. "It's not for me to be sayin' what you do, don't y'know, but I wonder if you've thought on this?"

"What do you mean?"

"Well, there's plenty o'children in your class who've lost fathers to the Sioux and Cheyenne, including three o'me own."

"Patrick and Sheila's father was killed in action?"

"No, their father was my second husband, damn his soul. He drowned in his own vomit after pourin' a gallon o'whiskey down his throat. It was my first who took a Sioux arrow through the neck at the Battle of Yellow Gorge, back in '59."

"I didn't know."

"No, and how should you?"

Mary's reassuring smile faded. Memories put shadows in her faded blue eyes.

"He was with Company D, 3rd Infantry. They'd been ordered from St. Paul to Fort Wadsworth, on the Minnesota River. I was six months along and travelin' in an ambulance wagon at the rear of the column with the rest o'the women. An early storm hit and caught us in the open. Bitter cold it was, with snowdrifts up to the men's chests. The third night out, two of the mules froze where they stood. On the fourth day, the Sioux attacked our column. Me husband only had time to pass me his pistol and warn me to keep low in the wagon before he went down."

The airless heat inside the neat quarters dewed Julia's skin under her layers of clothing, but Mary's quiet recital chilled her to the bone. She could almost feel the snowy cold on her face, almost hear the shots and screams of the wounded.

"I laid there all that day, coverin' my babies as best I could with my body. The Sioux weren't no match for army carbines, don't y'know, but they rallied long enough to drive our boys back."

With a faint rattle of china on china, she set her cup in its saucer. When she met her guest's gaze again, her eyes held a bleakness that stilled Julia's breath.

"We had to retreat to higher ground and leave the dead and wounded where they lay. Two privates burrowed a tunnel through the snow that night and managed to drag six o'the wounded back behind our lines.

"When the battle was over and we claimed the rest o'our men's bodies, I almost didn't recognize me own husband. They'd taken his hair, o'course, to hang from a coup stick. They'd also cut out his tongue, ripped open his belly and severed his hamstrings so he couldn't talk, eat or walk upright in the next world."

"Dear Lord!"

Julia had read of these atrocities. Eastern newspapers had published bloodcurdling accounts of attacks on wagon trains and isolated outposts for decades. Every traveler who headed west was warned by wagon masters and trail guides that they risked the same fate. Hearing the details of an Indian attack from a woman who'd experienced them firsthand, however, wasn't quite the same as reading about them in the newspapers.

"I'm not sayin' our troopers haven't taken some hair themselves on occasion," Mary said. "And I've heard of some would brag about skinning a papoose. It's not what I or any decent soul would hold with, mind you, but you can understand why we don't want our children learnin' the ways of the Sioux."

Julia felt compelled to offer a token protest. "Yet Little Hen and other children from the tents attend class and learn our ways."

"That's as it should be," the laundress said with a logic that wasn't open to argument.

*   *   *

Colonel Cavanaugh echoed Mary's sentiments when he summoned Julia to his office the next day, but used far less restraint in both his language and his remarks. Julia's ears burned by the time he dismissed her with strict orders to keep to the books supplied by the Army and not contaminate the children by teaching them the ways of "heathen red devils."

With Andrew out on patrol, she had no one else to turn to on the matter. By the time he returned four days later, she'd abandoned the idea. She was to remember the colonel's scathing remarks in the weeks to come, though.

For as matters turned out, it wasn't Julia who contaminated the children on post, but a toothless, leather-skinned mule driver by the name of Jackdaw Bill. He stumbled into Coffee's Hog Ranch some three miles from Fort Laramie one evening in early August, already falling down drunk and roaring for the big-breasted whore who'd given him such a good jiggle when he'd passed through last year on his way to Adler's Gulch.

While he waited for Fat Sarah to become available, he stood the troopers at the hog ranch to a round of drinks. Private Rafferty was among the blue-jackets who bellied up to the bar. In addition to downing several glasses of the watered whiskey, Rafferty pumped the mule driver for information about Adler's Gulch. The trooper's ears perked up when the mule skinner admitted as how he'd come across a Frenchy by the name of Bonnet or Bonnville or some such.

By the time it was finally Jackdaw Bill's turn with Fat Sarah, his bowels were churning from the bad whiskey. At least he thought it was the whiskey. Whatever the cause, he was sweating so profusely he could hardly keep from slipping and sliding right off the good-natured whore's massive belly. He managed to get his jiggle, then stumbled back to the bar to drink away the rest of the night.

No one paid him the least heed when he lurched out of Coffee's clapboard-and-tent establishment the next morning, hitched up his mules and dragged himself up onto his wagon. Dizzy and weak from the runs that had soiled his britches and kept him lurching to the privvy all night, Jackdaw Bill drove out of town. He made it as far as the Platte, where he stopped to take another squat and fell facedown in the muddy water. He drowned about the time Andrew went to inform Julia that Philip Bonneaux was dead.

12

Andrew crossed the parade ground, heading for the wooden building at the west end. A brisk breeze tugged at the flaps of his uniform jacket. The wind blew down from the north, carrying the first promise that the sweltering summer would soon end. Although the calendars showed it was just the first week in August, winter could descend at any time.

Snow didn't usually blanket the blue bulk of Laramie Peak rising some forty miles away until October, but Andrew had learned the hard way not to try to predict the weather on the plains. Early storms had been known to howl down from the mountains as early as August or September, though, stranding hunters and travelers alike far from shelter. The weather played heavily on his mind as he mounted the steps of the wooden structure that housed the adjutant's office, library and schoolroom. Julia would have to leave within a few weeks to avoid the dangers of winter travel if she decided to return east after Andrew told her what Private Rafferty had learned at Coffee's Hog Ranch last night.

That "if" ricocheted around in his mind like grapeshot fired from a cannon. The thought of Julia packing up and departing Fort Laramie carved a fist-size hole in his chest. He'd lost her once to another man. He was damned if he was going to lose her again. This was hardly the time to tell her so, though. Right now, his task was to inform her that the husband she'd traveled so far to find had died in a barroom brawl.

His jaw set, Andrew strode past the adjutant's office, acknowledging the orderly who leaped to his feet with a curt nod. His boot heels rang on the plank flooring and announced his arrival well ahead of his perfunctory knock on the schoolroom doorjamb.

Julia stood at the chalkboard Sergeant Schnyder had reblacked for her. She wore her cherry-striped silk skirt and a demure, high-necked white blouse with puffy mutton sleeves. The sunbeams slanting through the windows picked up the blue-black tint to the hair braided in its usual neat coronet. She glanced up when Andrew appeared at the door. A slight flush washed into her cheeks.

"May I speak with you a moment?" he asked. "Privately?"

"Yes, of course. Peggy, will you take the class, please?"

Mary Donovan's oldest left her desk and came to the front of the room.

"Help the little ones with their letters," Julia instructed her assistant. "Those of you in fourth and fifth form may work on your compositions."

A frowning Suzanne squirmed around in her seat to watch her mother leave. Andrew had made some strides with the girl during their sessions at the stables, but had yet to completely overcome her hostility. There was more than a passing possibility that now he never would.

"We can talk in the library," he told Julia, standing aside to allow her to precede him into the room across the hall.

The scent of stale tobacco and musty volumes gave the place a stuffy, closed-in air. Hundreds of well-thumbed books lined the shelves, while month-old newspapers lay in a neat stack on the sturdy reading table Sergeant Schnyder had ordered constructed for just that purpose. This early in the day, the library was unoccupied, although a dozen or more bored, restless men would crowd into it after the evening meal.

Julia drifted to the table, rubbing one hand with the other nervously as Andrew closed the door behind them. When he turned to face her, a worried certainty darkened her violet eyes.

"It's Philip, isn't it? You've received word from him?"

"I've received word *of* him."

He dragged off his broad-brimmed campaign hat, turned it round and round in his hands. The telling was proving harder than he'd anticipated during the walk across the parade ground. Or maybe it was the waiting to hear what would come after the telling that corded his muscles.

"Private Rafferty came to see me this morning. He was off duty last night and spent a few hours at Coffee's. While he was there, he talked to a mule driver who spent last winter in Adler's Gulch."

Julia's breath hissed in. Catching her lower lip between her teeth, she waited.

"Rafferty asked him about your husband."

Her worried eyes dug into him like needle-sharp spurs. Hellfire and thunderation! There was just no easy way to do this.

During his time in the Army, Andrew had written dozens of letters, delivered countless last messages to wives and parents. He should have found the right words of comfort over the years. Instead, the news seemed to come harder each time he delivered it.

"The mule driver told Rafferty he remembered a Frenchified faro dealer at the Bucket of Blood Saloon named Bonnet or Bonnville or something like that. He said he was a sharp man with the cards."

Julia's nervous hands stilled instantly. Pain flooded her eyes. "Philip swore before he left he wouldn't gamble any more. Those were his last words to me."

"Julia..."

Andrew took a step toward her. A sad resignation replaced the pain, halting him in his tracks.

"I didn't believe him," she said softly. "I wanted to. Fool that I am, I wanted desperately to believe

Philip. I should have learned the lesson you taught me all those years ago.''

He deserved that, Andrew acknowledged silently, although admitting as much sure as hell didn't make the gall any easier to swallow.

"According to the mule driver, your husband's gambling days are over," he said quietly. "A drunken miner claimed he pulled a card from his coat sleeve. The miner shot him through the heart."

"Mon Dieu!"

Wrapping her arms around her waist, she turned away to stare blindly at the leather-bound volumes. Moments crept by with only the faint clip-clop of horses on the parade ground outside to disturb the musty silence.

Andrew stood with his hat fisted in his hands. The need to comfort her tugged at him, yet he knew any condolences would sound as false to her ears as they would to his own. He couldn't pretend to be sorry she was free of a man he'd never met. Nor could he deny that her freedom made no difference to either of them. Still, he wasn't prepared for the stubborn tilt to her chin when she swung back to face him once more.

"Philip never cheated at cards in his life. If he had, he might have won a little more than he lost."

"The mule driver didn't say he cheated, only that a miner thought he did."

"Whatever the circumstances, I don't believe he's dead."

"What?"

"I *won't* believe it," she corrected, "until I see proof with my own eyes."

"How the devil do you intend to obtain that proof? Press on to Adler's Gulch to view his grave marker... assuming there is one?"

"If I must."

"For pity's sake, Julia! You haven't heard from him in over a year. Now you've received confirmation of sorts that he was killed. Would you drag Suzanne across three hundred miles of Sioux and Cheyenne territory to stand on her father's grave?"

Her chin tipped up another notch. "Don't dare to tell me what I should or shouldn't do, or what I should or shouldn't believe! I once saw you lying in a pool of blood. I believed my uncle when he told me you were dead. I refuse to believe secondhand tales about Philip."

"Secondhand tales?" Fury rose hot and fast in Andrew's chest as the implication of her words sank in. "Do you think I made up this mule driver? Or that I would lie to you about your husband?"

"I don't know what to think right now," she shot back, "although..."

"Although what?" he asked dangerously.

"We both know you've lied to me before."

If she'd grabbed an ax handle and beaten him over the head with it, Andrew wouldn't have felt the blows any harder than that one. He stalked forward, his anger exploding like grapeshot in his veins.

Julia's bruised heart welcomed the rage she saw

blazing in his eyes. She deserved his anger, and worse. Far worse. As long as she lived, she'd never forgive herself for her spurt of relief upon hearing that her agonizing uncertainty about Philip's whereabouts was over at last.

Or for her sudden, guilty realization that she was free to love again.

Guilt had made her lash out at Andrew. Guilt now held her stiff as a poker while he fought to control his fury.

"This isn't the time or the place to say what needs to be said between us," he ground out. "But it will come, Julia. And soon."

"This is as good a time or place as any. Say whatever you wish to me."

"No, you need time to—"

"Say it, Andrew! Straight out. No lies. No shading the truth."

For a moment, she thought she'd goaded him into loosening the rein he held on his temper.

"You need time," he growled again. "We'll talk later, when our emotions have cooled."

His words rang in Julia's head for the rest of that long, heart-wrenching day. Somehow, she finished the morning's classes and composed herself during the noon break, but the afternoon passed in a blur of worry over what to tell Suzanne about her father.

The sympathetic look on Mary Donovan's face when she called at Julia's quarters after supper settled the matter. Rumors were already flying around the post, the laundress confirmed. Since it was only a matter of time until her daughter heard some version of the story, Julia knew she had to tell her.

As she'd expected, Suzanne took the news of Philip's possible death with a storm of tears.

"No, Mama! No! Papa's waiting for us in Montana Territory. You said we'd go there and find him."

"I'm sorry, *ma petite*."

"He's not dead!" Tears streamed down her cheeks. "He's not! He's *not!*"

Julia held her in her arms and rocked her until she'd cried herself out and dropped into an exhausted sleep. Wishing she could do the same, she tucked the girl into bed and prowled about her quarters until guilt and wrenching doubts about the future left her too exhausted to think.

Thankfully, the next day was Saturday. With no school to teach, Julia spent the day with a red-eyed and tearful Suzanne. The next few days saw a steady progression of callers.

A solemn Little Hen and her mother brought a mourning gift of pemmican cake. Walks In Moonlight said little, but Julia appreciated both her gift and her soothing companionship.

The laundresses followed in her wake, one after another, offering awkward sympathy. Maria Schnell and the officers' ladies came, as well. Even Victoria McKinney made the trip to Suds Row after tattoo one evening. Julia had just taken down her hair with a thought to washing it when a baby's squawling cry announced the latest visitor. Hastily, she rebuttoned the top buttons of her chemise and pulled her blouse back on.

Victoria's false sympathy and curiosity to know Julia's plans shredded her hostess's nerves. The visit lasted less than twenty minutes. Ushering Victoria out with more firmness than courtesy, Julia walked down to the end of the row quarters and knocked on Mary's door.

"Could Peggy come and watch Suzanne? I need to walk and think a bit."

"O'course. Are you needin' someone to talk to? I'll get my shawl and come with you."

"No, thank you. I—I just need to think."

The early evening air carried a soft coolness. After seeing Peggy settled with a candle and her books, Julia grabbed her own shawl and walked along the riverbank. Bullfrogs sounded their deep, croaking chorus as she struggled with the guilt that still threatened to choke her.

Why couldn't she grieve for Philip?

Why did she feel only this empty numbness?

Although she'd told Andrew she wouldn't believe her husband dead until she saw proof with her own eyes, she knew in her heart he was gone. Knew, too, that he'd been lost to her for more than the two years since he'd left to find the fortune that always seemed just out of his reach. For all his charm and careless smiles when he was home, Philip's gambling had taken him away more and more with each passing year.

In his absence, Julia had been the one to deal with the angry shopkeepers and impatient creditors. And it was Julia who'd sold off their belongings, piece by piece, until nothing remained but her husband's empty promises and grandiose schemes. Now even those were gone.

What should she do now? What *could* she do?

There was no going back to New Orleans. Or to Mobile. She had no family left to take her and Suzanne in, and Philip's relations had cut him off years before Julia had met him. Nor could she go on to Adler's Gulch. Despite her angry words to Andrew, she wouldn't drag her daughter through three hundred miles of hostile territory to view a grave.

That left only here, she realized with a lump in her throat. At least for now.

She stood on the bank, chewing on her lower lip. Farther down along the river, the lights of the main post winked in the early dusk. The square, solid bulk of Old Bedlam rose above the other buildings and loomed against the purpling sky. Julia stood still and silent, staring at the golden light that spilled from its windows.

Night had blackened the sky when Old Bedlam's front steps creaked under her feet. From her previous visits, she knew Colonel Cavanaugh's quarters and offices took up the south wing. Andrew occupied two rooms in the north. To reach them, she traversed a long, dimly lit central hallway that smelled of tobacco and boot polish.

Private O'Shea answered Julia's tentative knock. The striker's brows soared when he saw who stood on the other side of the threshold. She forced a small, polite smile.

"I'd like to talk to the major."

"He's upstairs with the other officers, missus. Will you come in and wait while I go fetch him?"

Nodding, she stepped inside. O'Shea snatched his uniform jacket from the back of a chair and scrambled into it before hurrying out.

Left alone for a few minutes, Julia glanced around curiously. Although the officers on the post held frequent parties and soirees in their quarters, she'd refused the invitations she'd received over the past months. She'd been too tired after bending over the tubs all day, for one thing. For another, the awkwardness of her situation had made her uncomfortable in social gatherings. Consequently, this was her first glimpse of how the bachelor officers lived.

If Andrew's quarters were any indication, they lived as austerely as the rest of Fort Laramie's residents. The quartermaster had obviously furnished the cast-iron stove and wood plank table, but Andrew had supplemented the government-issue furnishings with pieces of his own. A thick buffalo skin rug covered the floor. Crossed sabers hung on one wall, and a framed print of West Point on another. Folding campaign chairs provided more than adequate seating, while shelves held a collection of leather-bound books and mementos.

One in particular caught Julia's eye. Moving closer, she peered at the exquisitely painted miniature. The woman in the oval portrait had Little Hen's dark hair and eyes, matured to a stunning sensuality. Yellow Buckskin Girl, Julia guessed, oddly disconcerted at putting a face to the legend.

Creaking floorboards in the hallway warned her of Andrew's approach. She turned, swiping her palms down her skirt front. Sudden nervousness attacked her. She should have delayed this visit, she thought. Taken more of the time Andrew had insisted she'd needed.

No, time would change nothing, except perhaps to dull the aching emptiness in her heart. She couldn't afford the luxury of waiting for that to happen. Mentally, she rehearsed what she intended to say to the major in her mind, but the man who entered the room a moment later looked so little like the officer she'd grown used to seeing that the words fled.

He still wore his boots and blue uniform pants with the cavalry stripe down each leg, but his suspenders stretched over an undyed broadcloth shirt. Open at the neck and rolled up at the sleeves, the well-washed fabric molded his shoulders. Small swirls of chest hair showed above the unfastened top buttons of the shirt, russet-dark against his tanned skin.

He closed the door behind him, his blue eyes searching her face. "Are you all right?"

"Yes. Better than I was the last time we talked, anyway."

She drew her tongue along lips gone dry with nervousness. It had just occurred to her that this was the first time she'd been alone behind closed doors with Andrew since their wedding night so many years ago.

Dear Lord in heaven! How could she remember that night in every, searing detail, yet struggle to recall Philip's face? Racked by the guilt that heaped onto her shoulders once more, she plunged into the matter that had brought her there.

"You were right, Andrew. I wasn't thinking coherently that day in the library."

"That's understandable given the circumstances."

"I can't seem to think any more coherently even now." Twisting one end of her shawl around her fingers, she played with the black fringe. "I've been walking down by the river, trying to decide what I should do."

His expression became still and watchful. "What did you decide?"

"Nothing yet. I—I needed to talk to you first." Gathering her courage, she lifted her chin. "You said there were matters that needed saying between us. I need to hear them, Andrew. Now, before I can determine what I must do next."

He was silent so long her nerves came close to unraveling. She was considering a bolt for the door when he tossed the challenge she'd thrown at him back at her.

"Do you want it straight out?"

Her heart pounded so hard against her ribs she was sure he could hear the thuds. "Yes."

He moved toward her then, one slow step at a time. His intent gaze raked her face. "I want you, Julia. In my arms. In my bed. Despite the years and the hurts that lie between us, I want the woman you've become as much—no, more than I ever wanted the girl I knew in New Orleans."

It was what she'd expected. No more. No less. The truth, without paint or varnish. He wanted her. The blunt admission demanded an equally honest answer. Swallowing the lump in her throat, she forced her reply through stiff lips.

"I don't love you. I'm not sure I can ever trust you again, but I…"

A muscle jumped in the side of his jaw. "You what, Julia?"

"I…"

So much for her noble intentions! She couldn't lay herself bare, couldn't admit that she needed him, that she craved his touch and his strength. That she longed to lose herself in the desire he made no effort to disguise. For just a moment. Just a night.

For Suzanne's sake, she'd struggled for so long, held her head up proudly when she wanted to slink away and hide. For now, for this small bite of time, she needed someone stronger than she was, someone who demanded nothing more from her than what she was willing to give.

What she *wanted* to give, God help her!

Mercifully, Andrew didn't seem to need to hear the words. A fierce light sprang into his eyes. She recognized it immediately for what it was. A mix of triumph, of satisfaction, of male desire so raw and potent Julia's womb clenched.

She barely had time to absorb the shock before he closed the distance between them. She felt his heat, the tension that leaped from his body and hers. Then he curled a hand under her chin and tipped her face to his.

13

Andrew intended only a taste. Just enough to satisfy the ache that threatened to leave him permanently crippled.

He recognized his folly the instant Julia wrapped her arms around his neck. Like a tumbling mountain stream swollen by early spring thaws, the feelings he'd tried so hard to keep locked away burst their chains.

This was Julia pressed against his chest and groin and thighs. Julia whose mouth opened so urgently under his. The woman he'd come as close to hating as he had to loving. The wife he'd done his damnedest to forget.

She didn't love him. She didn't trust him. But she wanted him with the same raw hunger he wanted her. He could feel it in the way she strained against him, taste it in the greedy tangle of their tongues and teeth.

He told himself to go easy. Actually believed a mere kiss would satisfy the ache. Like a fool, he even tried to draw back when he hardened with swift, painful intensity.

"No. Don't pull away. Please, Andrew."

Half whispered, half moaned against his lips, the plea shattered any thoughts he had of sparing her or himself.

She didn't love him.

She didn't trust him.

But she wanted him.

Widening his stance, he wrapped an arm around her waist and hauled her body hard against his. He'd handled her so gently the first time. Taken such care not to bruise her creamy skin or give her any hurt after the first, hard thrust. This time, the need to claim her, to leave his mark, roughened his mouth and his hands.

She welcomed his assault with a fierceness that matched his, as if she, too, wanted no reminder of how things had been before. This was no sweet, tender exploration, no slow fanning of the flames. This was a flash of heat, a greedy match of mouth to mouth and hip to groin.

Twisting her flowing hair around his fist, Andrew dragged her head back. Her neck arched. Her hips canted even more intimately into his. He felt the swell of her mound against his groin and had to tear his mouth from hers or he would have dragged her to the floor then and there. His eyes raked her flushed cheeks, the slant of her coal-black brows.

"This is how I remembered you," he growled,

more to himself than to her. "When I let myself think of you at all."

He hadn't intended it as a barb, but she flinched and opened her eyes. Old angers and hurts shaded them to dark purple.

"If we're to talk of the past, I should tell you this is *not* how I remember you."

With a wry smile, Andrew shifted her in his arms, just an inch or two, only enough to rock her mound against his corded thigh.

"Then we'd best not talk, Julia."

"No," she gasped, the heat rising in waves in her throat and cheeks. "No talking."

She was panting when he brought her head up and her mouth to his again, but the touch of their lips was no longer enough for either of them. Her hands clutched his shoulders, her fingers dug into his muscles. His tangled in the fringe of her shawl. Impatiently, he yanked it off and unhooked the bone fasteners that closed the collar on her blouse.

Holding her head anchored by that heavy twist of hair, Andrew trailed kisses down the underside of her jaw to her throat. Her skin was hot under his lips. The scent of starch and eager woman filled him with an immediate need to rid her of the rest of her clothes. He went to work on the next button, but the hand she slid down his chest to the flap of his trousers shoved the breath back down his throat and destroyed his coordination. His whole being was centered on the press of her fingers against his hard, ridged flesh.

Within seconds, her busy hand came damned close to destroying his command over his own body.

With a sound somewhere between a groan and a growl, Andrew caught her up and carried her to the back room. Like the front, it was sparsely furnished, boasting only a bed, a washstand and a clothes press. Pegs held his dress saber in its silver-tipped sheath, a cartridge box and Colt pistol in its leather holster. His hunting and sporting rifles were mounted on pegs above his military-issue Sharps carbine. Another buffalo hide rug covered the wood plank floor.

Andrew had spent his first years on the frontier battling the barbs and fleas that inhabited the straw-filled ticking furnished by the quartermaster. It had cost a month's pay, but he'd had the sutler freight him in a mattress sewn with horsehair and stuffed with goosedown. He gave fervent thanks for that extravagance now. In a fever of anticipation, he envisioned Julia's soft, sinuous body sprawled across the imported mattress.

As matters turned out, they never put it to use. Lowering her to stand on the curly-haired buffalo rug, Andrew set about removing her clothes. Each layer revealed another smooth curve of flesh, another soft target for his kisses. Her blouse yielded the slopes of her high breasts. The half corset, her narrow waist. Mercifully, she wore only two petticoats under her skirt, but the strings knotted under Andrew's impatient fingers.

Interspersing kisses with curses, he went down on

one knee to tug at the damned knot. It finally gave and the petticoats fell away, leaving only the barriers of her cotton underchemise and the drawers riding low on her waist. He couldn't resist the patch of bare skin peeping between the two. Curling an arm around her waist, he drew her closer.

At the touch of his tongue on her belly, Julia jumped. She stood awkwardly while he used his tongue and his lips and his hand to smooth and stroke and arouse. Her heart stuttered and skipped. Her breath came in little pants. She looked down at his dark head, at his broad shoulders, and ached to put her arms around him and clutch him close. It was so intimate, this moment, so incredibly tender.

Then his hand found the slit in her drawers and all thoughts of tenderness fled. Gasping, she tried to jerk away from his touch. He held her easily, murmuring assurances between the kisses he dropped on her breasts, her hips, her belly. All the while his skilled fingers probed intimately between her thighs. Within moments, she was groaning. Moments more, and she gushed hot and wet.

Her knees gave out then, or perhaps she just dropped. Julia didn't know and didn't care. All she wanted, all she needed was the feel of his body on hers. In hers.

Knee to knee, mouth to mouth, she yanked down his suspenders and attacked the buttons on his shirt with the same urgency he ripped away her chemise and drawers. When they were naked enough for flesh to meet flesh, Julia fell back atop the scattered clothing, dragging him down with her. They rolled onto the buffalo rug, legs tangling, hips grinding. She felt him stiff as a pole against her belly. Wiggling, she wedged a hand between their straining bodies.

He filled her fingers, thick and hot and bone-hard. Two strokes and his panting grunts matched hers. Four, and the velvety head dewed in her hand.

She'd been married long enough to recognize the urgency of his need even before he rolled her onto her back and thrust a knee between her legs to pry them apart. A part of her cried with want, with an intense longing for just a few moments more of this pulse-pounding play, but she opened for him and prepared to satisfy his need.

The muscles of his forearms tightened as he positioned himself. She felt the head lodge, felt his buttocks clench under her fingers, but the hard thrust she expected didn't come.

"Open your eyes."

The hoarse command dragged her from the feverish depths. She blinked, surprised and questioning. With her legs spread wide and his body penetrating hers by only a maddening inch or two, she felt so vulnerable, so...so trapped.

"I want to watch you when the pleasure takes you," he growled.

She arched her back, every nerve in her body screaming as he pushed in another inch. Only another inch. Her head went back. Her womb clenched. She tried to squirm down, to impale herself. He moved with her, giving her only that part of him already inside.

"Look at me, Julia," he ordered again, his muscles quivering.

His intent burst on her feverish mind. He wanted her to see him, to know who it was whose body claimed hers.

"For God's sake, Andrew!"

Half angry, half insane now with her own need, she writhed under him. Either the sound of his name or her fierce urgency satisfied him. Whatever the cause, he flexed his buttocks and thrust into her, not hard and fast, as she wanted so desperately, but slowly, deliberately.

Julia had never experienced such intense desire, never felt so wholly and completely at the mercy of her own raging need. Nothing in her marriage to Philip had prepared her for this. No remembered moments from the times she'd bedded with Andrew could compare.

With each slow push, the muscles low in her belly clenched. With each withdrawal, her mind screamed in protest. When she could stand no more, she wrapped her legs around his corded thighs and set her own pace.

Any thoughts Andrew had of holding back, of watching Julia's pleasure take her before he attended to his own, disintegrated at that moment. He drove into her, his hips ramming into hers. She arched under him. Head back, hips lifted, she bent like a young sapling, ready, quivering. A raw groan ripped from far back in her throat.

"Andrew! Now, Andrew. Please!"

With a growl that matched hers, he fastened his mouth on hers and slammed into her again. He felt the hot spurt come and pulled out, spilling his seed onto her belly. With so much yet to be resolved between them, he couldn't ask her to bear his child. Yet.

Julia lay limp and unmoving long after her waves of pleasure faded. Gradually, other sensations besides the pulsing of her own blood intruded on her senses.

Andrew's sweat-slicked body weighted her down. Stiff, curly buffalo hair tickled the skin at the small of her back. Wadded clothes formed an annoying lump under one shoulder.

Yet she couldn't bring herself to move. A thousand emotions held her pinned to the rug. Fierce satisfaction. Joyous relief. Wonder. Guilt.

It was an odd sort of guilt. More remorse over the fact that she didn't feel more disloyal to Philip's memory than true regret for having dishonored him by lying with another man.

No, not with another man. With Andrew.

Frowning, Julia squirmed. The inert weight atop her shifted immediately in response.

"I'm sorry," he murmured, rolling over. "I'm too heavy for you."

Arms and legs still entangled with his, Julia rolled

with him and landed on his chest. She raised her head and saw something of her own contradictory emotions reflected in his face.

He wore the look of a well-satisfied male. But she couldn't interpret his crooked smile when he lifted a hand to tuck her tangled hair behind her ear.

"Don't look so worried, Julia. We've just proved we can contrive well enough without love or trust."

She reared back, stung by the echo of her own words. Her mouth opened, but a sudden hammering on the door cut off her reply.

This time it was Andrew who frowned. Easing Julia aside, he rolled to his feet and tugged his pants from under her.

She should have looked away. Despite this frenzied coupling, the years had made them strangers. Yet she found herself unable to turn her head. His muscled arms, so tanned where rolled-up sleeves had bared them to the sun, held her gaze. As did his flat belly and lean, muscled flanks...until he angled his hip and stepped into his trousers.

"Dear Lord!"

Her horrified gasp stilled his fingers on the button flap. She'd never seen such brutal scars. Puckered ridges crisscrossed his thigh where it joined his hip, some white and faded, others still brownish-red.

She had imagined what he must have suffered, first from the bullet her uncle put into his thigh, then from the rifle butts Private O'Shea had said the guards at Andersonville slammed into him.

Her imagining had come nowhere close to reality. Stricken, she raised her glance to his.

"Andrew, I—I—"

What could she say? After all the years and all the hurts, what on earth could she say that would in any way make up for the pain he'd suffered?

Once more, the urgent pounding on the door in the other room relieved her of the necessity of saying anything. A muffled call accompanied the round of knocking.

"Major Garret, sir? Are you in quarters?"

"Yes. I'm coming."

He closed the door to the bedroom behind him to shield her from curious eyes. The rough plank door gave her privacy to dress, but didn't block the hurried exchange in the other room.

"Colonel Cavanaugh's compliments, sir. He's received a telegraph from Fort Phil Kearny."

"Regarding?"

"He didn't say, sir, but he requests your presence immediately."

"All right. Tell the colonel I'll report as soon as I pull on my uniform."

"Yes, sir."

Julia had scrambled to her feet and dragged on her drawers by the time he returned. Unaccountably shy, she pulled her sleeveless chemise over her head and thrust her arms through the openings before turning to face him.

''Wait for me,'' he instructed, yanking on a boot. ''We need to talk.''

Julia borrowed the phrase she'd just overheard. ''Regarding?''

He shoved his other foot into a boot. The heel thudded against the bare planks as he stomped it in place. Snatching his uniform shirt from a peg, he jerked it on as he crossed the floor.

''Regarding us.''

With that succinct reply, he wrapped an arm around her waist and pulled her close for a swift, hard kiss.

''Wait for me,'' he ordered again.

Grabbing his leather holster and cap on his way out, he left Julia in the middle of the room. The outer door slammed a moment later. The uneven flooring in Old Bedlam's long hallway groaned under his footsteps before all sounds faded away.

Julia stood where he'd left her, her bare toes curled into the buffalo hide. The most ridiculous urge to cry suddenly gripped her.

As Andrew had pointed out, they'd just demonstrated they could contrive well enough without love or trust...on either side.

Angrily, she bit down hard on her lower lip. What had she expected from him, for pity's sake? Flowery phrases? Passionate declarations? She'd come to him, hadn't she? As brazen as any whore at one of the hog ranches scattered around the post, offering herself in exchange for...

For what? What did she want of Andrew Garrett

now? For the life of her, Julia couldn't sort through the overwhelming needs that had driven her across the moonlit parade ground to his quarters.

She was still trying to understand what this stolen hour might mean to them when he returned. She was waiting as ordered, fully dressed and in the sitting room. One glance at his face told her any discussion between them would have to be postponed indefinitely.

His eyes grim, he crossed to where she stood. "I'm taking a column out at dawn. I'm sorry, but I'll have to meet tonight with my company officers and lay out the marching orders."

"What's happened?"

"Some five- to six-hundred Cheyenne and Bad Face Ogalalla Sioux attacked a woodcutting party near Fort Phil Kearny earlier today. Our men routed them, but Colonel Cavanaugh thinks this may signal a new wave of attacks on the posts strung out along the Bozeman Trail. I'm escorting three companies of infantry up to reinforce the Forts Reno, Kearny and Smith."

Her blood chilled. "Dear Lord!"

"It's not as bad as it sounds," he said in an obvious attempt to alleviate her fear. "Initial reports indicate Spotted Tail's Brulé band didn't participate in the attack, nor did Sitting Bull and his braves. My guess is that Red Cloud was returning from the summer dance ceremonies and stumbled across a target of opportunity."

"Was anyone killed?"

"We lost three troopers and four civilians who'd been hired to help with the woodcutting. Captain Powell, commander of the detail, reports sixty hostiles killed and a hundred or more wounded. His men were just issued a new, breech-loading Springfield rifle," Andrew explained, his brow furrowed. "No one, me included, had any idea of its effectiveness until this incident."

It sounded like far more than an incident to Julia, but his next comment drove the thought from her mind.

"I've given Private O'Shea instructions to help you and Suzanne move into these quarters."

"I beg your pardon?"

"There's no need for you remain on Suds Row any longer. O'Shea will come for your things tomorrow."

Astounded that he would order her life so arbitrarily, Julia gaped at him.

"I've got to go. The officers are gathering in the mess."

He grabbed her arms and kissed her, as swift as before, but with his mind already clearly on the immediate tasks ahead of him.

"Andrew! Wait! I can't just take up residence in your quarters."

"Why not?" A slashing grin relieved the tightness around his mouth and eyes. "If you're worried about appearances, there's no need. Most of the people on the post think we're still married. They don't understand how our union was simply put aside. Neither do I, for that matter, but it's a moot point now.''

"What do you mean?"

"I told you we'd contrive, Julia, and so we will. Very well, I'd say after tonight. We'll take care of the formalities when I return. Wait here for O'Shea. He'll take you back to your quarters."

He was gone before Julia could gather her whirling thoughts enough to protest further.

Andrew and his troop rode out at dawn without the fanfare of flags and drums this time. Julia didn't join the sleepy well-wishers who turned out to see them off. Her emotions were in too much turmoil, and Suzanne had awakened colicky and complaining of stomach cramps.

Julia kept the fretful girl in bed and sent a plea to Corporal Gottlieb to arrange for someone to cover classes for her that day. Suzanne's indisposition also gave her a convenient excuse to turn Private O'Shea away when he came to move Julia and her daughter to Old Bedlam.

The striker muttered about the major having his hide if he failed to follow orders, but left.

He returned to Suds Row early the next morning. Julia froze when she opened the door and saw him standing outside, his expression grave beneath the bill of his forage cap.

"I'm afraid I've got worrisome news, missus."

Her nails dug into the door frame. Andrew's patrol!

They'd been attacked! Fear for him clogged her throat, and with it came a regret so deep and sharp she couldn't breathe.

"Jules Escoffey asked to see Colonel Schnell this morning," the private informed her.

Wetting her lips, Julia croaked out a query. "Who is Jules Escoffey?"

"He and his partner run the, uh, establishment three miles down river."

It took her a moment to understand the reference. "Coffee's Hog Ranch?"

"Yes, ma'am."

"Did they have some news about the major and his column?"

"The major? No, ma'am. Jules came to report that Fat Sarah died."

Totally bewildered, Julia stared at him. "Who's Fat Sarah?"

"She's one of his girls."

"I'm sorry to hear she died, but what has her death to do with me?"

"Nothing directly, ma'am." Worry dug deep creases in the New Yorker's brow. "But the doc says what took her sounds like cholera, and seeing as how half the troopers on post have laid with Fat Sarah some time or another, the sickness might start going around. I thought I'd better tell you, missus, since the major instructed me to watch out for you while he was gone."

Julia barely heard his last few sentences. The fear

she'd felt for Andrew a moment ago paled beside the terror that now poured into her. Her blood pounding in her ears, she turned.

Her daughter frowned from across the room, her brown eyes dark pools in a flushed, feverish face.

14

Six days later, Julia slumped against the center pole
of the canvas tent, wondering what she or any of the
others in this makeshift hospital ward had done to
deserve this hell on earth.

She hadn't slept for more than a few minutes at a
time in almost a week. Couldn't remember the last
time she'd eaten. The stench of vomit and the watery
diarrhea that filled the buckets beside the rows of cots
would clog her nostrils for the rest of her life.

Sweat poured down her neck. Her soiled blouse
stuck to her skin. Suffocating heat filled the tents that
had been thrown up to shelter the stricken. The August sun that beat down on the canvas coverings was
bad enough without the cooking fires burning right
outside the tent flaps adding to the suffering inside.

But the fires were a necessary evil. The only treat-
ment that seemed to provide the moaning patients any
hope of recovery at all was to force boiled saltwater
down their throats until they purged their stomachs

and their bowels. That done, it was necessary to swaddle them in blankets and apply hot water bottles, bricks wrapped in blankets or even baked ears of corn to their feet to sweat out the sickness.

Some retched up the salt water immediately, broke into a sweat and recovered within a few hours. Others had died before they even made it to the tents, having displayed no symptoms at all. A few had lingered on for almost a week now, parched, lethargic, skin dry, eyes sunken in their sockets, discharging fluid as fast as their nurses could pour it into them.

Like Suzanne.

She lay on a cot in the center of the tent that had begun as a ward for women and children, but now sheltered whoever needed tending. Her coffee-brown hair lay lank and lusterless against the folded blanket that served as a pillow. Her eyes stared unseeing from the face of a near skeleton. By contrast, the cheeks of the porcelain doll tucked in the crook of her arm bloomed with obscene, painted health.

If Julia had thought about such matters at all, she would have supposed she'd become numb with the passage of so many desperate hours. Instead, her heart broke all over again each time she bathed her daughter's emaciated body or emptied the bucket beside her cot.

No wonder the French called cholera *mort-de-chien,* a dog's death. The vomiting and diarrhea drained so much from the victims that they became shrunken caricatures of their former selves. The pain that racked their joints drew screams from even the strongest men. No one, even the lowliest, flea-bitten cur, deserved to suffer like this.

"How's the little one doing?"

With the slow, awkward movements of an old woman, Julia turned to greet Mary Donovan.

"She's holding on."

"I don't know how. Poor little thing."

The Irish laundress looked as ravaged as Julia felt. Her strawberry red hair hung in lank tendrils about her face. Grief had carved deep lines around her eyes and mouth. Her youngest, Molly, had been stricken and recovered, but she'd lost her boy Patrick three days ago. Now her husband was down.

"How about the sergeant major?"

"His eyes have gone glassy. I doubt he'll make it through the night."

Wordlessly, Julia held out her arms. Mary walked into them, too numb and weary to cry. The two women clung to each other. They'd shared so much in their brief acquaintance. Had so many roads yet to travel, Julia feared. Shuddering, she forced the thought from her mind. All they could do was take each hour, each day, as it came.

At the far end of the tent, the trooper pouring salt-water down a moaning private's throat lifted his head. His glance flicked to the two women. Silently, he turned his attention back to his task. Death was too common an occurrence these days to borrow anyone else's grief.

Mary pulled away, her blue eyes bright with unshed tears. "I have to get back. Walks In Moonlight is tendin' to Sean now. We just wanted to know how Suzanne did."

How sad that it had taken an epidemic to bring down the artificial social barriers separating the women on the post. Cholera held no respect for rank or skin color. Sleeves rolled up, skirts pinned out of the way, officers' ladies, laundresses and native wives all toiled side by side with the troopers detailed to hospital duty.

Those ladies who hadn't fled, that is, or barricaded themselves inside their homes and fought frantically to keep the sickness away by burning feathers dipped in sulfuric acid and dosing their families with calomel and tincture of opium. Julia didn't blame Victoria McKinney and the handful of other women of all ranks who refused to come near the hospital tents. If Suzanne hadn't been stricken, she wasn't sure whether she would have risked carrying the disease back to her own child, either.

Luckily, Walks In Moonlight had sent Little Hen to her people at the first sign of illness. Suzanne's playmate was safe, thank God.

Her arms still wrapped around her friend, Julia rested her cheek against Mary's. "Can I do anything to help you with Sean?"

The laundress pulled back. Blowing out a weary sigh, she shook her head. "You're doin' enough. I heard you sat with Mrs. Powers and the captain last night."

Julia nodded, glancing toward the cot where the infantry officer had breathed his last just hours ago. His exhausted wife had stayed with him through his final, agonizing moments. She'd only left to tend to her frightened children when Julia promised to help the orderly wash the captain's body and prepare it for the coffin makers.

"You've got to rest," Mary reminded her. "You can't tend to Suzanne and all the others, too."

"I'm here," Julia said simply. "I do what I can, just as you do."

With another hug, Mary left to go back to the sergeant major. Wearily, Julia resumed the task she'd interrupted to check on her lethargic daughter. Moving from cot to cot, she gathered the wooden buckets that needed emptying. The fishy odor of the white, watery bowel discharge no longer gagged her, but the bluish tint to the nails and the terrified expressions of those who sensed the end approaching still wrung her heart.

"Tilda?"

A glassy-eyed young recruit grasped at her apron. His breath rasping and labored, he dragged at Julia.

"Ist du, Tilda?"

Wearily, she set down the buckets to ease him back onto his cot.

"Shhh. You must rest easy."

He gabbled something in German and clung frantically to her apron.

Sighing, she sank down on the beaten grass and smoothed his hair back from his forehead. From somewhere she found the energy to hum the same lullaby to him she sang to Suzanne. It was all she could do for him at this point. For any of them.

She left the recruit a little more at peace, dreaming of his Tilda, she hoped. After another check on Suzanne, she resumed the backbreaking task of hauling the buckets down to the newly dug sinks. After dumping their noxious contents, she swilled them clean at the river.

She returned to find the young recruit dead and Victoria McKinney waiting for her. White-faced with fright, the lieutenant's wife stumbled forward.

"He won't wake, Julia! Dear God above, little William won't wake. Please, help me!"

One glance at the baby clutched to her chest sent Julia's stomach plunging to her boot tops. His lips were blue. The awful rictus of death was already contorting his tiny features into a mask.

Setting down the buckets, Julia scrubbed her hands down her apron front. "Let me take him."

Whimpering with fright, the young mother handed over her child. "Colonel Schnell said to bring him to you. He said you'd know what to do."

There was nothing she could do. Nothing anyone could do, except make the baby as comfortable as possible and hold the hand of a mother facing the loss of her child. She hadn't thought her heart could hurt any more, but it ached for the spoiled young wife stripped bare now of everything but a mother's terror.

"Come, we'll lay him on the cot next to Suzanne."

"Thank you," Victoria whispered raggedly. "Thank you!"

She followed on Julia's heels, almost tripped over her in her pathetic eagerness to see her baby cared for.

"I'm sorry I was so hateful to you when you first arrived, Julia. I—I don't mean to be, but…"

"Oh, Victoria, it doesn't matter. Nothing matters now but little William. Here, I'll show you how to dose him."

William McKinney II died the next afternoon. Julia rocked the ravaged Victoria in her arms for what seemed like hours after the baby slipped away, murmuring the wordless noises women across time have offered to each other at such times. The young wife clung to her, racked by sobs, until a haggard Mary Donovan poked her head in and persuaded the lieutenant's lady to go home and get some rest. She could make the necessary arrangements for his burial later.

Grasping brokenly at Julia's promise to wash William's tiny body, the weeping Victoria stumbled out of the tent with Mary. Heartsore, Julia performed the all too familiar ritual and carried the tiny bundle to the carpenters.

They'd set up a shop not far from the hospital tents.

A special detail had been dispatched to cut wood and haul it from the mountains forty miles away. Julia knew she would never again breathe in the tang of resin and green-cut wood without feeling her heart begin to weep inside her chest.

She left her tiny bundle with the red-faced, sweating carpenters and hurried back through the maze of tents set high on the bluffs above the fort. She hadn't been away from Suzanne's side for more than a few minutes at a time since she'd carried the limp, moaning girl into the sweltering tent.

Lifting the flap, she ducked inside to find an officer coated head to foot with trail dust standing beside her daughter's cot.

"Andrew!"

Her ragged cry wrenched him around. His eyes met hers across Suzanne's emaciated body. Julia read the shock in their silvery blue depths. She stumbled forward, unmindful of the fact she must look as wretched as her patients. She didn't care, couldn't spare a thought for anything except the need to lose herself in his strength.

Andrew rounded the end of the cot in three swift strides. He moved instinctively, driven by a primal need to comfort his woman. If the old lies and hurts that lay between them hadn't already faded into insignificance in his mind, this glimpse of Julia would have killed them instantly. She looked so exhausted, so close to despair, that his first, his only thought was to spare her and her daughter more pain. Given the chance, he would have gladly sacrificed his life in exchange for Suzanne's.

She all but fell into his arms, digging her fingers into his sleeves, burrowing her cheek against his crossed cartridge belts.

Neither spoke. Amid the rustle and moan of patients, the shuffle of the orderly moving from cot to cot, Andrew felt her heart thud against his chest. Her whole body trembled, whether from fatigue or fear he couldn't tell. The stench of vomit and urine permeated her hair, her blouse.

Finally, she drew her head back and looked up at him with eyes that would haunt him for the rest of his days.

"When did you get back?"

"A few moments ago."

"Did you…?" She shook her head, as if trying to remember what had taken him away. "Did you get the reinforcements to Fort Reno?"

"Yes." His jaw worked. "That's where they gave us the news."

As long as he lived, Andrew would remember the terror that had ripped through his gut when Fort Reno's commander rode out to meet the weary relief column with the news that cholera had broken out back at Fort Laramie. Twenty dead so far, the grim-faced colonel had reported. Sixty or more down. The disease was sweeping across the plains. Forts Larned and Riley in Kansas had also been hit. A fourth of Custer's Cavalry was stricken.

Andrew had known fear before. Any soldier who claimed his bowels didn't turn to water before a battle lied through his teeth. Those who had survived hell-holes like Andersonville carried another special set of demons on their backs. But Andrew had never experienced anything like the fear that knifed into him on that high, windswept plain.

He hadn't needed the news that Colonel Cavanaugh had ordered for his immediate return to galvanize him into action. Nor had his troop needed exhorting to slough off the weariness of six days' march. The fear that their wives or children or barracks mates might be among the dead or dying had spurred them on relentlessly. They'd left the infantry at Fort Reno, hurriedly resupplied and set out within an hour to retrace their steps.

Sleeping and eating in the saddle, they'd dismounted only long enough to feed, water and walk their mounts. The grueling march had cost them three horses, one to laming, one to snakebite and one to the "thumps," the sudden, palpitating heaves that could drop an overheated horse in its tracks without warning. Four men had had second thoughts and deserted rather than return to a camp swept by cholera. One had rejoined the column the next day.

The grim, silent troops had ridden past the post cemetery less than an hour ago. No regimental bands had turned out to welcome them when they reached the parade ground. Without fanfare they dismounted and dispersed to check on families and bunkmates.

The company commanders had been waiting for Andrew with their reports. His muscles as tight as bailing wire, he'd listened while they reeled off the losses. After approving on the spot extra pay for the troops who'd volunteered for hospital and burial duty, he put off all other matters until he'd consulted with the post surgeon.

Andrew hadn't drawn a whole breath until an exhausted Henry Schnell confirmed that Julia wasn't among the stricken. The surgeon had then proceeded to cut the ground out from under his feet with the news that Suzanne had been among the first to take ill.

Looking down at her small, wasted body, he couldn't imagine how the girl had found the strength to cling to life. He'd seen so many seemingly strong men curl up and die after only a few weeks in Andersonville. On the other hand, walking skeletons had survived months of near starvation and repeated bouts of dysentery, himself among them. The incomprehensible vagaries of life and death were the only comfort he could offer Julia now.

"She's made it this long," he murmured, stroking the dark head resting wearily against his shoulder. "Stronger men have succumbed, but she's held on."

"I don't know how."

The ragged whisper tore at his heart. With a visible effort, Julia raised her head. The hollows around her eyes made his chest ache.

"Do you know Private Rafferty died?"

"Yes."

"And little William McKinney?"

"Yes."

"Mary Donovan's son, Patrick, is gone." Grief darkened her eyes. "The sergeant major's down, too."

"I know."

To lose any of his troops was a blow. To lose a man with Sean Donovan's experience and calm head in a crisis would leave a gaping hole in the regiment.

"Henry Schnell said Colonel Cavanaugh has recovered enough to return to his quarters," Andrew told her, his voice gruff. "I have to give him my report and get him moved to Old Bedlam. I'll come back soon as he's taken care of."

With a tortured effort, she shrugged off her fatigue. "No, I'm not thinking. You shouldn't have come at all. It's too dangerous."

He didn't bother to respond.

"You could take the sickness," Julia cried, waking belatedly to the danger he'd exposed himself to.

Pain lanced into her, as sharp as a sword. She couldn't lose Suzanne and him, too. Dear God, not both of them!

A gloved thumb feathered across her lips, stilling her incipient panic.

"You're about to drop where you stand. You need sleep. I'll come back and watch Suzanne while you get some rest."

"I can't leave her."

''What use will you be to your daughter if you keel over in exhaustion?''

Or if she started cramping, or hearing the noises in her head that signaled the onset of cholera? The possibility that the disease might yet strike Julia had Andrew sweating under his uniform jacket.

''I'll be back,'' he promised grimly.

15

She couldn't leave.

Despite Andrew's stern orders when he returned, Julia refused to go back to her quarters to rest for fear Suzanne might slip away while she was gone. The most she would agree to was to curl up for a few hours on the cot emptied by the young private's death.

True to his word, Andrew took over Julia's nursing duties while she rested. The trooper detailed to help in the tent seemed somewhat awed by the sight of his major with sleeves rolled up, lifting patients to help them use the buckets and wrapping scraps of blanket around heated bricks to tuck at their feet. The barriers of rank between major and trooper soon fell away, however, just as the social barriers between the women had. Julia sank into an exhausted slumber to the murmur of Andrew's questions and the experienced nurse's firm responses.

She had no idea how long she'd slept when she woke, groggy and disoriented. A flicker of lamplight against the canvas tent wall sent fear bolting through her. Terrified that Suzanne might have lost her fragile hold on life, she rolled over.

The sight of Andrew seated on an upturned bucket beside her daughter's cot, murmuring to the girl while he bathed her face with a damp rag, left Julia limp with relief.

He'd taken off his uniform jacket in concession to the heat but still wore his riding boots and dark-blue pants with their yellow cavalry stripe. Suspenders stretched over his white linen undershirt that was already soiled. Whiskers shadowed his cheeks and chin, and his short, rumpled hair stood in spikes, as if he'd thrust a hand through it.

Seeing this tall, lean man bent over Suzanne closed Julia's throat. For all his joy in his daughter, Philip Bonneaux had considered it a mother's responsibility to change nappies and tend to childish complaints.

Shoving aside all thoughts of how different things might have been if Andrew, and not Philip, had fathered her child, Julia pushed off the borrowed cot and made her way down the center aisle. Two heads turned at her approach, one so slowly and painfully Julia's heart squeezed.

"Mama?"

The hoarse whisper wrung her soul. "I'm here, *ma petite.*"

As if that reassurance was all she needed, Suzanne's lids drifted down over sunken eyes.

"She drank a little boiled rice water a few hours

ago,'' Andrew said quietly, relinquishing his seat on the bucket. ''So far, it's stayed down.''

''Thank God!'' Dragging a hand through her hair, Julia tried to shake the last vestiges of sleep from her mind. ''What time is it?''

''A little after midnight.''

''Where's Private Connors?''

''The patients had quieted down, so I sent him to get a good meal and some rest. I don't suppose I can convince you to go down to the mess tent for a decent meal, too.''

''No, I won't leave Suzanne.''

''I figured as much.'' Retrieving a cloth-covered plate from a makeshift table in the corner of the tent, he pushed it into her hands. ''I asked Private Connors to bring you something before he headed back to his barracks. It's only cold beans and pork, with a little buttered bread,'' he warned.

Julia hadn't eaten in so long even cold beans and pork made her mouth water. Murmuring fervent thanks, she sank down onto the bucket.

Andrew disappeared and returned just as she was sopping up the last of the bean juice. Steam curled from the two tin mugs he carried. The wondrous aroma of hot, black coffee acted like a cattle prod on her numbed senses.

He passed her one of the cups, brought another bucket over, and squatted down beside her. They sat side by side, shoulders brushing as they downed the bitter brew, ears tuned to the mutters and occasional groans of their patients. Twice, Julia leaned forward to check her daughter's shallow breathing and sponge her face. Once, Andrew got up to help a whiskered infantryman roll over and piss into the bucket beside his bed. The veteran dropped back on his cot, exhausted by effort, and drifted into restless sleep.

"You're so good with them," Julia murmured when he reclaimed his seat.

Fort Laramie's other officers had dutifully come to check on their men, but had left the menial tasks of caring for them to the troopers on hospital detail. Andrew shrugged aside her surprise that he didn't do the same.

"We learned to take care of each other in Andersonville."

In the quiet of the night, with everything stripped from Julia's soul but prayers for her daughter and the others in the tent, she could finally ask Andrew about his past without stirring old hurts.

"How did you end up in prison? No—start earlier, before that. What happened that night in New Orleans? I heard the shot, and watched you fall. I saw the blood," she added hoarsely. "There was so much of it. My uncle swore you'd died of your wound."

"I almost did."

Leaning back against a tent support, he stretched out his legs. The tin mug nested loosely in his hands.

"I bled like a stuck pig," he admitted with a wry grimace. "The ball shattered my thighbone and knocked me out. Luckily, Justin didn't think it necessary to waste another shot. He had two servants drag me into the back of a wagon with instructions to cart my carcass off to the swamp. My guess is they were supposed to feed me to the alligators and spare a military tribunal the trouble of hanging me as a spy.''

Spare Justin the shame of having his name associated with that of a Union spy, Julia corrected silently. Her uncle had made it clear when he shipped her off to Natchez the next day that she'd better keep her mouth shut. With luck, his scheme to annul her marriage to Andrew would quash any rumors before they began to circulate.

That, and the fact that he'd disposed of Andrew's body.

''How did you get away?''

''I managed to throw myself out of the wagon as it drove along a levee. I landed in the Ponchetrain.''

His careless shrug made light of the agony he must endured in that fall.

''The damned river carried me almost to the Gulf. I hid out in the swamps for a few weeks, then eventually made it back to Union lines. My spying days were over, so I returned to my company. Two years later, what was left of my regiment marched into Andersonville. Eleven months after that, less than twenty of us crawled out.''

The sparse tale omitted so many details. The weeks of crawling through a swamp with a shattered thighbone. The battles he'd fought. The horror of the prison camps.

"I didn't know any of this," she whispered. "Justin bundled me onto a paddle wheeler and shipped me off to stay with friends in Natchez the very day after I— After you—"

"The day after I came back for you," he finished quietly. "It's all right, Julia. I don't blame you for showing your uncle the note I sent you. Nor do I blame him for shooting me down in the street."

Not any more, perhaps. He'd blamed her once, though, and hated her. Just as she'd hated him.

"I was a fool to entangle you in my dangerous games," he said. "An even greater fool to think I could protect you when I couldn't even tell you the truth about why I was in New Orleans in the first place."

"You weren't any more to blame for what happened than I was. I wouldn't listen when you warned me there were things about you I didn't know."

The ghosts of old passions, old hurts drifted through the tent. They left no bitterness in their wake, only a fleeting sadness for all the wasted years.

Downing the rest of his coffee, Andrew set the tin mug aside. Metal chinked against wood, rifling through the quiet.

"How long did you stay in Natchez?"

"For the rest of the war. I never went back to New Orleans. I couldn't live with my uncle any longer."

Or with the way Justin Robichaud's avid gaze had

followed her every move. Even after all these years, she couldn't put into words what she'd been too naïve—or too ashamed—to recognize at the time. Incest left as foul a taste in her mouth now as it did then.

Locking away the memories of her uncle in the darkest corner of her mind, she stared down at the coarse-ground coffee beans at the bottom of her mug.

"Is that where you met Bonneaux?"

She nodded, remembering the first time she'd bumped into Philip. She'd been staying with her cousin Dorothy and was on her way back from a ladies' auxiliary meeting at Monmouth Plantation, set high above the river. Fingers aching from hours of rolling bandages, she hadn't even noticed the dashing young officer making his way up Silver Street until an uneven paving stone tripped her and she pitched forward, right into his arms.

"He'd just assumed command of an ironclad."

The knowledge Philip gleaned from his gambling days aboard a succession of Mississippi riverboats had stood him in good stead during the war. Familiar with the river's twists and turns, its shifting sandbars and treacherous currents, he'd sallied out in his flat-topped, iron-plated gunship to stalk and sink enemy supply barges.

After each hazardous mission, he'd return to port in Natchez to woo the woman Julia had become. She'd married him within the year.

From the perfect perspective of hindsight, she could see now the real reason she'd accepted Philip

Bonneaux's persistent suit. He was everything Andrew Garrett wasn't.

Southern born and river-bred, Philip wore his gold and butternut gray with a jaunty pride. He kept no secrets from Julia, freely admitting to his past career as a gambler with fervent promises of reform. And his kisses roused only a gentle hunger instead of hot, mindless greed.

"After the war, we returned to his home in Mobile," she told Andrew. "That's where Suzanne was born."

He sifted the details through his mind, mulling them over in the quiet. So many happenings, Julia thought. So many roads traveled to get them to this isolated outpost on the plains. She wouldn't have believed it all those years ago, when a laughing, careless sixteen-year-old had caught a stranger's glance across a whirl of dancers and felt her breath quicken.

"I searched for you after the war."

Startled, she lifted her gaze to find his shadowed blue eyes on her, unreadable in the flickering light of the oil lamp.

"You did?"

"I went back to New Orleans. Justin was dead, and no one knew what had become of you."

The knowledge that he'd returned for her a second time started a little ache just under Julia's ribs.

"I finally ran down one of your old house servants. Tante Bettina, I think her name was."

"Our cook," she murmured. How long ago those days of servants and gracious living now seemed.

"She said she'd heard you'd taken up with a riverboat gambler."

"Is that the tale that got back to New Orleans? I'm not surprised. Philip used to ride the paddle wheelers before the war. He—he had a fondness for the river."

His fondness was for the deep games of chance played aboard those paddle wheelers, but even now Julia couldn't bring herself to reveal her husband's weaknesses to anyone. Not to Suzanne. Certainly not to Andrew.

Not that it needed revealing. Andrew had guessed her straightened circumstances within hours of her arrival at Fort Laramie.

God, was that a mere—what? Two months ago? Three? When had she left Mobile? In late May. It was now August. August what?

Lifting a tired hand to rub her neck, Julia tried to pinpoint the exact date she'd clutched Suzanne's hand in hers and boarded the train that took them both away from all that was familiar. It seemed so important to keep the weeks from blurring together, although she couldn't think why until she remembered that Suzanne's birthday came in early September.

A moan clawed at her throat. The fear she'd fought to hold at bay these endless days and night swam to the surface.

Please, Dear Lord! Please! Let her see another

birthday! I'll pay whatever you ask for my sins when it's my time to die. Just let her live.

Her nails dug into the back of her neck. Tears stung her eyes. She squeezed them tight, refusing to give in to the anguish that tore at her insides, unable to bear the sight of her daughter's emaciated form.

"Here, let me."

Andrew shifted on his bucket. A strong hand peeled away her fingers. Slowly, surely, he began to knead her shoulders, her neck, the base of her skull.

Julia's knotted tendons screamed in protest, but she welcomed the pain. Desperately, she fastened on the fire in her aching muscles, on the strength in Andrew's hands, on anything but the terrifying possibility that her daughter might not live to celebrate her sixth birthday.

Gradually, the knots loosened. Slowly, the fear receded. For long moments, there was only the steady rhythm of Andrew's breathing behind her. Almost boneless now with a week's worth of accumulated fatigue, Julia slumped on her bucket.

"Lean back. Rest against me."

The invitation rumbled low and seductive in her ear. She had no shame left, no defenses. She needed to draw on his strength. Wanted to ease into his arms and let him shelter her. For a moment. For...

For forever.

The truth seeped slowly into her consciousness. Wary as a kitten, it crept soft-footed into her mind. She'd loved the handsome rogue she'd known in New

Orleans with all the passion of her youthful heart. Now she craved this man's strength and solid support with every particle of her woman's soul.

She didn't love him. She no longer believed in that ephemeral, illusive emotion. But this…this was as close to love as Julia ever expected to feel again.

"Andrew."

It was a whisper, a plea. Her head tipped back on his shoulder, his angled down to meet her gaze. She could see every bristle in his cheek. See, too, the question in his gray-blue eyes.

Like one in a dream, she lifted her lips to his. His mouth fit over hers, so right, so sure.

"Mama?"

The hoarse whisper wrenched Julia's head around. She jerked forward on her bucket, her heart pounding. Brown eyes too dry and sunken for tears stared up at her in distress.

"Darling! Are you in pain?"

"Were you…kissing him?"

The raspy query cut straight to Julia's heart.

"No, sweetheart, we were only—"

Suzanne's small face scrunched in dismay. "You *were* kissing him."

Clearly agitated, she plucked at the blanket swaddling her thin body. In an agony of fear that she would use up her pitiful store of strength, Julia tried to soothe her.

"Be still, *chèrie*. Please."

Her daughter pushed at her restraining hands with weak fists, working herself into an agitation.

"I don't like this place! I want to go home!"

"We will, darling. We'll go back to Suds Row as soon as you get well."

"No! I want to go back to Mobile, to our own house!"

She thrashed disconsolately on the cot, forcing Andrew to rap out a command.

"Be still, Suzanne!"

Startled by the brusque order, she quieted for a moment. But only for a moment. Her lower lip trembling, she fixed sunken, resentful eyes on the major.

"I don't like you. You mashed Daisy. You're a bad man." Her small chest heaved. "I want my papa."

The pitiful cry closed Julia's throat. Swallowing the coppery taste of fear, she dropped to her knees beside the cot.

"Papa's gone, darling. Remember, Mama told you?"

"I want to go home." Sobs racked her daughter's thin frame. "Back to Mobile. To papa's house."

"Dear God!" Smoothing the lank brown hair from her daughter's forehead, she fought to calm the agitated girl. "Shhh, sweetheart. Shhh."

"Please, Mama. Promise me we'll go home."

The hoarse cry ripped Julia's heart out of her chest and shredded it into small pieces.

"I promise," she whispered, blinking fiercely to hold back hot, desperate tears. "Just get well, my little one, and we'll go home."

16

The spectre of death hovered above Fort Laramie throughout the rest of August.

Julia followed the funeral cortege too many times to count as people she now considered friends were laid to rest. Private Rafferty, who had succumbed during the first week. Sergeant Major Sean Donovan, buried with full military honors. Private Lowenstahl of the flowing blond mustaches and innate grace. He'd waltz no more, except with angels.

And the children. Julia's heart grieved with each small, freshly dug grave. Six died in addition to Patrick Donovan. Mary Donovan had taken her loss with dry-eyed stoicism, but Victoria McKinney had thrown herself atop her baby's coffin, sobbing hysterically, and had to be dragged away by her friends. Julia stayed with her whenever she could snatch an hour or two away from Suzanne's bedside.

The patients who survived recovered their strength, some quickly, others more slowly. Bit by painful bit,

Suzanne's thin frame fleshed out, but her sunken eyes and pallid skin haunted Julia. Little Hen's return to Fort Laramie helped spur her daughter's recovery. So did Andrew's reminder that her pony waited for her.

Julia made a point to avoid all appearance of partiality or friendship with Andrew during his visits to the invalid. The memory of that awful night when Suzanne had almost sobbed away the last of her strength would remain forever seared in her heart...along with the grim expression on Andrew's face after she'd promised the sobbing daughter that she'd take her home to Mobile.

Andrew didn't bring up the subject of their departure while Suzanne remained in the sick tent, for which Julia was profoundly grateful. Her own strength had stretched almost to the breaking point. She couldn't deal with anything but her daughter's day-to-day condition.

Nor did Andrew reopen the subject of moving them into his quarters. When Suzanne recovered enough to move her back to their apartment on Suds Row, he carried her down from the hospital himself. But Julia knew it was only a matter of time until they would have to discuss her promise to Suzanne. Sick at heart, she dreaded the moment Andrew would force her to defend her choice of her daughter over him.

Mary Donovan got the story from Julia one evening when the laundress came bearing a gooseberry pie for the invalid. While Mary's six remaining children crowded around Suzanne's bed and helped her devour the tart treat, the two women sat side by side on the bench outside.

They talked first of the still sick and the dead. Julia could only admire the way Mary had buried her grief along with her son and her husband.

"It does a body little good to mourn," the older woman said simply.

"Will you stay here?"

"Here, or at some other post. The Army's me home, don't y'know?"

Hands folded loosely in her aproned lap, the laundress lifted her gaze to the spectacular sunset painting the sky with pinks and golds.

"I'll marry again," she said after a moment, her eyes fixed on the swirl of colors. "I've already had three offers."

The old Julia, the Julia who'd grown up in a culture that expected women to don unrelieved black and retire from society for a full year after the death of a close family member, would have been shocked. The woman who'd emerged from the sick tents merely nodded.

"'Tis a matter of choosin' which o'the three will make the best father to me children," Mary mused. "And to the babe I'm carrying."

A strangled sound of joy and sadness escaped Julia. A new baby could in no way compensate for the loss of a son and a husband, but she could only thank God He'd seen fit to give Mary this bit of happiness to see her through the bleak days and weeks ahead.

"What about you?" the laundress asked. "Will you and the major be marryin' again?"

"No."

"Whyever not?"

A flight of geese swooped over the rooftops. Long black necks extended, wings flapping, they splashed into the river to break their journey south for the night. Their raucous honking gave Julia the time she needed to frame a quiet response.

"As soon as Suzanne regains enough strength to travel, I'm taking her back to Mobile."

"Why? What's waitin' for you there?"

Nothing but empty yesterdays, she admitted silently, and the promise of Suzanne's tomorrows.

The laundress wagged a finger under her nose. "Now you listen to me, missus. The major's daft about you, don't y'know? You and that little girl, both."

"You don't understand. I promised Suzanne I'd take her home."

"Well glory be, *un*-promise her!"

"It's not that simple. I bargained with God, too." The pledge she'd offered over and over again in the darkest hours echoed in her mind. "If he spared my daughter's life, I swore I'd—I'd—"

"Give up anything that smacked o'sin or worldly pleasure and live a pure, repentant life," Mary finished dryly.

"More or less."

"The major, o'course, being your greatest temptation to sin?"

She didn't bother with a denial. Mary wouldn't believe it, in any case. The mere thought of those stolen hours in Andrew's arms before the epidemic struck raised telltale heat in Julia's cheeks.

They'd coupled like wild, jungle beasts. Without love, without trust, with no thought to marriage or the moral obligation to procreate. Driven by a hunger their joining hadn't begun to satisfy. If anything, that taste had only made her crave him more. Now, it seemed, she'd pay a heavy penance for her all too brief descent into insanity.

The ever-pragmatic Mary dismissed such philosophical considerations with an impatient wave of her hand. "What man or woman doesn't make dire promises in times o'stress? Didn't I swear I'd be a meek, humble wife to the sergeant major if only the Lord would leave him on this earth a bit longer? It wasn't meant to be."

Julia picked at the threads of her skirt. "Maybe Andrew and I aren't meant to be, either. We made a mockery of the sacrament of marriage the first time we tried it. This time, my first consideration has to be my daughter."

"Well, Suzanne will be some time yet gettin' her full strength back. And winter blows in early out here on the plains, don't y'know? Come spring, I'm thinkin' you and Suzanne might both have changed your minds about leavin'…if the blizzards and snow blindness don't drive you mad first.''

On that cheerful note, she called to her noisy brood and went home.

In her own, far more reserved way, Walks In Moonlight echoed Mary sentiments when she, Little Hen and Lone Eagle came bearing a buffalo calf's liver wrapped in oiled cloth. Lone Eagle stood behind her with arms crossed, saying little while his daughter clambered up to sit cross-legged on Suzanne's bed. His wife shared her recipe for liver stew with the patient's mother.

''Boil the meat long with wild onions. The broth will help to thicken Suz-anne's blood.''

Assuming Julia could get it down her daughter's throat. The girl's weak, fretful state hadn't diminished her fussiness.

''Thank you.''

Placing the dripping bundle in a bowl, she wiped her hands and offered her guests a glass of the gooseberry wine. Walks In Moonlight glanced to her husband for guidance before declining gracefully. The barriers were coming back up, Julia thought with a stab of regret.

They talked for a few moments more, then Lone Eagle called to his daughter. Affection softened his granite features when the girl came skittering across the room. Reaching out a big hand, he tugged one of her braids. Giggling, she wrapped her arms around his naked thigh.

When Lone Eagle looked up, a smile passed between husband and wife, so fleeting and so intimate that envy dug sharp fangs into Julia's breast. She had to fight to keep it from her face when Walks In Moonlight turned back to her.

"Is it true you will leave Fort Laramie when the little one recovers?"

"Yes."

"Does your heart take you away?"

"I—I must go. I promised Suzanne."

The Sioux cocked her head to one side. Her dark eyes searched Julia's.

"Each woman must find her own path," she said softly. "I will pray to the Great Spirit that you find yours."

To Julia's relief, Suzanne accepted that it might be some weeks before she was strong enough to travel. The mere prospect of returning to her familiar world seemed to satisfy the still lethargic girl, although she reminded her mother of her promise whenever the opportunity arose. In the meantime, she had Little Hen to keep her company and the books her mother borrowed from the classroom to help her learn her letters.

September swept in on a rush of cooling days and momentous events. The residents of Fort Laramie were goggle-eyed with the news that Colonel George

Armstrong Custer, flamboyant hero of the War of the Rebellion and commander of the 7th Cavalry Regiment, had been recalled to Fort Leavenworth to face a court-martial board. The rumor was he'd ordered his officers to shoot deserters in cold blood. Not only that, he'd left his troops in the field without authority. Like so many other men, he'd feared for his wife Libby's safety during the cholera outbreak and had rushed home to move her out of harm's way. Unlike so many others, he'd abandoned his troops to do so. A military tribunal sentenced him to one year's suspension from the Army without pay.

The officers and men at Fort Laramie either rejoiced in or cursed Custer's dismissal. Colonel Cavanaugh saw it as one more victory for the Sioux and Cheyenne, who hated "Yellow Hair" for his savage attacks on their encampments. Others, Andrew among them, viewed Custer's court-martial as one more strand in the complex tapestry of the plains. Like Red Cloud's attack on the woodcutting party at Fort Phil Kearny last month—now known as the Wagon Box Fight for the way the woodcutters had circled the wood wagons to fight off the attack—Custer's dismissal held political undertones.

Andrew suspected the real reason Congress was more interested in peace than in continuing the war against the Plains Indians had to do with cold, hard cash. Quite simply, it cost more than they wanted to pay to maintain the posts along the Bozeman Trail, particularly with alternate routes to the Montana gold fields now available.

His suspicion hardened into certainty when General Sherman confirmed that the Army would not retaliate for the Wagon Box affair. Nor would the army brass allow Captain Powell's success in repulsing the attack be touted in the eastern press as a major victory.

Instead, Colonel Cavanaugh received word that the newly appointed peace commission would gather in St. Louis prior to setting out for Fort Laramie in early November, weather permitting. Andrew dispatched messengers to all the major bands, apprising their chiefs of the commission's expected arrival. Spotted Tail sent word that he would meet with them, as did Sitting Bull. Red Cloud and Crazy Horse didn't reply.

Julia absorbed all of these events only peripherally. Her main focus remained on happenings closer to home. The second week in September, Mary Shaunessy O'Dell Donovan married Private Robert Mulvaney in a quiet ceremony attended only by her family and a few friends. The brawny, bull-necked private was five years Mary's junior and as much in awe of his new wife as he was amazed by his incredible good fortune in winning her. He didn't have the rank or the presence of her late husband, Mary confided frankly to Julia, but Sean Donovan had considered Mulvaney the hardest working and most sober of all his troops. That, she declared roundly, was sufficient recommendation for her.

Her own affairs somewhat in order, Mary decided

Julia needed a break from nursing and urged her to resume classes. With a tart reminder to the other laundresses that it was their children who benefited from Julia's school teaching, she marshaled them into shifts to care for Suzanne during the day. And it was Mary, Julia discovered, who sternly advised Andrew that the mother was looking as peaked as the daughter. She needed to put some of the late September sunshine into her cheeks.

Obedient to Mary's crisp order, Andrew appeared at the schoolroom just after Julia dismissed her students for the afternoon. She glanced up, her hands stilling in their task of scrubbing the slate board.

"You didn't keep any pupils after school to do that?" he asked with a smile.

"No, not today."

"Good."

The uneven floorboards creaked under his boots as he strolled down the aisle between the desks. Removing his hat, he held it in one gloved hand. Sunbeams slanting through the window picked out the russet tints in his hair.

"Can you leave for a while, Julia? I've got a gig outside. We could take a short ride."

"Yes, of course."

Her calm reply disguised a sudden nervousness. They hadn't talked, really talked, since that night in the tent. Andrew's visits to check on Suzanne and convey Daisy's wishes for her speedy recovery had,

of necessity, been conducted under the child's watchful eyes.

He'd known better than to press Julia when her
daughter's health still weighed heavily on her mind.
From the way his hands lingered on her waist when
he lifted her into the high-seated buggy, it was evident
that time had now passed.

She gathered her shawl about her shoulders, more
to hide her fluttering pulse than for protection against
the playful breeze that snapped the flag against its
wooden pole. The same breeze tugged at the hair
she'd caught back in a loose bun at the nape of her
neck. Wishing she'd brought a bonnet to keep the
wayward strands from flying about her face, Julia
slanted Andrew a curious glance.

"Where are we going?"

"You'll see."

He handled the reins of the buggy with the same
ease he did his chargers. Neatly maneuvering around
the troops walking guard, he tooled the gig along the
dirt track circling the parade ground. Old Bedlam's
two-story bulk swept by, as did the surgeon's quarters
and the sutler's store.

At first Julia thought their destination might be the
cavalry stables at the north end of the post. Perhaps
he wanted her to see for herself how Suzanne's pony
fared, or discuss its disposition when she and her
daughter returned East. The mere thought of leaving
put a lump in her throat.

To her secret relief, they swept past the stables and

followed the curve of the Laramie River. Once clear of the outbuildings, the breeze chased away the earthy odor of horse manure and the clang of farriers' hammers against iron anvils. Another bend of the river cut off all echoes from the fort completely.

A few moments later, the gig swept up a slight, sloping incline to the bluffs above the river. Julia's jaw dropped in sheer astonishment.

A sea of purplish-blue spread before her delighted eyes. Acre after acre of tall spiky flowers poked their heads above the grass and bowed proudly in the breeze. They were the most extraordinary color, so deep an indigo as to make Julia think of the fabled royal purple of ancient kings.

"They're glorious," she breathed. "What are they?"

"Private Cooper identified them in one of his botanical lectures as prairie gentian, but the troopers call them Johnny-jump-ups."

"Because they jump right out of the grass like that, I suppose," she murmured, gazing in awestruck wonder at the spectacular display.

"I think it has more to do with the fact that the dried leaves make a sort of tobacco." A lopsided grin tugged at Andrew's mouth. "It has certain, er, stimulating effects when smoked."

An answering chuckle tickled Julia's throat. "Leave it to your inventive cavalrymen to discover a practical use for all this beauty."

How good it felt to laugh, she thought ruefully.

How wonderful to simply sit here in the sun amid all this glorious color. Sighing, she clasped her hands loosely in her lap and let her gaze roam over the rippling sea of indigo.

With a sideways glance at her face, Andrew brought the buggy to a halt. Her unabashed wonder lit little fires of satisfaction just under his skin. So many of Fort Laramie's residents hated life on the Plains. They saw nothing but relentless miles of dun-colored hills baked by sun in summer and heaped with snow in winter. Only a few, like Andrew, had learned to appreciate the subtle beauty of the area.

Showing Julia its transitory magnificence was part of his deliberate campaign to erase the horror of August from her mind...and to convince her to abandon any plans of returning to Mobile.

He'd lost her once. She didn't know it yet, but he had no intention of losing her again.

He allowed no hint of his determination to show in his face when he climbed out of the gig and walked around to lift her down. He'd laid out his campaign in deliberate steps. The first was to get her out in the sun, away from the fort, amid this riot of color and heady scent. The feel of her narrow waist under its layers of stiffening and whalebone propelled him directly into phase two.

He lowered her slowly, sliding her body down between his and the wagon wheel. When he didn't step back, her gaze lifted to his. He smiled down at her, fighting to control the sudden pounding in his blood from the brush of her breasts against his chest.

"The jump-ups only bloom for a few weeks. Each time I saw them I'd try to decide if they were the same color as your eyes. Then I'd curse myself for thinking about you at all."

"Andrew..."

"Your eyes are a deeper violet, Julia. And I've given up trying to keep you out of my thoughts."

His blunt admission sparked an answering desire, quickly overlaid by distress.

"Don't look so worried," he told her gently. "I would never come between you and your daughter. You have to do what's best for Suzanne."

"You heard her, Andrew. She was so weak, and I was so frightened that I might lose her."

"I know."

"I would have promised to put her on my back and climb to the moon, if she'd asked."

"She won't be strong enough to travel to the moon or anywhere else for weeks yet." Reaching up, he tucked a wayward strand of inky black silk behind her ear. "Anything can happen in those weeks, sweetheart."

With a wavery smile, she clutched at the temporary reprieve. "That's true."

"Like this," he murmured, bending to take her lips.

Fire raced through her. As swift and greedy as a

prairie fire, it set her skin to burning. Groaning, she flung her arms around his neck.

Julia had never made love under the open sky before. Never dreamed she would lie amid a crush of purple blossoms, her clothes cushioning her back and bottom while the breeze raised goose bumps on her bare skin and Andrew's clever, busy mouth teased her nipples into aching peaks.

This wasn't her. This greedy wanton who refused to think beyond this moment, beyond the feel of Andrew's mouth and hands on her flesh, bore no resemblance to the convent-bred Julia Robichaud Bonneaux. To Julia Robichaud *Garrett* Bonneaux, she reminded herself fiercely. The silly, naïve virgin who'd convinced herself a few vows exchanged in a dim chapel cloaked in propriety the passion Andrew roused in her.

She knew better now. There was nothing proper or decent or polite about this all-consuming hunger. No vows could tame it, and none were offered or exchanged this time.

A few weeks, she thought desperately as Andrew's mouth found the damp heat between her legs. They had a few weeks yet of this glorious autumn. Then she'd carry the memory of these crushed blossoms and wild, windswept plains back East with her, to hold forever in her heart.

17

Andrew implemented the next phase in his campaign to sabotage Julia's return to Mobile the Sunday after their trip to the meadow.

His brief visits to Suzanne and intelligence gathered from various sources indicated the girl had put back on some of the flesh she'd lost. She could now walk a bit, but became winded after only a few steps. She'd also grown fretful at her confinement. A planned concert by the 2nd Cavalry regimental band would cheer her considerably…and provide Andrew with just the opportunity he'd been waiting for.

On a bright, breezy Sunday afternoon he rigged out in his blue dress uniform complete with gold epaulets and Prussian-style helmet sporting a high horsehair plume. A wide yellow sash weighted on its fringed ends fell in neat folds beneath his dress saber. With a final pass of the polishing rag over his boots, he headed for the stables.

Company C's farrier was waiting for him. The

brawny sergeant had shed his leather blacksmith's apron and cleaned the grime from beneath his nails. Like the major, he'd decked out in his best uniform for the afternoon's concert.

"Is she ready to go?"

"All set, sir."

Grinning, the farrier led Suzanne's pony out of the stables. To the merry tinkle of bells, the little pinto clip-clopped into the sunshine. She was harnessed between the shafts of a pony cart and looked about with bright, intelligent eyes, happy to be out of her stall.

"Well, Major? What do you think of the rig?"

Andrew ran an appraising eye over the cart. He'd commissioned its construction the day after he'd carried a weak, listless Suzanne back to Julia's quarters on Suds Row. The farrier, also an accomplished carpenter, had been only too happy to supplement his pay with this extra project.

As the vehicle began to take shape, half the company had become involved in the project. The annoyed farrier received advice on everything from the size of the wheels to the correct angle to set the shafts. His well-intentioned advisors had voted on the paint scheme and accouterments, too. As a result, the cart now boasted a coat of bright-blue paint, cavalry yellow trim on the wheels and a strand of jingling bells across the harness holder. The street-tough Private O'Shea had added the finishing touch—a spray of painted daisies on either side panel.

"You've done a fine job," Andrew said sincerely. "Very fine."

So fine, in fact, that the major became the object of goggle-eyed stares as he paraded through the post. He felt more than a little foolish returning the troopers' salutes with one hand while grasping the pony's leading rein with the other, all done to a silvery chorus of bells. He was sure none of the men in his company had ever thought to see their commander all spiffed up in his best uniform and leading a little spotted pinto and blue cart instead of mounted on Jupiter's broad back.

After the third or fourth such encounter, he shrugged off the astonishment he generated. Surely his reputation as an officer and a decorated veteran would survive a blue-and-yellow pony cart.

He'd sent a note earlier offering Julia and Suzanne his escort if they wished to attend the band concert. Her brief reply expressed heartfelt appreciation. Both mother and daughter needed relief from each other's company, Andrew guessed. They were waiting for him when he arrived at their quarters, trailed by a following of wide-eyed children lured along by the bells and the cart.

Suzanne's delight when she glimpsed Daisy more than compensated for Andrew's brief embarrassment during his march across the post. Julia's gratitude when she saw the gaily painted rig repaid him tenfold.

"Oh, Andrew, how thoughtful of you!"

"I take full credit for the cart," he told with a grin,

"but the flowers on the side panels were Private O'Shea's contribution. Consider this an early birthday present for Suzanne from the entire troop."

Julia's violet eyes glistened with moisture. "You're so good to us."

His grin took a wry twist. Bending, he murmured a few words for her ears alone.

"Don't credit me with too chivalrous a nature. There's deliberate intent behind this pony cart, as I think you understand."

Julia blinked back her silly rush of tears. Of course, she understood his intent. He'd made it clear enough that afternoon among the Johnny-jump-ups. He didn't want her to return to Mobile, any more than she wanted to go.

That didn't mitigate the extraordinary generosity of this gesture, though. She might have told him so if his next murmured comment hadn't completely stolen her breath.

"I can't sleep for wanting to whisk you back to the meadow. Or my quarters. Or the hay barn. Or anywhere else."

Mercifully, Suzanne didn't notice the sudden blaze of color in her mother's cheeks, and Andrew moved away before she did.

How absurd that two adults should have to whisper like this, Julia through ruefully. Or be held hostage to a promise made to a girl just turning six, an evil voice in her mind whispered. Only then did Julia realize how much she'd come to regret that rash promise.

She didn't want to leave. Nor could she deny the catch just under her heart when Andrew unlatched the pony cart's door, clicked his boot heels and bowed to Suzanne.

"Your carriage awaits, milady."

The girl turned to her mother. Desire to climb onto the leather seat and take the reins clearly battled with her instinctive wariness of the major. He represented everything foreign and strange to her, Julia knew. Everything she'd lost in the past few months. Clinging stubbornly to memories of Philip and Mobile, the girl resented the major's attentions to her mother. Swallowing a sigh, Julia gave her daughter an encouraging smile.

"It's all right. You're strong enough to take the ribbons. Major Garrett will hold the leading reins, just in case."

"I want you to hold them," was the petulant reply.

"Suzanne..."

"It's all right." Andrew passed the leads to Julia with unperturbed calm. "We'd better start for the parade ground. We don't want to miss the concert."

Closer to being out of patience with her daughter than she'd been at any time since her illness, Julia tugged the pony into a sedate walk.

Suzanne and her little cart provided almost as much entertainment as the regimental band.

The post's entire population had turned out for the afternoon affair, as if determined to let the music lift spirits still heavy from so much grieving. Parasols and bright-colored shawls fluttered in the breeze. Officers in helmets and dress swords strutted amid enlisted personnel similarly spit-shined and polished. Rows of chairs had been arranged for the ladies, who reverted back to rank now that the crisis had passed, Julia saw. The officers' wives occupied one end of the front row, the laundresses the other.

After so many weeks and so many shared hardships, Julia seemed to have bridged the gap between the two classes. Victoria McKinney, still wan and drawn from the loss of her baby, begged her to take the chair next to hers. Maria Schnell waved a plump hand and offered to make space for her. Mary Donovan and the other laundresses called friendly greetings.

Their warm overtures filled Julia with a sense of belonging that intensified the little ache just under her heart. Now, just when she was coming to feel at home and count so many of Fort Laramie's residents as friends, she would leave them.

Hiding her thoughts behind a smiling facade, Julia chose to stand with Walks In Moonlight beside Suzanne's pony cart. Lone Eagle towered behind his wife, erect and proud in fringed buckskin leggings, dark-blue army jacket and gray slouch hat with its single eagle feather. Andrew returned the scout's greeting and turned to Walks In Moonlight. In a voice as soft and melodious as her daughter's, she asked a question of him in her native tongue. He answered with a shake of his head and a few words of Sioux.

Catching Julia's curious glance, Walks In Moonlight smiled apologetically. "We speak of my father's cousin, Spotted Tail. I asked the major if he has heard yet whether the chief will meet with the new peace party when they arrive at Fort Laramie."

Julia slanted Andrew a curious glance. "Will he?"

"He's said he will."

"What about the other chiefs?"

"We don't know."

"I'm surprised the commission would travel all the way to Fort Laramie without firm assurances that the other chiefs will come in to parlay."

"The commission is remaining in St. Louis for the present, debating how best to proceed. In the meantime, they're sending George Beauvais as a sort of advance ambassador."

Lone Eagle's eyes gleamed with interest at the news. "Beauvais? It is good. He knows the ways of the people."

"He's an old hand," Andrew explained to Julia. "A trader who's long held the respect of both the Sioux and the Cheyenne. He helped craft the treaty of '51, and forced the recall of one of the agents who stole goods and supplies that were supposed to go to the Sioux under the terms of the treaty. General Sherman's hoping his weight added to Spotted Tail's will convince Red Cloud to come in and negotiate."

Lone Eagle shook his head. "Red Cloud will not talk peace until the White Father agrees to burn the forts to the north. More blood will yet spill."

The talk of war dimmed the brightness of the afternoon. A shiver rippled down Julia's spine. She clutched her fringed shawl a little tighter around her shoulders.

Andrew caught the little gesture and changed the direction of the conversation. "Suzanne has found her shadow, I see."

The women's gazes turned to the pony cart, where Suzanne had invited Little Hen to join her for the concert. The two girls sat with their heads together, whispering and giggling while lively marches and martial beats filled the air. They made such a marked contrast, Julia thought. Suzanne in her Sunday dress of bordered muslin and bonnet to match, Little Hen in her finest beaded and fringed dress. Yet the girlish delights and fantasies they shared made them closer than sisters.

So close, in fact, that Julia had to quietly prompt Suzanne to give the other children a ride in her cart during the brief intermission. Julia guided the pony for two lengths of the parade ground before relinquishing the rein to Andrew's striker. Private O'Shea took the lead willingly enough, but shook his head when he surveyed the cart's occupant.

"I don't know, missus. Doesn't seem right, her driving an army wagon without the proper uniform."

"This isn't an army wagon," Suzanne protested. "It's got daisies on it!"

"Sure it does, darlin', because I put them there. But this conveyance was built on army property, out of army scrap lumber. Don't know what the major was thinking of, putting a civilian in the seat."

As reluctant as she'd been to accept the cart, Suzanne wasn't about to relinquish her prize now. Her agonized glance darted to Andrew.

With a dry look at his striker, he stepped into the breech. "As it happens, the same thought occurred to me."

Reaching inside his uniform jacket, he extracted a flattened forage cap. A brisk shake gave the hat its proper shovel-front tilt. The brim had been polished to a glossy black, Julia noted, as had the chin strap. The crossed swords and regimental insignia embroidered on its crown caused an uneasy flutter in her breast. She'd never thought to see her daughter wearing the cap of a Yankee officer.

Suzanne had no such qualms. With a squeal of delight, she untied the strings of her bonnet and tossed it into the back of the cart. When Andrew set the cap at a jaunty angle on curls that were only beginning to regain their luster, the girl actually dimpled up at him.

"How do I look?"

An answering smile softened the major's rugged features. "Like a regular trooper."

Julia drew in a swift breath. The unexpected moment of harmony between the daughter she loved and the man she was coming to crave held her spellbound. Like uninvited guests, tantalizing possibilities crept into her mind and refused to leave, but she allowed none of them to take specific shape. The connection between Andrew and Suzanne was too fragile to attach any significance to it.

Julia reminded herself of that salient point repeatedly over the days that followed.

With a diet supplemented by wild game, haunches of venison and the store-bought delicacies Andrew and his troopers insisted on sending to the quarters in Suds Row, Suzanne steadily regained her strength. She soon progressed from sitting docilely in her pony cart to wanting to handle the ribbons herself. In a remarkably short time, the residents of Fort Laramie became used to the sight of a diminutive trooper with a forage cap tipped over her curls tooling about the post in a blue-painted cart, her boon companion beside her more often than not.

The troopers in Company C seemed to have adopted her as a sort of a mascot. Daisy never wanted for grooming or attention, and was waiting patiently between the shafts when "the little soldier girl" arrived at the stables after classes. Andrew assured Julia he would see that Suzanne didn't overtax her strength.

If the sharp nip of fall brought a hint of color back to Suzanne's cheeks and a quiet joy to her mother's heart, that joy was increasingly tempered by the knowledge Julia would have to decide soon when they would return to Mobile. If she waited much longer, the threat of winter storms would make travel across the open plains too dangerous.

After his flat assertion that day in the meadow that he would never come between Julia and her daughter, Andrew didn't bring up the matter of their departure. Yet she knew it weighed as heavily on his mind as it did on hers. With the inexorable press of time, she no longer tried to deny her hunger for the man she'd once hated as much as she'd loved.

The craving left her tossing restlessly at night when she laid in bed beside Suzanne. The same craving fired her blood during those few hours she could steal away to lie under...or atop...or entwined around Andrew. With a wantonness that shocked her when she had breath enough to think about it, she rode him like the most savage, untamed beast would ride its mate. Other times, she would writhe in pleasure when he rolled her over, yanked her up on all fours, and plunged into her from behind with the same ferocity.

When she finally understood that he refused to spill his seed in her body to spare her a pregnancy, Julia took him in her mouth. She'd never performed such a service before, had never dreamed of performing it. Now she could only wonder why!

The simple act bestowed the most incredible power on a woman and reduced even a man of Andrew's iron will to a state resembling quivering pork jelly. When she said as much one afternoon during a stolen hour in his quarters after classes, a rumble of laughter started low in his belly.

"This is the kind of power a man gives a woman most willingly."

"Is that so?"

She glanced up at him from her reversed position. He lay like some foreign potentate, smug in his nakedness, while she sprawled along his length. She knew his body now almost as well as she knew her own. Scars and hard ridges marred his skin, but the muscles beneath were sleek and smooth to her touch.

Very sleek and smooth.

With a smug smile of her own, she took his rigid shaft in her hand. Catlike, she rasped her tongue along the satiny length.

"It doesn't seem to me that this is so much something you give—" she paused for another delicate lick "—as something I take."

Grinning, he clasped his hands behind his head. "I'm hardly in a position to argue the matter right now."

"No," she murmured, scraping her teeth along a blue-ridged vein, "you're not."

His grin vanished on an indrawn hiss. To her delight, his rod jumped in her hand.

"Julia!"

"Mmm?"

"Be careful, woman. I don't... I can't..."

"Can't what, Andrew?"

Her only answer was a strangled grunt.

The heady knowledge that she could bring him so quickly from lazy playfulness to incoherence flowed through Julia's veins like heated wine.

She'd been so young, all those years ago. So untutored. Andrew had initiated her to a woman's passion with what she now recognized as incredible gentleness. But this...this was a journey to uncharted lands, a voyage to erotic delights she'd never imagined.

Andrew showed no shame in his reactions to her touch, allowed her no shame in his. To sprawl head to toe like this, in the light of day no less, without so much as a stitch of clothing between them, went beyond anything Julia had experienced. Philip had never played with her like this. He'd bedded her with such gentleness, always so careful of the proprieties. She couldn't remember ever removing her nightdress in his presence, either in bed or out.

The feel of Andrew iron-hard and flame-hot in her hand, against her lips, in her mouth, drove all thoughts of Philip from her head. Drove out everything, in fact, except the growing dread of leaving Fort Laramie, and leaving Andrew.

That dread added a spur of urgency to her need. Her fingers tightened on his shaft. Her body arched over his. As her lips closed over the hot, satiny flesh, she knew she'd take the taste of him with her whenever she left, wherever she went.

18

George Beauvais arrived at Fort Laramie on the second of October. The whole post buzzed with speculation about the details of the one-time trader turned peace ambassador's mission…and with the fact that he came accompanied by several freight wagons hauling gifts for the Sioux and Cheyenne chiefs who would agree to meet with the commission.

Andrew and Colonel Cavanaugh stayed closeted with Beauvais for hours on end. The colonel made no secret of his opposition to the peace mission. Nor did Cavanaugh hesitate to deride Beauvais for kowtowing to the "heathen savages." The more agitated the colonel became, the more he laced himself with laudanum. Finally, Andrew was forced to step in and issue the necessary orders for the couriers Beauvais wanted dispatched to the various chiefs. The post rang for a day and a half with the sound of bugles announcing the patrols' departures.

All this Julia learned in bits and snatches from Andrew. He came by Suds Row each evening to check on her and Suzanne, but the press of duties made his visits brief. Not until the following week, when Julia encountered him by chance after classes, did they have time to talk privately about the rocky start to the peace negotiations.

She was alone. Suzanne and Little Hen had already made their way to the stables, where they'd find Daisy harnessed to the pony cart and ready for her afternoon trot. Julia had voiced doubts about letting the girls drive out this afternoon, as the day had turned gray and restless, but Suzanne had pleaded her cause with such a marked return to her old self that her mother couldn't refuse.

Great, humped clouds now galloped across the sky like a herd of ghostly buffalo. A frisky wind tugged tendrils of Julia's hair loose from its braided coronet as she made her way along the path fronting the white clapboard buildings of Officers' Row. She was on her way to the surgeon's quarters to visit Maria Schnell. If Maria's husband was there, Julia would consult with him about the tincture of cinnamon water infused with two drops of creosote and a half-ounce of thick mucilage he'd prescribed for Suzanne. Now that the color was blooming in her daughter's cheeks again, Julia wondered how much longer she'd have to force the noxious mixture down her throat.

Strange how eager she was for the day the surgeon would pronounce Suzanne fully recovered…and how reluctant she was to admit that day had almost arrived. A hollow sensation formed in the pit of her stomach at the thought of packing her belongings in her humpedback trunk, climbing into a wagon and driving away from Fort Laramie.

And away from the man who emerged onto Old Bedlam's lower veranda just as Julia approached.

Her pulse skipped when she caught sight of him. Tall, lean, the brim of his campaign hat pulled down low on his forehead, he stood at the top of the steps. He didn't see her at first, which gave her time to note the square set to his chin. Another session with Cavanaugh, she guessed. Five minutes with the colonel could wind Andrew tighter than a bullwhip.

His expression lightened when he saw her, but not even his slow, welcoming smile could disguise the tight lines bracketing his mouth.

"Out for a stroll?" he asked.

"I have an hour while Suzanne's exercising Daisy. I'm on my way to visit with Maria Schnell."

The smile eased into his eyes, and with it came something else, something so tender that Julia's heart thumped against her stays.

"I have an hour before the buglers sound watering call. Care to visit with me instead?"

As quickly as that, she knew she'd come full circle. Once again, she'd lost her head as well as her heart to Andrew Garrett. She didn't want to love him, had convinced herself this greed for his touch sprang from the desire he could always wake in her, nothing more.

Yet mere desire couldn't explain her sudden, fierce

urge to retire to his room, sit him down in a chair and knead the tension from his shoulders. Lust didn't explain her burning wish to ease his mind with light-hearted chatter, or kiss away the lines of strain on his face, or provide any of the homey comforts a woman can give her man.

"Yes," she answered with an ache in her throat. "I'd far rather visit with you."

Gathering her skirts, she mounted the front steps. The veranda's weathered boards creaked as Andrew escorted her inside. Now-familiar scents of tobacco and boot polish welcomed Julia, as did the lieutenant who tipped his hat respectfully when they passed him in the hall.

This early in the day, Private O'Shea was still at his military duties, as were most of the other officers and their strikers. Undisturbed quiet surrounded her and Andrew when he ushered her into his sitting room and closed the door. Still gripped by the overwhelming need to ease his tension, she tossed her shawl on one of the folding campaign chairs and ordered him to take the other.

She knew her way around his apartments well enough now to feel comfortable reaching for the decanter on one of the shelves. In deference to Julia's less hardened palate, Andrew had filled the decanter with port instead of the turpentine that passed for whiskey on the frontier.

"Can you take a little wine, or are you still on duty?"

His hat joined her shawl on the chair.

"I'm still on duty, but with the colonel swimming in laudanum and George Beauvais crawling up my back, I'm damned if I'm going to worry about a glass of port."

"Why is Mr. Beauvais angry with you?"

"I put one of his drivers in leg irons." Shaking his head in disgust, Andrew claimed one of the chairs and thrust out his legs.

"The driver and his scurvy friends got drunk as wheelbarrows last night and busted up the billiard table at the sutler's store."

"It's been broken before," Julia commented mildly. "Every payday, I understand. You usually just fine the men involved and make them pay enough to cover the cost of repairs. Why did you put this particular culprit in leg irons?"

"Most likely because he didn't take kindly to the officer of the day's suggestion that he open his pockets to pay for the damage. He jumped on the captain's back and took a bite out of his ear before the troopers could haul him off."

"Good Lord!"

"It took three men to subdue him. He won't be biting down on anything else for a while," Andrew finished grimly, accepting the tumbler Julia handed him.

"Why in the world would Mr. Beauvais hire someone like that to accompany him on what's supposed to be a peace mission?"

"George swears he had no choice. After the Wagon Box incident last month, few civilians are eager to climb up behind a team of mules and risk their scalps out here in the heart of Sioux country. Beauvais emptied the jail cells in St. Louis to hire this lot. I had to request he bivouac them upriver, away from the main part of the post, and keep them there. But enough of Beauvais and his crew."

Hooking an arm about her waist, he drew her down to his lap.

"Let's talk about other things. Or better yet," he murmured, pressing the tumbler to her lips, "let's not talk at all."

The suggestion sent the wine down the wrong pipe. Andrew waited politely until Julia had finished coughing to set the glass aside.

"You're tired," she protested when he nuzzled her neck. "And we have only an hour."

"I'm not that tired, and we've made good use of less time than that. Here, turn around a bit on my lap and let me show you one of the cavalry's more interesting mounts."

"This chair's too rickety for such maneuvers!"

"It'll hold us," he said with more confidence than Julia felt the wobbly chair legs warranted. "We just have to distribute our weight evenly."

She grabbed at his shoulders for balance while he spanned her waist and lifted her up and around. "Andrew, this won't work!"

"We won't know until we try. Hook your leg over

mine, sweetheart. There, just like that. Wait, let me remove my pistol. Raise your bottom a bit.''

"And your sword," she protested, laughing helplessly. "It's at a most awkward angle."

"All right, but you'll have to—"

The sudden crash of thunder just outside the window caught them both by surprise. Julia jumped a good three inches in the air. Andrew smothered an oath and looked past her to the shuttered window.

Twisting around, she saw that the tiny bits of sky visible through the slats had darkened to an ominous gray. Wind rattled the windows and had gathered so much force that Old Bedlam's timbers began to groan in protest. Another earsplitting crack brought Julia scrambling off Andrew's lap.

"I'd better find Suzanne and Little Hen. I don't want them caught out in her pony cart in a storm."

"I'll come with you."

When they stepped outside, the force of the wind knocked the breath back in their throats. Dirt and bits of debris whirled through the air. The sky roiled like an angry gray sea. Lightning forked, fast as a serpent's tongue and twice as deadly.

The first, fat bullets of rain fired down as Andrew and Julia fought their way along the dirt path that divided the row of officers quarters from the parade ground. Within moments, they were both soaked.

"I'll check the stables," Andrew shouted over the wind when they reached the fork in the path. One branch curved around the north end of the parade ground, past the long, single-story infantry barracks, to the river. The other led to the cavalry barracks and the stables beyond.

"You go back to Suds Row," he yelled. "The girls would have seen the storm coming. They're probably huddled safe and snug at home."

Julia certainly hoped so. Flinching at another flash of lightning, she picked up her skirts and abandoned her dignity to make a dash for the laundresses' quarters.

Suzanne wasn't at their quarters. Nor, Julia discovered when Andrew appeared at her door fifteen minutes later, was her daughter at the stables. None of the men had seen either her or Little Hen since they'd driven off in the pony cart a half hour earlier.

"They must have taken shelter," Andrew said, his deliberate calm in direct contrast to Julia's increasing worry. "I've got men out looking for them. The pony cart will be easy to spot."

"I hope so."

"I'm going back to join the search. I just rode over to make sure they weren't here with you. You'd better change," he suggested when shivers racked her. "You're soaking wet."

"So are you."

He'd thrown an India rubber poncho over his uniform to deflect the rain, but water dripped from his broad-brimmed slouch hat in a series of continuous splats.

"Just get changed and stop worrying," he ordered
brusquely. "Every trooper on the post knows the little
soldier girl by now. They'll watch out for her and
Little Hen."

Julia forced a smile and lifted her face for his
quick, hard kiss. He left her with a promise to return
soon with the girls.

Chewing on her lower lip, she started for the bedroom area behind the partition. The thought that the
girls might have taken shelter with Walks In Moonlight had her changing directions. Snatching up her
sopping shawl, she draped it over her head and went
out into the storm again.

Mud weighted the hem of her skirt and petticoats
as she dashed across the footbridge. Blinking in the
heavy rain, she wove her way through the tents and
tipis strung along the riverbank. A few wretched dogs
slunk past her, ears flattened against the rain, tails
tucked between their legs. Refuse floated by on the
rivulets that had already formed in wagon ruts.

By the time Julia reached Walks In Moonlight's
tipi, she was panting with the effort of dragging her
feet out of the mud with each step. Larger and more
artistically decorated than any of the other tents,
Walks In Moonlight's home reflected her status as
both niece to a chief and wife to an army scout.

Answering Julia's anxious call, the Sioux woman
raised the buffalo hide tent flap with one arm. "Come
inside."

Ducking under the flap, Julia pulled the dripping

shawl from her head and breathed a sigh of relief at escaping the rain. Although she'd visited Walks In Moonlight several times, the efficient use of space inside the buffalo hide tent always amazed her.

Beds draped with buffalo robes circled the inside walls. Backrests made from peeled willow twigs and supported by wooden tripods converted the beds to comfortable chairs. Colorful, beautifully decorated calfskin storage pouches, such as the one Walks In Moonlight had made for Julia, hung from antelope gut lacings above the beds. Lone Eagle's spare saddle and bridles were kept on the "men's" side of the tent, Walks In Moonlight's cooking utensils on the other.

Julia scanned the neat, orderly interior quickly. Her initial relief at escaping the rain turned instantly to disappointment.

"Suzanne and Little Hen aren't at my quarters or at the stables," she told Walks In Moonlight. "I'm worried they may have been caught out in the storm."

"A wetting will not harm my daughter. She is as strong as a young sapling. But Suzanne..." Concern flickered in the Sioux's dark eyes.

"Andrew—Major Garrett—and some of the men are out looking for them."

"Do they look north along the riverbank, where the rivers join?"

"Why would the girls go there?"

"Little Hen promised earlier she would gather the moss I need for yellow dye. For the new saddlebags I make for Lone Eagle."

With a graceful gesture, Walks In Moonlight indicated the square of buffalo hide pegged out in the workspace at the center of the tipi. Intricate vermilion squares already decorated the hide. Like the other bags, shields and personal items hanging throughout the interior of the tent, this bag would reflect Walks In Moonlight's exquisite artistry.

"The moss grows best where the two rivers join," she explained.

Julia swung the dripping shawl back over her hair. "I'll look there."

"I will go with you."

Snatching a decorated buffalo calfskin from one of the low beds, Walks In Moonlight pressed it on Julia.

"Here, cover yourself with this instead of your wet cloth. The hide is oiled. It will protect you from the rain."

With a murmured word of thanks, Julia traded her sopping shawl for the furry robe. Draped over her head and shoulders, it proved a very effective shield as she and Walks In Moonlight hurried across the footbridge and turned to follow the Laramie to its juncture with the Platte. Swollen by the rain, the mountain stream bubbled and frothed. Julia gave a silent prayer that Suzanne and Little Hen hadn't strayed too close to the rain-soaked banks and tipped into the rushing water.

Thankfully, the rain lessened to drizzle as the two women passed the quartermaster's warehouses and the sinks, malodorous even after this downpour. From the corner of one eye, Julia spotted a stand of freight wagons on the bluffs above the river. Shaggy-looking mules were picketed behind the wagons, their ears flattened against the rain.

George Beauvais's freight wagons! Remembering what Andrew had told her about the drivers' characters, Julia's heart began to thump with painful intensity. Surely, *surely,* even the most hardened dregs of humanity wouldn't harm two little girls.

She almost sobbed with relief when a few more turns of the riverbank brought an exclamation from Walks In Moonlight.

"Look! There they are."

Peering out from under the calfskin, Julia saw at once the girls' predicament. The rain had indeed softened the bank, so much so that one wheel of the pony cart had sunk almost to its yellow-painted hub. Two disconsolate girls sat cross-legged on the ground beside the cart, partially sheltered from the storm by its tipped side. Daisy, bless her, stood docilely between the tilted shafts.

"Mama!" With a glad cry, Suzanne scrambled out from under her makeshift shelter. "We got stuck."

"So I see." Now that her worst imaginings had come to nothing, exasperation put a bite in Julia's voice. "Why didn't you unhitch Daisy and all of you come in, out of the storm?"

"Her harness got tangled. We couldn't get her loose."

"You could have left her and gone for help."

Suzanne stared at her mother in shocked reproof. "The major says a trooper's first duty is to care for his mount."

"Oh. Well. If that's what the major says."

"We knew he would come looking for us when we didn't return to the stables," she explained. "He always looks out for us."

"Does he?"

"Yes. Us and Daisy." She hesitated a moment, then lifted her gaze to Julia's. "I don't think he really meant to mash my other Daisy, do you, Mama?"

"No, darling, I don't."

Secretly delighted by this sign of lessened hostilities between her daughter and Andrew, Julia swallowed any further scold.

"Perhaps if Walks In Moonlight and I put our shoulders to the cart, we can push it free of the mud. Take Daisy's lead, *ma petite*."

The folded calfskin provided a useful pad when Julia leaned into the cart. A few minutes of strenuous rocking succeeded in freeing the vehicle from the softened earth. It also succeeded in splattering both women with mud.

Suzanne walked beside her pony's head to lead her away from the soggy bank. A thoroughly bedraggled Julia knelt to untangle the harness straps, then ordered both girls into the cart.

"You've got mud on your face, Mama. In your hair, too."

Their giggles had Julia rolling her eyes and Walks In Moonlight smiling.

"We take them home and warm them with willow bark tea. They will come to no hurt."

Plodding along beside Daisy, Julia was looking forward to the hot tea when a turn of the river brought them face-to-face with a new, and far more chilling danger than the rain.

"Well, lookee here."

The thin, scarecrow of a man with a pockmarked face and blackened stumps for teeth had obviously taken advantage of the storm's cessation to relieve himself. He buttoned the flap of his filthy canvas trousers and shouted over his shoulder toward the freight wagons circled some distance away.

"Hey, boys! It's them squaw wimen I told you I'd seed go by."

19

They were drunk. Every one of them.

Julia needed only a glance at the bloodshot eyes and staggering gait of the men who straggled out from the circle of wagons for her blood to ice in her veins. Evidently last night's brawl and the arrest of one of their companions hadn't broken up their revels.

Realizing she had mere moments to escape a dangerous situation, she infused her voice with steel and addressed the driver who'd planted himself squarely in front of the pony cart.

"Please step aside and let us pass."

"You talk pretty fancy for a half-breed squaw." His lips cracked into a grin. "Under all that mud and buffalo skin, you look pretty fancy, too."

"Let us pass."

"Well, now, maybe I will."

He ambled to the side. Julia drew in one swift breath of relief before he snaked out a hand and twitched away the painted calfskin.

"'N maybe I won't," he smirked, his avid gaze devouring her whole.

She stiffened, all too aware that the rain had soaked her clothing down to her skin. Her wet blouse clung to her breasts. Her skirt dragged tight around the outline of her hips. From the leer on this *canaille*'s face, she might as well have been standing before him in her corset and drawers.

One of the men staggering toward them gave a long whistle. "You done flushed us a whole covey o'quail, Brewster. Bet they's gonna taste as juicy as they look."

Julia darted a look at the woman beside her. Walks In Moonlight's face was tight and closed, but her dark eyes telegraphed a grim message.

"I want the half-breed," one yelled.

"Fine with me," another snorted. "I got a hankerin' for a bit of red meat, myself."

"I flushed 'em," the one called Brewster snarled. "I gets first choice."

To Julia's horror, the driver's gaze drifted to the two girls.

"The little ones are always the juiciest."

With a sickening jolt, she knew she had to act. Whipping her hand up, she slapped it down hard on Daisy's flank. Startled, the little pony lurched forward. The two girls almost tumbled off the seat and into the cart.

"Take up the reins, Suzanne! Head for the stables!"

Brewster made a grab for the pony's harness as it went past. Julie threw herself at him, hitting him square in the chest with a hard shoulder. Cursing viciously, he went down.

The momentum carried Julia forward as well. She managed to avoid tripping over the sprawled driver, but her muddied skirts tangled around her legs and brought her to her knees.

From the corner of one eye, she saw the other men break into a run. Frantic, she fought to get her feet under her.

"Drive, Suzanne! Drive fast!"

"Mama!"

The girl squirmed around on the seat. Fear and indecision twisted her face.

"Find the major!"

Walks In Moonlight added her urgings to Julia's.

"Go, daughter! Go now!"

With a poke in the ribs from Little Hen as incentive, Suzanne slapped the reins down on Daisy's flanks. The pony cart rattled off with its two frightened occupants.

Walks In Moonlight half dragged, half pushed Julia to her feet, only to release her the next moment. Whirling, she clawed at the man who'd grabbed one of her braids from behind. Her nails scored his unshaven cheeks. Blood welled instantly.

With a foul oath, he yanked his hand down, jerking her head along with it. Walks In Moonlight gave one, small grunt of pain before his knee came up with brutal force and smashed her full in the face. She crumpled to the mud, blood spurting from her nose and split lip.

"Stupid bitch," her attacker snarled, fingering the welts on his cheek. "You'll pay dearly for marking me. Come on, boys, bring the other one and let's have us some fun."

He started for the wagons, dragging Walks In Moonlight by the one braid. She writhed at the end of the painful tether, feet thrashing, hands reaching up behind her head to yank at the rope of hair.

Horrified, Julia lunged forward to aid her. Before she'd taken more than a step or two, a vicious backhanded swipe caught her beside the head and knocked her sideways. The gray afternoon dimmed to black. Pinpoints of bright light whirled in front of her eyes. Then a hard hand grabbed her wrist and twisted it up behind her back.

"Move yer feet, woman, 'lessn you want us to drag you, too."

There were seven of them. Julia's terror-filled mind managed to make the count as she was shoved toward the freight wagons. She and Walks In Moonlight couldn't hope to fight off seven, nor did the drivers look the kind who would listen to reason. Still, she tried.

"Let us go," she gasped. "Now, before you make even more of a mistake than—"

"Your friend's the one what made the mistake, half-breed."

"She was just protecting herself."

"Looks like we need to learn her that she can't go around markin' up white men."

"Listen to me! You can't do this!"

"Sure we kin."

To prove his point, he gave Julia's arm another savage twist. Fire shot into her shoulder socket. Gasping, she blinked back burning tears of pain. When the haze cleared, one of the drivers danced beside her. He was hardly more than a boy, she saw with a shock, but the feral gleam in his eyes terrified her.

"I want this one, Brewster."

"I found her, I'm having her."

"Yer gonna share, ain't ya? Hell, I shared that skinny little bit of crow bait I dragged away from her mama and papa in St. Louis. You rode her ass while I was jammin' it in her mouth, remember?"

"I remember she bled like a stuck pig when you sliced her throat to stop her screechin'," the man behind Julia snarled. "I'm having this one. You kin take what's left after I'm done...if there's enough left to take."

"Yeah, well, we's all gonna have fun with the squaw first," the boy said with a fiendish glee. "We'll make her squeal some for diggin' them welts in Kinkaid's face."

Walks In Moonlight died an agonizing and soundless death.

Her refusal to make so much as a whimper of pain

drove the men who brutalized her to a frenzy of cruelty. They stripped her naked, pinned her to the ground and lashed her arms and legs to picket stakes with rawhide thongs. Obscenely spread, she was at their mercy.

No amount of begging or pleading or shouted threats from Julia could stop what came next. Her frantic attempts to aid her friend earned her a roundhouse punch in the stomach. Dazed and gagging, she thrashed ineffectively at the younger driver—the boy—when he dragged her to her feet. He threw her back against a wagon bed and tied her wrists above her head to the seat support, pulling the rawhide up so tight it cut into her flesh and left her dangling with only the tips of her toes skimming the earth.

Sobbing, shouting, cursing, she was forced to watch every indignity, every degradation forced on her friend. The drizzle continued, washing the blood that soon welled from the knife cuts on Walks In Moonlight's body to a pale pink.

Julia grew hoarse from pleading, from shrieking threats and promises, from begging Walks In Moonlight to give her attackers what they so obviously wanted...acknowledgment of their power over her.

"Do like she says," the one called Kinkaid sneered, digging the tip of his hunting knife into his victim's throat. His flanks quivered as he leaned over her. "Let's hear you sing out sweet and loud, redbird."

The Sioux raised her head an agonizing inch or

two. The blade cut into her jugular. Crimson spilled down her neck and stained her buckskin blouse. Her black eyes glittering with hate, she spat in her attacker's face.

With a howl, Kinkaid drove the knife through her throat and pinned her to the earth.

"Nooo!"

Caught up in the spectacle of Walks In Moonlight's death throes, none of the men paid any attention to Julia's anguished scream.

20

❦❦❦❦❦

"Look, major! It's them!"

Twisting in his saddle, Andrew followed Dennis O'Shea's outstretched arm. Their vantage point on the low bluffs above the post gave them a panoramic view of the flats below...and of the pony cart that came careening around a bend in the river. Andrew's heart plunged to his boots when he spotted the two girls jouncing precariously on its leather seat.

Digging his spurs into Jupiter's sides, he sent the chestnut plunging down the low bluff. Private O'Shea's bay was a half stride behind. Their mounts' iron-shod hooves threw up clods of mud as they raced across the flats to intercept the cart.

Andrew reached the galloping pony first. Bending low in the saddle, he grabbed Daisy's harness. He was shaking with relief and fury when he dragged the laboring little pinto to a halt. Swinging out of the saddle, he stalked back to the cart.

A single glance at the girls' frightened faces took

some of the edge from his anger, but he intended to administer a dressing down Suzanne wouldn't soon forget for setting her pony to such a headlong gallop.

Before he got out a single word, the girl flung herself off the seat and into his arms. Her small body shook with sobs as she poured a stream of stammering incoherence into his ear.

"Shhh," Andrew soothed, awkwardly patting her back. "Don't cry."

The feel of her small body pressed against his chest gave him a funny jolt. He'd carried the girl back to her quarters from the sick tents, lifted her on and off her pony often enough. But this was the first time she'd clung to him with desperate, clutching hands, as if he were a safe port in a storm.

With a wrench, Andrew realized that's exactly what he wanted to provide for her. A safe haven. A home port. Another being she could come to with her problems, her secrets, her woes. Her sobs tore at his heart and eliminated all thought of taking her to task for her recklessness.

"We won't tell your mama about this," he promised, "as long as you swear you'll never…"

She wrenched back in his arms. Her brown eyes bright brimming, she spilled a torrent of sobs and half phrases.

"Mama! Sh-she's th-there!"

"Slow down, Suzanne. Take a deep breath. I can't understand you."

"Mama's back there!" She beat at his chest with

a fist to make him understand. "By the river! With Walks In Moonlight and the bad men."

His gut twisted. Swinging the girl to her feet, he hunkered down onto a knee before her. His hands gripped her arms and held her steady.

"What bad men?"

"They were dirty and wouldn't let us go by."

Over her head, Andrew met his striker's hard blue eyes. It was the freight drivers. It had to be. Dammit, he should have ordered the whole cursed lot of them thrown in the guardhouse last night.

"One of them tried to grab Daisy," Suzanne sobbed, tears streaming down her dirty cheeks, "but Mama slapped her flank and made her bolt. She shouted at us to come find you."

Clutching at his uniform sleeves with frantic hands, she pleaded with him. "Please, Major, please. Go get my mama and Little Hen's mama and—"

Andrew didn't wait to hear more. Flinging an order at O'Shea to take the girls back to the stables and assemble a squad, he raced back to the patiently standing charger.

He heard the scream above the rushing roar of the Laramie and the hammering of his own heart.

With a vicious curse, Andrew dug his heels into Jupiter's sides. The charger's ears went back. His stride lengthened. Mud flew in huge clumps from his hooves.

When the circle of wagons came into view, all it

took was the press of a knee to aim Jupiter away from the bank and straight up the slope. Shifting the reins to his left hand, Andrew reached across his middle and unsnapped the flap on his Colt .45 with his right. He wore it butt forward, army style, and whipped it out with the deadly precision that only came with long years of practice.

After the incident at the sutler's last night, he had expected the worst. Even so, he wasn't prepared for his first glimpse of Walks In Moonlight's naked body sprawled in the mud. Blood trailed from the gaping wound in her throat. Her scalp had been half torn from her head.

Nor was he any more prepared for the sight of Julia writhing frantically on the ground. One man knelt behind her head, holding her lashed wrists, two others at her widespread ankles. A fourth crouched between her thighs and ripped at her clothes, while three more huddled close, shouting raucous suggestions and encouragement.

The rain-softened earth combined with the men's shouts to swallow the drum of Jupiter's hooves. None of the drivers noticed Andrew's approach until he burst inside the ring of wagons, the Colt roaring.

His first shot hit the man pawing at Julia and spun him around. His second, a gangly youth who lurched toward a rifle propped against one of the wagons.

With savage deliberation, Andrew emptied the Colt at the men scattering in all directions. One howled and grabbed his thigh, but kept going until the next shot brought him to his knees. Another went face-down in the mud. A third slammed into a wagon bed, then dropped like a stone. The rest leaped over wagon tongues to head for the river.

Whipping his Spencer from its scabbard, Andrew raced after them. He pumped out two shots, hit one fleeing target, missed another, then let them go. He didn't know how badly the others were injured, and wasn't about to leave Julia alone with them. Wounded and enraged, they might kill her...or try to barter her life for theirs.

Which was clearly the intent of the rawboned youth Andrew's second shot had hit. Blood seeped from the wound in his side and drenched his dirty white shirt, but the blade he held to Julia's throat gleamed sharp and lethal.

"Drop the rifle," the youth shouted hoarsely.

"No, Andrew!"

She was on her knees, chest heaving, a rawhide thong dangling from her lashed wrists.

"Hold easy!"

The terse shout was for her as much as the wild-eyed boy pressing the blade to her throat. He'd buried a bloody hand in her hair. The other gripped the knife handle with white-knuckled determination.

"Drop the rifle!"

"Don't do it!" Julia cried. "He's a killer. He murdered a girl in St. Louis. Neither one of us will leave here alive if you—"

"Shut yer mouth!"

The vicious yank on her hair was exactly what Julia had been hoping for. She thrust back and butted her head into her captor's injured side with all the force she could muster.

Howling, he staggered backward. The hand fisted in her hair took her with him, but she managed to throw herself sideways just long enough for Andrew's Spencer to spit fire.

Hot blood gushed over Julia. A dead weight fell onto her shoulders. Wild, animal sounds burst from her throat as she fought to free herself from the smothering weight.

Suddenly, it was gone. Just as suddenly, she was in Andrew's arms. Sobbing, she grabbed his uniform jacket with both lashed hands and buried her face in the wool.

21

Circling his hands around Julia's waist, Andrew lifted her onto Jupiter's broad back. A firm grip on her thigh steadied her until she found her seat.

"Can you hold on for a moment?"

Limp and shaking uncontrollably, she nodded.

As anxious as he was to get her away from the scene of such carnage, Andrew had other tasks to perform first. Leaving her safely atop Jupiter, he strode through the mud and callously rolled over one of the wounded drivers. Blood poured from the hole in the man's shoulder.

"Help me, Major."

Fighting the urge to smash his fist into the man's face, Andrew unknotted his neckerchief and threw it at him.

"Stuff that in the hole."

"Ya gotta get me to a sawbones," the driver whined, scrabbling in the mud for the scrap of yellow. "I'm bleedin' a river here."

"The only reason I'd waste a doctor's time on you is to keep you alive long enough to dance at the end of a rope."

He found the second injured driver on his belly, crawling through the grass in a frantic attempt to escape. With a total lack of sympathy for the wound in the man's thigh, Andrew dragged him back and used a length of rope he found in one of the wagons to lash him to a wheel.

Two wounded, two dead.

Three, he amended with a glance at Walks In Moonlight's body.

His jaw working, he drew out his knife. Four quick slashes cut the thongs on her ankles and wrists. Resheathing the knife, he gently drew her limbs together, then covered her with his India rubber poncho.

Those bastards would pay, Andrew vowed, spinning on his heel. Every one of them.

"We can't leave her like that," Julia whispered.

"We have to. The others might come back and make another try for their weapons. I'll bring a squad to retrieve her body as soon as I have you safe."

She nodded, but a film of tears glazed her eyes. Vicious bruises were already blossoming on her skin where it wasn't coated with blood. The little that was left of her blouse hung in tatters. Swallowing a curse, Andrew ripped open the brass buttons of his uniform jacket. Swinging into the saddle behind her, he wrapped the jacket around her shoulders, then reached for the reins.

Halfway to the post proper, they met a squad of mounted men. Dennis O'Shea rode at the head of the troop alongside Sergeant Kostanza, a reedy, whiskered veteran of Shiloh and Antietam. Shock and anger filled the men's faces as they took in Julia's bruises and tattered clothing.

"The girls are at the stables," O'Shea reported.

"Good. You'll find two wounded at the freight wagons and three dead, including Lone Eagle's wife, Walks In Moonlight."

"Murderin' bastards!"

"Three made a run for it," Andrew said curtly. "They're afoot, but desperate, so keep a keen watch."

"Yes, sir."

"Detail four men to escort the wounded to the guard house. The hospital steward can attend them there. Have them bring in the bodies with them. Send the rest of your men after the other three. I want them all. Every one of them."

"Yes, sir!"

The troop thundered past. Cradling Julia in his arms, Andrew urged Jupiter into an easy canter. She clung to his chest as tremors shook her.

He was no stranger to brutal violence, or to the shock of survival against all odds. He didn't know many men who wouldn't shake like bread pudding after a battle. That Julia should react the same after what she'd just experienced was natural—and ripped a hole in Andrew's chest.

When they approached the stables, she dashed an arm across her eyes and made a valiant effort to struggle upright.

"Sit easy," Andrew told her. "I'm taking you to the surgeon."

"But Suzanne and Little Hen—"

"You don't want your daughter to see you so bloody and bruised, and Little Hen's father should be the one to tell her what happened to her mother. I'll leave you with Henry Schnell, then see to the girls."

When they arrived at the surgeon's quarters, he carried her up the front steps, just as he had the night she'd arrived. This time it was Maria Schnell who opened the front door, shocked at the sight of the bruised and battered woman he carried in.

"Dear God above, what happened?"

"She was attacked by those scum Henry Beauvais hired to drive his wagons." Striding past Maria, Andrew headed for the parlor. "Is your husband to quarters?"

"He came home just moments ago. He's upstairs, changing his uniform. I'll get him."

As he had on that hot June night when Julia arrived at Fort Laramie, Andrew lowered her to the humpbacked sofa.

"Please," she begged. "Go find Suzanne. She'll be frantic."

"Not until I know you're all right."

"I'm just a little bruised."

A little! Angry marks circled her wrists and ankles.

A purple lump had formed on her temple. Her torn pantalets and ripped blouse would probably reveal cruel finger marks when they were removed.

She saw his jaw work as he eyed her torn clothing. Stumbling over the words, she tried to reassure him. "They didn't have time to—to finish what they started."

The reality of what would have happened if he'd been delayed another five minutes tied his gut into knots.

"They were so savage," she whispered, her eyes as bruised as her face. "So vicious. I couldn't help Walks In Moonlight. I couldn't—I couldn't stop them."

Her anguish brought him to his knees beside the sofa. "You got Suzanne and Little Hen away."

His gruff reminder broke her fragile hold on her emotions. Shuddering, she held out her arms.

"Hold me. Please, Andrew, just hold me."

"I have you, my darling."

The words came from deep within him. Waiting until the worst of the storm had passed, he growled into her hair.

"I have you, Julia, and I won't let you go. Not again. Not ever. I'll resign my commission, go back to Mobile with you and Suzanne. It will take time, but I think I can get her to accept me in place of her papa."

She pulled back. Tears still blurred the brilliance of her violet eyes, but Andrew detected the same desperate hope in their depths he knew must be reflected in his own.

"I don't think it will take as long as you think. Or that you'll have to resort to such drastic measures. Suzanne's first thought this afternoon was to find you." A wavery smile pushed its way to her mouth. "She even admitted that she doesn't think you meant to mash her prairie dog pup. With a little persuasion, maybe we can convince her to forget about going back to Mobile."

After the horror of the cholera outbreak and her near brush with brutal rape, Andrew couldn't imagine that Julia would even consider making her home on the frontier, much less raise her daughter here.

"Is that what you want, sweetheart? To stay at Fort Laramie?"

"No."

The hope that had surged into his chest died an instant and painful death, only to leap to life again when she gave him a shaky smile.

"I want to stay with you, Andrew. Here at Fort Laramie, or wherever your duties take us. We'll follow the bugles like a proper army family...if you'll have us."

"If I'll have you!" A strangled sound escaped him, half laugh, half groan. "I'd like to see either one of you try to get away from me now."

He gathered her to him, gently, so as not to add to her aches, eagerly, so as to satisfy his.

Julia lifted her mouth to his. For a moment, a moment only, she buried the horror of Walks In Moonlight's death. Blood and tears mingled, fusing their hopes, their hearts, their pasts, the future yet to come, until Henry Schnell's gruff exclamation pulled them apart.

"Save your kisses for later, man." The bewhiskered surgeon ran a quick, expert eye over Julia, scowling under his bushy brows. "Tell me what happened."

Andrew rose and related what he knew of the attack in a hard, tight voice. Maria Schnell bustled into the parlor during the telling, carrying a china washbowl and linen cloths. Shock blanked her plump features when she heard of Walks In Moonlight's death.

"You'll have two, possibly three wounded prisoners waiting for you at the hospital when the troop returns," Andrew told the surgeon.

"The steward can tend to them until I get there," Henry snapped. "Now move aside, and let me have a look at your lady."

The major turned back to Julia, his face grim. "I have to find Lone Eagle and tell him what happened before he hears it from someone else. Then I'll bring Suzanne to you."

He tracked the Arapaho scout down in the Company C mess. With the troopers detailed to kitchen duty banging pots and grumbling in the background, Andrew related the horrific event in the only way he

could. Sparsely. Succinctly. Without the detail Lone
Eagle would soon see for himself.

"I shot two, wounded two more," he finished, his
jaw working. "We have a patrol out searching for the
three who escaped."

Eyes as black as night stared straight through him.
Lone Eagle wore his dark-blue army blouse with its
double row of brass buttons over buckskin leggings,
but the major didn't make the mistake of thinking that
his years of service had in any way softened or tamed
him. A warrior stared back at him.

"We'll bring them in," Andrew promised.
"They'll pay for what they did."

Lone Eagle's hand moved to the knife handle protruding from an exquisitely beaded and fringed
sheath.

"Yes," he said in a flat tone that left no doubt in
the matter. "They will pay."

"Little Hen's at the stables with Suzanne. Will you
come with me to tell them what happened?"

"I will come."

They found the two girls sitting disconsolately on
upturned barrels just inside the large, open stall where
the farrier worked. The brawny sergeant wore his
blacksmith's apron over his canvas work uniform.
Soot grimed his face and big, meaty hands. He might
have frightened his charges if they weren't very well
aware that his affection for the little soldier girl and

her shy friend had, as he'd once confided wryly to Andrew, turned even his black heart to mush.

When Suzanne spotted Andrew and Lone Eagle, she hopped off the barrel and flew across dirt churned by the passage of hundreds of hooves. Her headlong rush propelled her straight into the major's arms. He swung her up, fighting the urge to crush her against his chest.

"Did you find my mama?"

"Yes."

"Did the bad men hurt her?"

"A little, but she's all right."

"What about Little Hen's mama?"

He glanced over her shoulder, watching while Lone Eagle took his daughter's hand and walked out of the stables without uttering a word.

"Walks In Moonlight was hurt, Suzanne. Badly." He couldn't think of any way to soften the brutal truth. "She died."

Shock, denial and fear shook the girl's small frame and found instant release in tears. Wrapping her arms around Andrew's neck, she buried her face in his shoulder. He patted her back, mumbling assurances until her shuddering sobs had eased enough for him to carry her out of the warm, earthy-scented stables.

He'd just lifted her onto Jupiter's back to take her to Julia when he spotted a solitary horseman bent low in the saddle and racing fast for the main post. Recognizing his striker, Andrew bellowed out to him.

"O'Shea! Over here!"

The private's gelding skidded to a halt a few yards from the major. "We got one, but the other two escaped."

His eyes burning with fury, the New Yorker dismounted and drew the major away.

"We followed their tracks to where the Platte and the Laramie come together. They went into the water and it took us a while to pick up their trail on the other side. We finally found it...right beside the bodies of two of our boys. One took a knife in the back. The other's throat was cut."

The oath that ripped from Andrew was short and savage.

"They took the troopers' mounts and lit out. Sergeant Kostanza and his men are going to stay on their trail, but he sent me back to get your orders."

"Find Sergeant Major Eastland," Andrew snapped. "Tell him I want a full squad ready to go in twenty minutes. They're to carry half rations, so we can travel fast, but tell him to issue twenty extra rounds per man."

"Yes, sir."

"Have them assemble on the parade ground. I'll notify Colonel Cavanaugh and join the squad there."

"Yes, sir."

Both men spun around and headed for their mounts. Andrew didn't even consider telling Suzanne what had occurred. Enough tragedy had heaped on the girl's still-fragile shoulders for one day.

Nor did he have time for more than a few words

with Julia. Scrubbed clean of the blood that had spilled over her and clothed in one of Maria Schnell's wrappers, she gathered Suzanne into her arms and hugged her so fiercely the girl squealed. Andrew schooled himself to patience until the tumult of their reunion subsided enough for him to be heard, then murmured a few quick words in her ear.

The little color that had returned to her cheeks washed away. Stunned, she stared up at him.

"They're riding mounts with army brands," he told her grimly. "We'll find them."

Mindful of Suzanne's tear-filled eyes, he squeezed Julia's arm in lieu of the kiss he ached to give her and turned away.

"Andrew!"

She hurried after him, her daughter still in her arms. The clear, piercing call of the bugle punctuated her soft farewell.

"Good hunting, and come home safe. I'll be waiting for you."

Rubbing a grubby fist in her eyes, Suzanne added a small, weepy chorus. "Me and Daisy, too."

The fugitives led them on a long chase.

Knowing their necks would stretch if captured—assuming they lived long enough to climb the gallows steps—the freight drivers must have figured they had nothing to lose by cutting north toward the Powder River country. If they made it through three hundred miles of plains hunted by hostile Sioux and northern

Cheyenne, they could lose themselves in the wilds of Montana Territory.

Sergeant Kostanza and his small detachment followed in determined pursuit. Anticipating that Andrew would follow with reinforcements, the frontier-savvy veteran sent another trooper back to meet them. He led them northwest on a quick march, directly into the heart of Sioux territory.

Lone Eagle and Arizona Joe Pardee ranged ahead on point. The Arapaho had shed his army shirt, slouch hat and boots, along with all other white man's trappings except the Sharps carbine snug in an exquisitely beaded and fringed scabbard. Red and black paint covered his bare chest. Similar markings circled his pony's eyes and striped its flanks.

Lone Eagle's abrupt transition from army scout to Arapaho warrior had set some of the troops to muttering, but Andrew didn't question it. He understood, for he sought the same kind of vengeance.

The rain-drenched ground made for heavy going, but the reinforcements caught up with Kostanza's small detachment as dusk began to darken the gray sky. Their mounts winded, the squad was forced to stop and rest them while Andrew took the sergeant's report.

"We got a glimpse of riders against the horizon 'bout a half hour ago," Kostanza reported, swiping his forearm across a face caked with mud and chaff from the prairie grasses. "The dark clouds made it hard to tell if they were white, red or in between."

Biting down on the urge to order his men back in the saddle immediately, Andrew nodded. "If they're the bastards we're after, they'll have to rest their mounts, too, or they'll end up on foot. Tell your men we're taking a fifteen-minute stop, then we'll ride as long as there's any light to see by."

Luckily, the clouds dispersed enough to take advantage of the last bit of dusk. The troop ate cold beans and hardtack in the saddle, washed down by swigs from their canteens, and covered another few miles before darkness forced Andrew to call a halt. Before ordering dismount and preparations for camp for the night, he joined Arizona Joe Pardee and Lone Eagle on point.

The major, the grizzled former trapper and the Arapaho warrior reined in their mounts atop a small rise. In the wash of the pale moon, the three men surveyed the darkness ahead. No campfires flickered in the distance. No sounds carried on the night.

"We'll make camp here," Andrew said after a few moments. "Lone Eagle, I want you and—"

"Major!"

Pardee's low exclamation swung him around.

"Look over there!"

Andrew's pulse jumped. Off in the distance, faint pinpricks of light flashed.

"I see them."

"If that ain't gunfire, I'll eat my hat." Pardee gave a hoot of glee. "What do you want to bet them two snakes we're chasin' done run smack into a war party?''

"Let's go find out."

The flashes grew sharper, but the rattle and thunder of an armed troop moving fast drowned out the crack of gunfire until they'd drawn close enough to charge. Interspersed with the rifle fire came the echo of whoops and war cries.

"I'm hearin' twelve, maybe fifteen," Arizona Joe shouted.

That tallied with Andrew's estimate. Unholstering his Colt, he shouted to the trumpeter riding beside him to sound the charge.

When the clear, sharp notes of the bugle pierced the night, their effect was exactly what Andrew had anticipated. The rifle fire sputtered out. The unmistakable sounds of retreat followed.

He let the war party go with orders for a small squad to trail them for a distance, but not engage with them unless fired on. He wasn't interested in the attackers, only those they'd attacked.

His blood pumping, he spotted several humped shapes darker than the night. The defenders must have shot their horses to use them as shields. With a quick command, Andrew split his remaining troops into two flanking columns and quickly circled the mounds.

The fact that the men crouched behind the dead animals didn't fire on the cavalry troop told him they probably weren't the freight drivers. Those bastards would know they'd fare no better at the Army's hand than they would at those of the Sioux. Still, Andrew wasn't about to take any chances.

"I'm Major Garret, 2nd Cavalry, United States Army. Come forward with your hands up and identify yourselves."

Two men jumped up from behind the mounds, rifles held high.

"We're a'comin'! Don't fire."

They drew closer, featureless in the pale moonlight until one of them flashed a smile.

"I never thought I'd be so happy to see a troop of blue-coats." His white teeth gleaming, the taller of the two grinned at Andrew. "My thanks for the timely rescue, Major. The name's Bonneaux. Philip Bonneaux."

22

The coffee was scalding hot and grub-root bitter, but Bonneaux and his companion didn't appear to mind. They guzzled the harsh brew as if it were mountain spring water, emptying their mugs in noisy gulps.

In the light of the campfire, Bonneaux caught Andrew's narrow-eyed stare. His quicksilver grin flashed above the rim of the battered tin mug.

"You must excuse our manners, Major. We ran out of coffee some days ago."

"Along with the rest of our supplies," his partner grumbled.

Andrew ignored the toothless, bowlegged miner. The man had barely registered in his conscious thoughts.

"I'll admit I'm damned tired of stringy jackrabbit and roasted buffalo tongue washed down with muddy creek water," Bonneaux said, throwing back his head to down another long swallow.

Jaws tight, Andrew took his measure. Most women

would call him handsome, he supposed. Beneath its coating of trail dust, his light-brown hair lay thick and wavy. A pencil-thin mustache gave him a rakish air. He was tall, close to Andrew's own height, and trim. Unlike the miner he traveled with, he wore a patterned silk vest under a dusty green frock coat instead of a calico shirt and rough canvas trousers.

As if sensing the tension that held Andrew in its iron maw, Bonneaux downed the contents of his mug and directed a considering glance his way. His brown eyes took in the unit designation above the crossed swords on the major's hat.

"You wear the insignia of the 2nd Cavalry. Were you at Shiloh?"

"Yes."

"Cedar Creek?"

"Yes."

The war years rose up like ghosts, dancing ghoulishly above the flames. In the flickering light, two former enemies regarded each other.

"Where are you posted now?"

"Fort Laramie."

"Fort Laramie! That's where I'm headed."

Bonneaux tossed the dregs of his coffee into the flames. Hissing and spitting, they almost drowned out his eager words.

"My wife's there, or she was when she wrote me a couple of months ago. Do you know her? Julia Bonneaux?"

The breath Andrew dragged in pierced his chest like an iron-tipped arrow. "Yes, I know her."

"And my daughter? Suzanne? She's there, too?"

"Yes."

"My little Suzanne." Bonneaux's face softened with a smile. "I haven't seen her in over two years. Is she still the dainty miss I remember?"

A dozen images crowded into Andrew's mind. Suzanne's shocked face when she found her mother entangled with a stranger on the stairs of the Schnell's house. Her accusing, tear-filled eyes when she saw her mangled pet. Her nose all scrunched up in disgust after she stepped in the pinto's droppings. Her emaciated cheeks just beginning to recover their bloom.

Even more vivid were the images of Suzanne's mother. Andrew could hear Julia's laughter, feel her smile. As if she stood next to him, washed in moonlight, he could see her hair tossed by the wind. Her violet eyes gleamed up at him from a bed of deep-blue flowers.

Bonneaux had no right to either of them! The savage thought slashed into Andrew like a fine-honed hunting knife. The man had deserted his child, left his wife penniless, sent no word back to them in two years. He had no right to ride back into their lives now. Not when...

Not when Andrew wanted to claim them. The mother, with a desperate need that ate at his heart. The daughter, with a fierce urge to protect and teach and watch over her while she grew to womanhood.

Only the bitter reminder that he, too, had once left Julia alone and desperate in New Orleans kept Andrew from telling Bonneaux to climb on a horse and hightail it, right now, for anywhere but Fort Laramie.

His iron-jawed tension communicated itself to Bonneaux. The gambler's voice roughened with worry.

"Why do you look so grim? Has something happened to my daughter?"

Andrew's chaotic thoughts narrowed to one, clear truth. He couldn't deny Suzanne her father any more than he could deny Julia her husband. He answered slowly, each word a twist of a knife in his belly.

"A cholera epidemic swept through the post in August. Suzanne took sick, but pulled through."

"Thank God for that!"

"She's was recovering her strength well until this afternoon."

"This afternoon? What happened this afternoon, major?"

"She and her friend were set on by drunken freight drivers. The girls got away. Their mothers weren't as fortunate."

"Holy Christ!" Bonneaux paled. "Is my wife all right?"

"She's bruised and battered, but sustained no serious injury. The other woman, a Sioux named Walks In Moonlight, took a knife through the throat."

A relieved breath whistled from the gambler. "Too bad about the squaw, but as long as Julia and Suzanne weren't hurt, that's all that matters."

"To you, perhaps," Andrew said coldly. "Walks In Moonlight's husband might not agree."

Bonneaux's shoulders lifted under the pale-green frock coat. "I've got enough troubles of my own. I can't go borrowing everyone else's, too."

The man had more troubles than he could begin to guess. Knowing Bonneaux would hear the rumors about the major and Julia soon enough, Andrew jerked his chin toward the strings of horses picketed beyond the tents.

"We need to talk. Come with me while I see to my horse."

A silent, stony-eyed Philip Bonneaux rode out of camp the next morning, accompanied by the toothless miner and an escort of ten heavily armed troopers.

Andrew watched them depart, his gloved hand grasping Jupiter's reins. For long, agonizing minutes, he'd debated whether to send a letter for Julia with one of the troopers. He finally admitted there was nothing he could say to her now. Nothing that hadn't already been said. Nothing that could change their damnable situation.

She knew how he felt, how he'd always feel about her. He didn't have to put that in a note, and it would make no difference if he did. Turning his back on the small detachment heading south, Andrew ordered the bugler to sound "to horse."

At the quick trill of notes, the men mounted. Moments later, the top sergeants led them out in ranks of twos. First the corporals, then the privates. They lined up in long columns, their mounts freshly groomed and fed, saddles and bridles cleaned of yesterday's mud.

"Call the roll."

While the orderly sergeant took each top sergeant's report, Andrew cast his eye down the line of troops. They were a ragtag lot. Some wore forage caps at jaunty angles, others had gray slouch hats or broad-brimmed campaign hats pulled low on their brows. Only a few had buttoned their blue wool uniform blouse up to the neck, as required. Like their major, most had left the top buttons undone and let the front flap open to keep the scratchy material from chafing their necks. With their collection of bushy mutton-chop sideburns, drooping mustachios and bandoleers slung across their shoulders, they more closely resembled a band of outlaws than a crack cavalry regiment.

Their shabby appearance didn't fool Andrew. He'd ridden long and fought hard with the veterans among them, had personally trained the new recruits. He knew what they were capable of, understood their fears and individual weaknesses. They were the closest thing he had to a family.

The closest thing he might ever have.

His jaw working, he swung Jupiter's head around and led them out.

They found what remained of one of the drivers three days later. The stench of burning flesh carried on the cool breeze and stung their nostrils even before they saw the thin spiral of black smoke.

Lone Eagle arrived on the scene first. Ranging far ahead of the main column of troops, the Arapaho reined in atop a slight rise. He sat unmoving in the saddle, his gaze on the sight below, until Arizona Joe joined him.

"What in the hell—!"

The driver was hanging head down from a tripod made of lashed poles. A slow-burning buffalo chip fire had burnt away what was left of his scalp and blackened his face and naked shoulders. His roasting carcass twisted in the breeze, pierced by twenty or more arrows.

A single warrior sat atop a painted war pony a few yards from the gruesome spectacle. He waited only until Arizona Joe had reined in to spur his horse to within shouting distance.

"I have a message for the long knives from Spotted Tail. Bring your officer forward."

Pardee shot a glance at Lone Eagle's granite face, spit out a curse and wheeled his horse around. He returned mere moments later, the major at his side.

Closing his throat to the acrid stench, Andrew kept his wary gaze on the emissary. "You have a message for me."

"I am Bear Claw, of the Bad Face band of Ogalalla Sioux. We find this one and another two days ago. They had with them the scalp of a Sioux woman."

Lone Eagle spoke for the first time. "She was my wife. Walks In Moonlight."

"This we have learned." Bear Claw spat on the ground. "You are Arapaho. She was Sioux. You stole her from her people and did not protect her, even after she was allowed to stay with you. Nor will you now avenge her."

"The Army will avenge her," Andrew promised grimly. "And the white woman who was attacked with her."

"The Army may avenge this other woman, but Sioux must avenge Sioux. The two we took swore they did not kill Walks In Moonlight, that one of their band named Kinkaid did. They said you have this Kinkaid now in your guardhouse."

"We do."

"Spotted Tail will give you this one, but will keep the other and make him weep many tears until the long knives turn this Kinkaid over to him."

With that, he yanked his pony's head around.

Charging straight at the slowly twisting corpse, he hefted a feathered lance and sent it flying. The spear drove clear through the driver's chest.

23

The last rays of the sun gilded the surface of the Laramie, still swollen after the torrential storms of the last week. Julia settled her hips more comfortably on the split-rail bench outside her quarters and leaned her shoulders against the rough adobe wall. Idly, she let her gaze rest on the rippling gold leaves. Crisp autumn air filled her lungs.

This was her favorite time of the day. She'd finished her after-school chores, was waiting her turn at the communal kitchens. All around her, Fort Laramie bustled with life. Children rolled hoops along the dirt path in front of the row houses or gathered in little knots to play at jackstraws. Women gossiped on their front stoops while suppers stewed and simmered. The buglers had sounded watering call. Soon the cavalry would finish stabling and watering their mounts and make their way to their barracks. The married men among them would peel off and head for home.

Home.

How strange that Julia now thought of this jumble of buildings on the lonely plains as home. It was where her heart resided, she admitted with quiet joy. Where she and Suzanne had decided to remain. With Andrew.

He'd been gone for over three days now. The patrol had ridden out with two weeks' rations and grain for the horses. One part of her prayed they'd find the men they hunted. She wanted to see the bastards hang, right alongside the two locked in the guardhouse. Another part of her just wanted the troopers back safe.

Walks In Moonlight's brutal murder had shocked the entire Fort Laramie community...and incensed the Sioux. The prospects for peace were now stretched thin. George Beauvais fretted openly that none of the chiefs would consent to meet with General Sherman and the peace commission already gathered in St. Louis for the trip west.

Resting her head against the adobe, Julia let her lids drift down. She couldn't think of the peace commission. Wouldn't allow herself to think of the horror of Walks In Moonlight's death. Andrew's image filled her mind. So lean, so hard, so different from the man she'd tumbled into love with all those years ago. And yet so very much the same.

"Papa!"

Suzanne's shriek jerked Julia upright on the wooden bench. Her eyes flew open. When she saw her daughter racing headlong toward the rider who'd reined in his mount a few yards away, her heart leaped straight into her throat.

"Papa!"

The rider dismounted swiftly. Catching the joyous girl up in his arms, he swung her in huge circles. His laughter soared on the clear autumn air, almost lost amid Suzanne's incoherent babbling. Then he clasped her close against his chest and buried his face in her hair.

Slowly, her every limb weighted with ice, Julia rose. She couldn't breathe, could barely see through the haze that misted her eyes.

That was how Philip found her. Frozen in place, her fragile hopes and dreams lying in a million pieces at her feet. Suzanne clung to him, her still-thin arms wrapped tight around his neck. Her face blazed with joy.

"Mama! It's papa! Papa's found us!"

Julia's throat worked. She couldn't force out so much as a squeak. Philip's brown eyes, so like his daughter's, held hers above Suzanne's tumbled curls.

"Hello, Julia."

He knew. She could see it in his face. The sorrow. The regret. The hurt. Fists buried deep in the folds of her skirt, she stood silent while he stepped forward and bent to brush a kiss across her lips.

They didn't speak of it until hours later, after Suzanne's jubilant emotions had drained her completely and she'd dropped like a stone into bed.

Night blacked the windows, shut tight against the chill. An oil lamp flickered on the table fashioned from army crates. Julia sat with her hands clasped tight. Philip stood across from her.

Andrew had told him the bald facts. That he was Julia's first husband, whom she'd thought dead. That he'd assumed responsibility for her and Suzanne since their arrival at Fort Laramie. That he'd come to love the woman he'd once been married to.

Slowly, painfully, she raised her eyes to Philip's. "I've come to love him, as well." She owed him the truth, as painful as it was. "I've given him my body as well as my heart."

He sucked in a swift breath. His face went pale behind his mustache, then flushed a brick red. Anger flooded into his eyes, followed swiftly by regret. He opened his mouth, snapped it shut. Tried again.

"I had time to think during the long ride to Fort Laramie." His voice was low, hoarse, hurt. "I've failed you many times over, Julia. You and Suzanne. I only want what's best for both of you. I'll divorce you, if that's what you wish."

Her fingers clenched. The short-trimmed nails dug into the backs of her hands.

"I—I have to think."

Two days later, Julia knelt in a spill of sunlight and folded her heavy green work skirt. Carefully, she laid it atop the items already packed in the humpbacked trunk. Her movements were slow, sluggish, as if massive weights hung from her arms and legs. Her limbs felt no heavier than her heart.

Everything inside her ached at the thought of her departure tomorrow. It was all arranged. The quartermaster was sending a detachment south to the railhead at Cheyenne to pick up supplies. Philip had secured places for her and Suzanne in the ambulance wagon that would accompany the detachment.

Sinking back on her heels, she stared blindly at the trunk's curved lid. She felt as though she'd aged fifty years in the short time since Philip had ridden back into her life. The old burdens heaped high on her shoulders again, the old uncertainties gnawed at her insides. Where would they live? *How* would they live?

Added to the old worries was a raw, new scar, one she knew would never fully heal. Philip only wanted what was best for her. Her and Suzanne.

As did Andrew. He'd sent her no word. Not a single line. He knew, as Julia did, that her daughter's needs must come first.

Suzanne.

If it weren't for Suzanne…

Squeezing her eyes shut, Julia propped her forehead against the trunk lid. If it weren't for Suzanne, she would willingly endure the shame and social ostracism that came with the disgrace of divorce. Even out here, where women lived by far different rules than the rigid Victorian code that defined their be-

havior back East, a divorced woman lost all rights to
her property, her name, her children.

Philip had assured her he wouldn't take Suzanne
away from her, but she couldn't, *wouldn't* bring such
onerous disgrace down on her daughter. Nor could
she tear her from the father she loved with every
ounce of her girlish passion.

Wearily, she turned her head toward the child sitting cross-legged on the bed, her shoulders slumped
dejectedly. When Suzanne caught her mother's gaze,
she gave a watery sniffle.

"Why can't Daisy come with us?"

"Papa explained that to you, darling. It's a hundred
miles to the railhead in Cheyenne. Your pony
couldn't make it that far."

"Yes, she could." The girl's lower lip jutted out.
"The major says she's of native stock. She's got
sound wind and lots of stamm...stammer..."

"Stamina."

"Yes, stamina. She'd make the trip easy, Mama,
and I could drive my pony cart beside the ambulance
wagon you'll be riding in."

"Daisy couldn't keep up. The ambulance is drawn
by four mules."

"She can go as fast as any stupid mule. The major
says she's—"

"Enough, Suzanne!"

Julia couldn't bring herself to admit the truth. After
two years in the gold fields, Philip had arrived at Fort
Laramie with barely enough in his pockets to pay

their train fare back East. They couldn't afford the additional cost of shipping a pony and cart.

Angry tears spurted from Suzanne's eyes. Folding her arms across her chest, she glared at her mother. "I don't see why we can't stay right here on Suds Row. There's room for you and me and Papa."

"These are army quarters." Julia held on to her lacerated emotions by a thin thread. "We can't remain in them indefinitely."

"The major would let us. He likes you, Mama, you know he does."

"Sweetheart..."

"If we stay, he could teach me to ride, like he promised, and you could help Mrs. Donovan when she has her new baby and Little Hen's grandma could bring her to play with me sometime." She ended on a helpless little wail. "I don't want to leave."

Oh, God! Neither did Julia. The idea of exchanging these wild, windswept plains for the crowded, garbage-strewn streets of an eastern city almost choked her.

"Come help me finish packing, *ma petite*. Will you carry your doll with you, or shall we wrap her in my skirt, to keep her from breaking?"

Still teary-eyed and mutinous, Suzanne picked up the porcelain-faced doll that remained her prized possession. Sniffling, she soothed the flaxen hair back from the painted face.

"I'm going to give her to Little Hen, 'cause she

put her doll in beside her mama when they wrapped her in buffalo skins and took her away for burial.''

Julia hadn't thought she could hurt any worse. Her daughter's forlorn face piled another ache on top of all the others.

"Oh, darling. That's very kind and thoughtful of you. Why don't you—?''

The clear, clarion notes of a bugle cut her off. Cocking her head, Julia listened intently. She could identify most of the signals now. It was too late in the afternoon for dismounted drill, too early for stable call.

Another ripple of notes brought her surging to her feet, her heart pounding. "They're sounding assembly. A patrol's coming in.''

Her daughter's face brightened. "Do you think it's the major?''

"It could be.''

"Let's go greet him!'' She scuttled off the bed and darted around the partition to the front room. "He'll talk to Papa and tell him Daisy can make it all the way to Cheyenne.''

"No! Suzanne, wait!''

Assuming a sudden deafness, the girl darted outside. Julia hurried after her, only to be caught up in the throng of laundresses who swarmed toward the parade ground. Any time a troop rode back in was cause for celebration.

Mary Donovan Mulvaney caught up with Julia and

hooked an arm through her friend's. Her keen eyes swept over the younger woman's face.

"I'm hopin' it's the major comin' back. You need to be sayin' goodbye to him before you leave, don't y'know?"

"I know."

"I'm also hopin' he won't let you leave at all."

"We've talked about this, Mary. Philip's my husband."

"You married the major first," the laundress pointed out with the bluntness so characteristic of her. "He has prior claim. There's plenty as don't hold with this business of annulments and such."

"Please don't make this harder for me than it already is. Philip is Suzanne's father. She loves him."

"Oooch, well, it's your choice after all."

Julia found herself echoing almost the same refrain to Andrew less than an hour later.

She stood stiff and unmoving, unable to squeeze out a single breath, when he rode onto the parade ground at the head of the dusty column. Tall and easy in the saddle, he reined Jupiter in and waited for the column to form ranks and center on him. Under the brim of his hat, his narrowed eyes swept the crowd. Julia felt the jolt of his blue, piercing gaze the moment he spotted her.

He knew she was leaving. She could sense it. Without a word passing between them, Julia felt his withdrawal, in spirit as well as body. That should have made what followed easier. Instead, it left her racked with pain.

Tearing his gaze from hers, Andrew returned the officer of the day's salute. Young, bewhiskered Lieutenant Stanton-Smith had the duty and relayed a message from the commander.

"Colonel Cavanaugh's compliments, sir. He requests you report to his quarters at once."

"Tell the colonel I'll be with him directly."

"Yes, sir."

The impatient wives and children waited only until the signal for dismount rang across the parade ground before rushing forward to greet their menfolk. Their commander swung out of the saddle and handed Jupiter's reins to one of the troopers with quiet instructions to rub the charger down well and give him an extra measure of grain.

Julia stood silent, her chest constricted with pain, as he limped toward her. His old injury had stiffened, the way it always did after long days in the saddle. Unsmiling, he slipped a hand encased in a leather gauntlet under her elbow.

"Walk with me."

Mutely, she matched her stride to his. He guided her past the barracks, down to the river. The Laramie bubbled merrily in the bright sunshine and rippled over its stony bed. Above its buff-colored banks, the sky was so clear and blue it added fiercely to the ache in Julia's chest.

"When do you leave?" he asked quietly.

"Tomorrow. The quartermaster's sending a detachment down to Cheyenne to pick up supplies. Suzanne and I will ride in the ambulance wagon."

His blue eyes held hers. "Is that what you want, Julia?"

No! She wanted to shout the truth, throw her arms around him and hang on forever. Her throat working, she answered the only way she could.

"Yes."

"Then it's what I want, too."

She tried to offer him the explanation he hadn't asked for. "Philip...Suzanne...I can't..."

He stilled her with a finger laid across her lips. "I told you I'd never come between you and your daughter. Nor will I come between her and her father."

"Oh, Andrew."

There was so much she wanted to tell him. About Suzanne's change of heart. About the way "The major says" fell from her daughter's lips ten or twenty times a day now. About the stinging regret that swept through Julia's blood whenever Philip had touched her these past few days.

Recognizing that those disclosures would only hurt him as much as they hurt her, she swallowed and offered instead a hollow echo of Mary's words.

"I have to make the best of my lot. For Suzanne's sake, as well as my own."

"I know, sweetheart."

He dredged up a smile. It crinkled the skin beside

his eyes and stabbed like a hunting knife into her belly.

"I never stopped loving you, Julia. Even during those weeks I dragged myself through the swamp, when I cursed your name with everything in me, I loved you. Take that with you when you leave tomorrow, and with it the knowledge that I'll always have you in my heart."

He wanted to kiss her. The need ripped at Andrew with the sharp, savage claws of a hawk. He ached to take her in his arms, to savor the taste of her that would have to last him for the long months and years ahead.

He wouldn't do that to her. Not here, in the bright sunshine, where anyone strolling by might see them and carry tales back to her husband. His smile tight and strained now, he tucked a silky strand behind her ear.

"Take care of yourself, sweetheart, and of the little soldier girl."

"I will."

Choking back tears, she whirled and hurried away.

24

Colonel Cavanaugh dragged his tongue across dry, cracked lips and glared at his subordinate.

"I won't release the prisoners."

Andrew stood in front of the colonel's desk, hands fisted inside his gauntlets. He'd tried his damnedest the day before to make his seperior see the justice in Spotted Tail's demand. He'd hoped the old man might be more willing to listen to reason after a night's reflection.

God knew, Andrew himself hadn't closed his eyes throughout the endless hours of darkness. The fact that Julia was leaving Fort Laramie that morning had kept him awake and staring into the darkness. He was in no mood to pander to his superior's bull-headedness.

"Walks In Moonlight was Sioux," he reminded the colonel bluntly. "The treaty of '51 states explicitly that a person or persons committing crimes against the Sioux in their own territories are subject to tribal justice.''

"Tribal justice be damned!'' Cavanaugh's red-rimmed eyes flamed with anger. "The woman was murdered on post. The Army has jurisdiction.''

"What difference in hell does it make who hangs Kinkaid, as long as he pays for what he did?''

"I'm not turning a white man over for those savages.''

Gritting his teeth at his superior's intransigence, Andrew tried another tack. "General Sheridan and the other commissioners will be setting out for Fort Laramie any day now. We'll jeopardize the entire peace effort if we deliberately antagonize Spotted Tail.''

A sly look entered Cavanaugh's eyes. Hooking his thumbs in his belt, he swayed back on his boot heels.

"We're not going to try Kinkaid at Fort Laramie. I've already given the order to prepare him and the other prisoner for transport to Cheyenne this morning with the quartermaster's detachment.''

"What!''

"From there, guards will take them by train to Omaha Barracks.'' His mouth twisted in the travesty of a smile. "Those pantywaists at departmental head-quarters are so anxious to pander to the Sioux. I'll let *them* assume responsibility for these murderers.''

His pulse skittering in alarm, Andrew abandoned military protocol. He leaned forward, both fists planted on the colonel's desk.

"You can't send Kinkaid across a hundred miles of open plains with only a twenty-man detachment as escort. That's tantamount to waving a red flag in front of Spotted Tail and inviting them to attack!"

"He'll be in for a surprise if he does. Our men will be equipped with the new breech-loading Springfields. We all saw how effective they were in the Wagon Box Fight. Twenty men are more than sufficient for this detail."

Cavanaugh's intent became clear to Andrew in a sudden, shattering rush. Stunned, he stared at his superior.

"You *want* him to attack! You're dangling Kinkaid like bait, hoping to goad him into a rash act, like Red Cloud's attack on the woodcutting party last December."

"I won't dignify that with an answer."

"The Wagon Box Fight didn't derail the peace process, but another savage battle might just do the trick."

Andrew didn't want to believe his superior capable of such malice, but the hate glittering in the man's eyes told its own tale.

"You can't do it," he said flatly. "I won't let you."

"You forget yourself, major."

He raked his superior with a glance of withering scorn. "I'm going to find George Beauvais. His charter as a member of the peace commission supersedes your authority in this matter."

"I'm in command here," Cavanaugh raged. "You'll keep your mouth shut, soldier."

"The hell I will."

"That's a direct order."

"One I refuse to obey."

His mind racing, Andrew started for the door. He had to get hold of Beauvais, convince him to override the colonel's orders. If necessary, he'd counter them himself. There'd be hell to pay afterward, but a court-martial was the least of his worries at the moment.

"Garret!"

The unmistakable snick of a pistol being cocked swung him around. His belly hollowed at the sight of the Colt leveled straight at his gut. From the drug-hazed glitter in Cavanaugh's eyes, it was obvious the resentment that had been building between them for months had now spilled into hate.

"I'm placing you under arrest for insubordination and refusal to obey a lawful order. You'll report to your quarters immediately and remain there."

"I'll report to my quarters after I talk to Beauvais."

"Damn you!"

The colonel's enraged bellow cannonaded off the walls. The hand gripping the Colt began to shake. Cursing, he whipped up his other hand to steady the first.

"I'll shoot you where you stand! I won't allow a mutiny in my command."

"You'd better think about this," Andrew said softly. "Even a decorated hero of the Cumberland campaign might have trouble explaining why he shot one of his own officers and incited another bloody war on the plains, all in the same twenty-four hours.''

Enraged, the colonel thumbed back the hammer. The Colt wove a wild pattern.

"Orderly!'' he bellowed. "Sergeant at arms!''

Andrew gathered his muscles, waiting for the barrel to veer another inch or two. One lunge, one fist to the jaw, and the old man would drop like a half full sack of feed.

A sharp rap on the door drew Cavanaugh's attention and provided the half second of distraction Andrew needed.

Laudanum might have dulled the senses of the decorated veteran, but it hadn't slowed his instincts. Cavanaugh whipped his head around just as his subordinate launched his attack.

The Colt barked. The force of the bullet spun Andrew sideways. He stumbled and went down, hitting the edge of the colonel's desk. Pain exploded in his temple, fire in his side. Through a dark haze he heard the orderly's astonished exclamation and Cavanaugh's terse reply.

"This man was resisting arrest.''

"Major—Major Garrett, sir?''

"Major Garrett, damn you. Summon the sergeant at arms, then fetch the surgeon.''

Grunting, Andrew fought the blackness. "Wait! Get—''

"Now, corporal!''

Slack-jawed with astonishment, the trooper gaped at the colonel. His goggle-eyed stare was the last thing Andrew saw before darkness claimed him.

Bright October sunlight beamed down on Philip as he paced the beaten dirt outside the shanty his wife and daughter had called home for four months now. Julia and Suzanne were almost ready to leave. They'd packed their few belongings in a single humped-back trunk, and were now making a last check of the quarters. Philip had dragged the trunk outside and hefted it onto the handcart that would convey it to the parade ground where the convoy was assembling.

Reproach and regret gripped him in a vicious vise whenever he eyed the innocuous piece of luggage. The wife he'd promised to drape in silks and jewels, the daughter he wanted to shower with every lavish toy and trinket, had packed everything they owned in one small trunk. It shamed him to his core that he had brought them to such a point, shamed him even more that he possessed barely enough funds to get them back East.

His luck had been so damnable these past months and years. It would change. It had to change. He'd find a game on the trip home, win enough to buy Julia another airy, spacious home and replace the furniture and jewelry she'd been forced to sell. He'd erase the lines of strain on her face. Erase, too, all memories of the man she was leaving at Fort Laramie.

Philip's hands clenched at his sides. The churning

resentment he'd battled every hour since Garrett had taken him aside heated his veins. As much as he fought to subdue his jealousy, he hated the thought of another man assuming responsibility for his wife and child. Hated even more the knowledge that Julia had shed her clothes and tumbled into Garrett's bed.

God knew Philip himself was no saint. Life in the gold fields was unremitting drudgery at best, and precariously brief for so many. A man snatched what relief he could with the whores who traded a sweaty, grunting slap and tickle for a few ounces of gold dust.

But Julia... Dear God, Julia was his bright, shining star. His lodestone. His conscience. Thoughts of her had kept him digging until he couldn't stand the mud and filth and icy water any longer, and traded his pick and pan for the slick, familiar feel of a deck of cards.

"Philip?"

The sound of her voice spun him around. She stood bathed in sunlight. Her silky black hair was braided and woven into a neat coronet atop her head, showing to perfection the clean line of her jaw and long, slender neck.

"We're ready."

She held Suzanne's hand in hers, and a sudden, fierce rush of emotion overrode the jealousy that ate at Philip's insides. This woman bore his name. Had born his child. She'd never complained once in all the years of their marriage, although he'd given her plenty of reason to.

He ached to reestablish himself in her affection, to

tease her into laughter, to see happiness instead of resignation shining in her lavender eyes. His chest tight, Philip smiled at his daughter.

"Suzanne, my pretty, I need to speak with your mama. Will you walk a little way along the river so we can talk for a moment?"

Clutching her precious doll to her chest, Suzanne looked at her father with wide, forlorn eyes. "I'll go say goodbye to Daisy."

Guilt stabbed into Philip once again.

"You can stay, Julia. You know that, don't you?"

Her throat worked. "Yes."

"I'd rather see you happy than hold you in a marriage against your will."

"We've talked about this," she whispered. "Suzanne loves you. Now that she has her father back, I couldn't take her away from you a second time."

He buried his hurt that she came with him only for their daughter's sake and caressed her cheek, trying to recapture what they'd once shared in the remembered feel of her soft skin.

"Perhaps we can start again?"

She swallowed, not pretending to misunderstand his meaning. They hadn't slept together since he'd arrived at Fort Laramie. Suzanne's presence in the bed she shared with her mother had provided a convenient excuse.

Her eyes held dark shadows when she raised them to his. The smile she forced to her lips ripped at his heart.

"Perhaps."

25

The bugles announced the assembly and imminent departure of the quartermaster's detachment. Like any event that broke the daily routine, the departure drew a crowd of spectators to the parade ground.

Julia climbed into the rear of the ambulance wagon and took one of the side-facing seats. A sniffling Suzanne took the other. Her woeful face and drooping shoulders earned her a sympathetic glance from her father.

"I'll buy you another pony, pet."

Her lower lip thrust forward. "I want Daisy."

Philip flicked a glance at his wife. He still hadn't quite accepted the fact that the delicate, adoring child he'd kissed goodbye two years ago had developed a will of her own. Spurring the horse he'd borrowed from army surplus stock for the march south, Philip rode forward to confer with the detachment commander, a doughty captain from Company A.

Sighing, Julia passed her daughter a clean handkerchief and leaned against the seat back. The wagon's canvas sides were rolled up to allow the morning breeze to circulate. The air was so clear it seemed to crackle, the sunshine so bright it hurt her eyes. Squinting, she searched the crowd for a glimpse of Andrew's tall, lean figure. They'd said their farewells beside the river yesterday, but she had thought...had hoped he'd come to see Suzanne off.

It was best that he hadn't, she told herself, swallowing the lump that threatened to choke her. She couldn't look back, wouldn't allow herself to dwell on what might have been. She'd take the years ahead one day at a time, she swore bleakly. One week at a time. She'd find some way to start over again with Philip, as he had suggested. Find some way, too, to make it through her final moments at Fort Laramie without breaking down into tears.

But that became impossible when Maria Schnell hurried up to the wagon. Breathless, she passed Julia a basket covered with a napkin. The tantalizing scent of fresh-baked bread rose from beneath the cloth.

"I put some cactus pear jelly in there," the surgeon's wife huffed. Her bright black eyes darted to the sniffling Suzanne. "And a can of peaches to cheer up the little one."

Julia bit down so hard on her lip she tasted blood. As if it were yesterday, she could hear Augusta Hottenfelder screeching at her husband, berating him for purchasing a tin of peaches at the sutler's store for Julia and Suzanne. How ironic, how achingly ironic, that she and her daughter would find themselves stranded at Fort Laramie because of a tin of fruit, and were now leaving with a gift of the same, precious commodity.

Fighting the tears that stung her eyelids, she pressed Maria's hand. "Thank you."

Mary rushed up just moments later. The two women had said their goodbyes earlier, but the laundress wasn't about to let her leave without a last word of advice.

"I've traveled from Arizona to the Dakotas and back in one o'these wagons," she announced, thrusting a down-filled comforter at Julia. "You and Suzanne will need this to pad your bottoms during the day, and keep off the chill come night."

Julia tried to refuse the hand-stitched quilt. "I can't take this. You told me it was a wedding gift."

"Ooooch, I've had so many weddings, I don't even remember who gifted me with this or when. You take it," she insisted. "The major wouldn't want you to set off across the plains without something to keep you warm at night. And speaking 'o the major..."

"He's not here," Julia said quietly.

"Mulvaney says there was some doin's over at Old Bedlam a while ago. A shot went off or something. The major must be sortin' the business out."

"A shot! Whatever happened?"

"No one knows for sure, but Mulvaney's guessin' it has to do with those rotten bits of crow bait." With a nod of her orangey-red head, Mary pointed out the carrion she referred to.

To her horror, Julia saw two men shuffling toward the lead supply wagon. Both wore heavy leg and wrist irons despite their bandaged wounds. Troopers with bayoneted rifles marched on either side of them, but the mere sight of their bruised and dirty faces made Julia's skin crawl.

One of the guards lowered the backboard on the canvas-topped wagon. The other prodded the prisoners inside. When the backboard had been latched in place again, the detachment commander called out an order.

"Bugler, sound to horse."

"Mary!" Her heart pounding, Julia twisted around to face her friend. "Why are those men being transported with us?"

"I don't know, unless it's because they're George Beauvais's men and he convinced the colonel to send them back to the States for trial."

It made no sense to Julia. Surely Colonel Cavanaugh could have exercised his jurisdiction over the criminals right here. The idea of traveling in the same convoy with the men who'd attacked her and murdered Walks In Moonlight made Julia feel nauseous. She was biting back the bitter taste of bile when the trumpeter's sharp, clear notes cut through the air.

"For-warrrrd, *harch!*"

With a slap of the reins and a few well-chosen insults, the ambulance driver urged the mules into motion.

Mary stepped back, her blue eyes misting. "Have a safe journey."

Others in the crowd shouted a chorus of final farewells.

"Good luck to you, missus!"

"Keep a straight back and a light hand on the reins, little soldier girl!"

Stunned by the turn of events, Julia barely heard their calls. A thousand thoughts whirled in her head, but only one emerged with crystal clarity.

She had to get to Andrew. He couldn't know of the order to send the prisoners south. He wouldn't allow it to happen.

She pushed off her seat, intending to grab the driver's coat or sleeve and demand he halt the wagon.

If the wheel hadn't hit a hard-dried mud rut, she might well have done just that. The sudden bounce caught her off balance. She went down to the wagon bed, hitting her knee with a vicious crack of bone on wood, and her boot heel caught in the hem of her cherry striped skirt.

By time she untangled herself and pushed back up again, the little cavalcade had started up the sloping incline that led to the bluffs beyond the post.

"Hold him steady."

"I have him, sir."

Andrew heard the voices through a thick, gray fog.

Fighting the haze, he tried to open his eyes. Sharp still lanced into his forehead. Instinctively, he flinched.

"Hold him still, dammit."

He forced his eyes open, saw only more gray. A pale blur swam into his field of vision, then disappeared. Sharp steel stabbed into his temple once again.

"There, that's the last stitch."

The blur returned and resolved into a scowling face framed by bushy gray muttonchop whiskers.

"Henry."

"You're back with us, are you?"

Andrew frowned at the surgeon and fought his way through the pain hammering in his head. Slowly, the gray fog receded. Images came back to him, hazy at first, then swift and sharp. Cavanaugh. A burst of gunfire. The orderly's shocked face.

He jerked upright, cursing when needles of fire lanced into his side.

"You'd best sit still," the surgeon advised. "The bullet glanced off your ribs. It didn't do any serious damage, but you came close to putting a permanent crease in your head. I had to set some stitches to close the gash."

Gritting his teeth, Andrew struggled to sit up. The clanking that accompanied his move drew another savage oath. He needed only a single glance at his wrists and ankles to identify its source.

The bastard had put him in irons.

Blinking to clear the pain splintering through his skull, he swept a quick look around. Apparently the colonel had realized he couldn't rely on house arrest alone to keep the major in line. He'd ordered Andrew confined to one of the dank, subterranean cells of the guardhouse.

"Be still while I bandage this."

Rinsing his hands in a bowl of bloody water, Henry pressed a folded pad to Andrew's temple. His chief hospital steward assisted by wrapping a gauze bandage around Andrew's head. That done, the surgeon turned a fulminating eye on his patient.

"Now suppose you tell me why in thunderation Cavanaugh put a bullet in your side, then clamped you in irons before he'd even let me tend you."

"I'll tell you later." Grunting, Andrew hunched one shoulder to test the wound in his side. It burned like hell, but wouldn't keep him down. "First I have to talk to George Beauvais."

"Beauvais? Why?"

"I don't have time to explain now. Just find him, Henry. Tell him it's imperative I speak to him before the quartermaster's detachment departs the post."

"You've been out cold, man. The wagons and their escort rolled out over an hour ago."

"Dammit!"

With a clatter of chains, he got his legs under him. Henry made a grab for his arm as Andrew pushed to his feet. The gray stone walls blurred. Grimly, he fought his way through the dimness.

"Did the two civilian prisoners we were holding go with the wagons?"

The surgeon shot a questioning glance at the sergeant at arms standing just outside the cell. The grizzled veteran nodded.

"Yes, sir. They was taken out just before we brung the major— Just before the colonel ordered—"

He stumbled to a halt, misery writ clearly on his weathered face. "I'm real sorry about them leg irons, Major. The colonel, he was all lathered up and insisted we put them on soon as we hauled you down here."

Andrew shrugged aside the abject apology. Muldoon had only followed Cavanaugh's orders, and those weren't the orders that consumed him right now.

"Find Beauvais, Henry. I've got to convince him to overrule the old man and bring the wagons back."

The surgeon's bushy brows shot straight up. "Beauvais is a civilian! He can't issue orders regarding military troop movements."

"He can if those movements directly affect his peace mission as dictated by the Congress and the President."

His jaw tight, Andrew relayed his suspicions regarding Cavanaugh's motives for sending Kinkaid and his cohort south with the quartermaster's detachment.

Schnell opened his mouth on a shocked protest, then snapped it shut. Like the major, he'd observed the deterioration in their supervisor over the past months.

"Find Beauvais," Andrew repeated. "Quickly."

Henry Schnell returned less than twenty minutes later—without the bearded fur trapper-turned-peace ambassador.

"Beauvais isn't here," the surgeon reported. "He got word that the agent for the Ogalalla was skimming profits off the supplies intended for the Sioux and left yesterday to check on him."

Andrew's stomach clenched. The Ogalalla agency was two days' ride from Fort Laramie. In the dim light of the cell, Henry's grim gaze met his.

"I sent a courier after him."

"If Cavanaugh hears of it, he'll have you in irons, too."

"I'll take my chances."

Morning crawled toward afternoon. Evening faded into night. Strung too tight to eat, Andrew let the rats have his supper of moldy salt pork and beans. The other prisoners—one a drunk still bleary-eyed from the effects of a wild night at Coffee's Hog Ranch, the other a deserter brought back and sentenced to five months of hard labor—huddled in their cells and left Andrew to his thoughts. They didn't quite know what to make of the fact that their commanding officer now shared their dark, dank quarters.

Andrew paid scant attention to them or his surroundings. He'd learned to shut down his mind in Andersonville, to close his ears to the moans and restless mutterings of his fellow prisoners. After the first few months, he'd even taught himself to wipe Julia's image from his consciousness to keep from going mad. None of his hard-learned discipline gave him any relief from the tension that had crawled up his neck and knotted his muscles.

For the second night in a row, he lay sleepless, staring at the sliver of the moonlight that penetrated the narrow, barred windows, feeling the dampness seep through his blanket into his skin, willing George Beauvais to return.

When the bugles sounded first call for guard mount the next morning, he was as red-eyed as Cavanaugh at his worst. Grunting at the pull in his side, he rolled to his feet and relieved himself in the bucket provided for that purpose.

Footsteps overhead signaled the start of the new twenty-four-hour shift. Some moments later, the sergeant of the guard appeared.

"Stand back, if you would, sir."

The cell door clanked open. A hulking trooper ducked his head and carried in the morning's ration of coffee, cold beans and bread.

"So you've got guard duty, Mulvaney?"

"Yes, sir." The hulking young Irishman aimed a glance over his shoulder at the noncommissioned officer behind him. "I asked Sergeant Muldoon to put me on detail, sir. Or rather, me wife did."

"Mary?"

He might have known the laundress would decide to get right to the bottom of things.

"We been hearin' rumors, sir. The whole camp's buzzin' with them."

He didn't doubt it.

"And there's news."

"What news?" Andrew asked sharply.

"The telegraph operator down to Cheyenne sent word one of the railroad crews spotted a large war party. They were all painted up and wearing their war bonnets. Two, maybe three hundred, heading north. They came whoopin' down on the track, but the railroaders beat the hell out of there and got away with all their hair intact."

"Sioux or Cheyenne?"

"Some of both, sir."

Andrew's gut clenched. "Any word from our detachment?"

"No, sir, but…"

"But what, man!"

"But Mary's thinkin' you should go after your lady, sir. Her and the little girl."

Andrew's glance cut to Muldoon. Without batting an eye, the grizzled noncom stepped inside the cell and drew a key from inside his uniform blouse.

"I'm thinkin' the same as Private Mulvaney, sir."

Kneeling down, he went to work on Andrew's leg irons. They fell away, followed by the wrist irons a moment later.

The sergeant would lose his stripes for this. And earn some time in the guardhouse himself. Neither possibility appeared to worry him as he unbuckled his gun belt and passed the holstered Colt to Andrew.

"Your horse is saddled and waiting for you outside, sir, along with a few of our troopers who don't want to see their bunkmates lose their hair over a worthless pile of buzzard shit like Kinkaid."

Nodding, Andrew buckled on the gun belt and headed for the stairs. He took them two at a time and burst outside, only to stop in his tracks.

Company C's red-and-white standard whipped in the morning breeze. The trumpeter sat with his bugle resting on his hip, waiting for orders. Behind them ranged almost the whole company, armed and ready to ride. Bewhiskered Lieutenant Stanton-Smith kicked his mount forward and whipped up a salute.

"I regret to inform you Colonel Cavanaugh is indisposed, sir. He took some, er, new medication the surgeon prescribed for him and felt dizzy and disoriented. He signed the order for your release just before he collapsed in his bed."

A flinty smile whipped across Andrew's mouth. Henry Schnell must have doped the old man to his gills to get him to sign such an order.

Swinging into the saddle, he ran an eye down the column. He knew every man jack of them, from the rawest recruit to the wizened scout who spit a brown wad through the stumps of his blackened teeth. Lone

Eagle sat beside Arizona Joe Pardee, his face stony as Andrew addressed the troop.

"There'll be hell to pay when we get back...if we get back. You know that?"

"Yes, *sir!*"

Despite the tension that corded his muscles, the major grinned at the deafening chorus.

"All right, men. Let's move out."

A mounted troop pushing their horses hard could cover three times the ground of a slow-moving detachment escorting mule-drawn wagons. With any luck, Andrew figured they'd catch the small cavalcade before nightfall.

As it turned out, they heard the distant rattle of gunfire just as the flaming ball of the sun started to sink into a sea of prairie grass.

26

As long as she lived, Julia would remember the terror that gripped her when the hills around their small cavalcade suddenly came alive. In almost the blink of an eye, an unbroken line of horsemen crowned the rolling hills. Their silhouettes were black against the flaming sun.

The column's scout first alerted the troop to danger. He came racing down one hill, bent low over his pony. The short staccato bugle notes that followed his report had the men reaching for rifles and pistols. As one, they broke ranks.

The ambulance driver knew just what to do, thank God. Whipping and cursing the mules, he pulled the team to the right and drew them up tight against the wagon in front, forming one side of a rough square. The moment their noses touched the wagon bed, he reached behind the seat to grab the picket stakes and jumped down to unhitch the team. With a stern order to the whimpering Suzanne to stay where she was, Julia scrambled down to help.

Philip rushed up a moment later. "When the attack comes, you and Suzanne lay flat in the bottom of the wagon bed. I'll let down the canvas sides. They should protect you from flying arrows."

Canvas wouldn't protect them from bullets, but neither she nor Philip would admit as much with their daughter peering over the side of the wagon with huge, frightened eyes. Mutely, the girl begged for more reassurance. Julia couldn't give it. Instead, she drew her husband a few yards from the wagon and held out her hand.

"You have a rifle. Give me your pistol."

His face grim, he drew out the heavy weapon and passed it to her. "Don't use it unless...unless you're sure it's necessary."

Julia grasped his meaning at once. Her eyes blazing, she wrapped her fist around the crosshatched grip. "I have no intention of shooting myself or Suzanne! I can survive being taken by the Sioux, and so can she. But I don't intend to let them take either of us without a fight."

Whirling, she stalked back to the wagon and climbed inside. With Suzanne's help, she rearranged their bundles to form an inner bullwork. That done, both mother and daughter stretched out on the hard floorboards.

Within minutes, the flurry of preparations was done. The troops' muttering died away. An eerie silence descended. Her heart thumping painfully against her stays, Julia lay wedged between the high-piled bundles and wished fervently the narrow space didn't feel so much like a coffin.

Beneath her, Suzanne whimpered softly. Murmuring meaningless nothings to the terrified girl, Julia closed her eyes. If she was to die, she prayed she'd die fast. From a quick bullet or an arrow through the heart.

But not her daughter.

Please, God, not her daughter!

With every fiber of her being, she clung to the knowledge that the Sioux more often took children captive than killed them.

Hope surged wildly when she heard a distant shout. They wanted to parlay! Surely that meant they wanted to parlay!

She didn't understand the Sioux phrases shouted across the plains, but the detachment commander's reply left no doubt in her mind.

"Tell Chief Spotted Tail I have no authority to release the prisoners."

Another string of angry phrases followed, then the sound of a pony galloping off. A few dozen heartbeats later, the earth beneath the ambulance began to rumble. What sounded like a thousand hooves thundered down from the hills, and the first volley of shots cracked through the air.

Company C chased the echo of rifle fire for a good twenty minutes. The sun was a ball of flaming red fast sinking into the waving prairie grass when they topped the last rise and saw the small, besieged square below.

"Sound the charge!"

The bugler had his trumpet to his lips before Andrew had bellowed the order.

"For...*ward!*"

Fifty troopers spurred their mounts from gallop to full charge. The earth thundered beneath two hundred pounding hooves. Seconds later, rifles and revolvers roared, spitting a wall of smoke.

The whooping riders circling the wagons jerked on their bridles, surprised by the attack from behind. They returned fire for a few moments before breaking off and wheeling in a dozen different directions.

Andrew was too experienced in the ways of the Sioux and Cheyenne to go after them. Their ponies were tougher and fresher than his men's mounts. A party of the attackers could easily lead the pursuing cavalry on a wild chase while the main body of warriors circled back to attack.

Instead, he aimed Jupiter right for the square. The chestnut sailed through the tight space between wagons, soaring over the barriers the besieged detail had thrown up. The rest of Company C followed, cursing and shouting warnings when their mounts knocked against each other or the picketed mules.

Whoops and cheers drowned out their shouts. As the last of the gunfire died away, the harried troopers sprang up to punch their rescuers' arms and pound hearty fists on their backs. The captain in charge of the detachment barely restrained himself from doing the same to Andrew.

"Sure glad to see you, Major! They were giving us a lively time of it."

"So I saw. How many down?"

"Two that I know of. One trooper, one civilian."

"Civilian?"

Andrew's chest hollowed. He had already started for the ambulance wagon when he saw Julia hunched over a sprawled body. She pressed a wad of torn petticoat against Philip Bonneaux's shoulder.

Blood stained the cloth and dribbled through her fingers. She glanced up at his approach and gave a sob of something that could have been joy or relief or pure terror.

"Andrew! Help me! Philip's been shot."

"Let me have a look at him."

Once the sun sank behind the hills, night descended swiftly. With it came a biting chill and a vast panorama of stars.

Julia tucked a blanket up around Philip's shoulders, then pushed to her feet. Wearily, she lifted the flap of canvas to check on the sleeping Suzanne. Between caring for Philip and calming her near hysterical daughter, she was too exhausted herself to feel fear.

The heavenly aroma of burnt coffee beans and sizzling pork fat drew her toward the campfire at one end of the small square. She recognized most of the men seated on stools and cartridge boxes around the fire, but it was the tall, lean officer who drew her.

Whiskers stubbled his cheeks and chin. The low-pulled brim of his hat covered most of the bandage on his forehead. He told her what had happened. If she hadn't seen the evidence of Cavanaugh's hatred with her own eyes—when he'd ordered her not to include the Sioux in her classes—she wouldn't have believed him capable of putting his whole troop at risk so deliberately.

Andrew rose and gave her his seat, then shoved a tin mug into her hand. "How's Bonneaux?"

He couldn't bring himself to call him Philip, Julia realized, much less refer to him as her husband.

"Better. The bleeding's stopped, and the laudanum the ambulance driver gave him finally put him to sleep."

Andrew's grunt could have signified anything. Sighing, Julia sipped the bitter brew. As if sensing the things that needed saying between them, the others at the fire drifted away one by one.

He settled a heavy weight over her shoulders. The blanket smelled of horse and prairie dust, but Julia was grateful for its warmth.

"Do you think the Sioux will come back?"

"Yes. Spotted Tail wants Kinkaid."

Her gaze shifted to the men huddled around the fire at the other side of the encampment. The two mule drivers still wore their chains. One had a dirty bandage wrapped around his thigh. The other showed a similarly soiled bandage under the rents in his filthy shirt.

At the time of the attack, the captain commanding the detachment had turned a deaf ear to their demands for guns to defend themselves, thank God. Andrew hadn't even bothered to listen to their whining pleas. The only concern he'd displayed for their continued existence was to send Lone Eagle out with Arizona Joe to stand silent sentinel. The Arapaho left with a look that promised Kinkaid he would return.

The freight driver looked up just then and caught Julia watching him. For a few moments, the night closed in on her and all she could see was Kinkaid carving Walks In Moonlight's flesh. As if reading her mind, he pulled his lips back in a smile, then smooched them up in a silent, nauseating kiss.

If she'd held Philip's pistol in her hand at that moment, Julia would have walked across the clearing and shot the man straight through his heart.

Shuddering, she whipped her gaze back to Andrew. "Will you give him to Spotted Tail?"

His jaw squared. Unshakable, implacable determination hardened his eyes. "Yes. I'll ride out with him and the other one at first light."

Julia could only guess the penalties Andrew would face for disobeying his commander's direct orders. At that moment, she didn't care. Clenching her fists, she uttered a short, savage wish.

"Good! I hope the bastard dies a long and agonizing death."

She got her wish, but not until the freight driver had taken two more victims to the grave with him.

Kinkaid made his move in the darkest hour before dawn. The banked campfires gave off only a dim glow. Sentries hunched behind their barricades, staring out at the inky blackness beyond the wagons. Those not on watch tossed restlessly on their bedrolls.

The mule driver figured he had nothing to lose. He'd seen the look in the major's eyes when he'd held that knife to the Bonneaux woman's throat back at the post. The same look that had come over his face tonight. Kinkaid knew damned well he wouldn't come out of this mess with a whole skin. If Garret didn't take him 'n Brewster back to Fort Laramie and put nooses around their necks himself, he'd give them up to the Sioux, sure as shit.

Well, Billy Kinkaid didn't figure to go to his grave without no fight. If the guard they'd set on him was dumb enough to give him the blanket he asked for, the stupid blue-belly deserved to die, too.

And die he did, without so much as a whimper. Muffling the sound of his shackles with the blanket the fool had given him, Billy slipped the trooper's knife out of its scabbard, clapped a hand over his mouth and thrust the blade in between his ribs. One quick twist, a single jerk of the trooper's limbs, and it was done.

It was a chancy kill, with half the troop at the barricades and the other half too jumpy to sleep in more than snatches, but Billy's luck held long enough for him to search through the blue-belly's pockets for the key to his irons.

"Kinkaid!"

The hoarse whisper jerked his head around.

"Unlock me, too!"

"Unlock yerself," he whispered, tossing the key at Brewster.

Thanking whatever devils owned his soul for the inky blackness, he tugged the dead trooper's hat from his head and pulled it down low on his brow. It wasn't much of a disguise, but he'd only use it for a few seconds. Just long enough to grab a horse and bust outta here.

Snatching up the dead trooper's pistol, he slipped through the shadows toward the picketed horses. The woman rolled up in blankets beside her husband snagged his narrowed glance.

The wounded Bonneaux represented no real threat. Billy had seen him go down, had seen his wife dose him with something to make him sleep.

Billy's avid gaze lingered on the woman. For a moment, only a moment, he was tempted to dig his fist into her hair and drag her along with him, like he done the squaw. Lordy, he'd like to hear her squeal.

Too bad he didn't have the time for that kind of fun right now. Seeing the two of them gave him an idea, though. What he needed was a hostage to make good his escape, and he knew just which one to take.

The rough hand that grabbed her arm brought Suzanne out of her sleep with a startled cry. Before the sound had even left her lips, she was dragged up and over the side of the wagon. With a frightened sob, she tumbled out.

"Suzanne! What—?"

The terrified girl saw her mother throw off her blanket and struggle up. An arm swung hard and fast. Her mother crumpled to the ground.

Then that same thick arm was around her neck, choking her, holding her high off the ground against a body that stank with sweat. Sobbing, she clawed at the relentless band. Her heels drummed against hard thighs. Something cold and round jammed into her temple.

"Let her go!"

The major's voice cut through the darkness. Other shouts rang out. Troopers scrambled to their feet. Through a red haze of terror, Suzanne felt the chest behind her rumble.

"What, this purty little thing? Nah, I think I'll take her along to play with."

"Dammit, Kinkaid, let her go!"

"You think I don't know you won't shoot me where I stand the second I do?"

"I won't, I swear it. Nor will any of my men."

"That right? Then why don't you prove yer honorable intentions, soldier boy? Unbuckle that holster and toss down yer gun. Slowly now! Use your left hand."

Through a sheen of tears, Suzanne saw the major reach awkwardly for his holster.

"The rest of you sons o'bitches do the same. Brewster, you get them guns and load them in this here wagon. We're takin' it and this pretty little thing with us."

Suzanne's fear-crazed mind registered only two stark facts. The man who held her had hurt her mama. And he wanted to take her away. With a frantic flail of her fists and heels, she tried to wrench free.

"Shoot him, major!" she choked out. "He's a bad man!"

The gun barrel jammed into her temple. Sobbing with pain, Suzanne thrashed even harder. The arm crushing her windpipe loosened just enough for her to drop her chin and sink her sharp little teeth into the sweaty skin.

"You little—"

The gun barrel whipped away. Suzanne bit down as hard as she could, locking her jaws, expecting to feel the pistol butt come crashing down on her head any second.

Suddenly, the bad man jerked backward. Suzanne went with him. Someone fell on top of her.

Papa! That was her papa's silk vest mashing into her face!

Still, she kept her jaws locked, like her little prairie dog the time he'd caught that garden snake. Crushed between her papa and the bad man, she could barely breathe. All the while her papa was grunting, the bad man was howling and trying to shake her loose.

Suddenly, the bad man flung his arm out. Suzanne went sailing through the air with it, still tethered by her unrelenting bite. She hit the ground hard, so hard she almost opened her mouth to scream with the pain of it. Her papa yelled something, then gunfire exploded right beside her ear.

Deafened and terrified, Suzanne squeezed her eyes shut. Something hot and wet poured over her. There was another shot, then another. Someone wrenched her up, or tried to. She wouldn't open her eyes, wouldn't unlock her jaw.

"Suzanne!" her mother sobbed. "Let go, *ma petite!* Please, let go."

Andrew rode out at first light.

Lone Eagle rode beside him.

Dawn pinwheeled across the sky, a swirl of gold and pink, dimming the glow of the hundreds of little fires that shot embers into the purple sky. The fires had danced in the darkness all night, constant reminders of the overwhelming force that waited patiently for daylight to renew its attack.

Andrew could only pray Spotted Tail rode at the head of the army of warriors, and not Red Cloud or Sitting Bull. If the old man would listen to reason, there was still some hope they could salvage the fast-shredding hopes of peace…and Andrew could honor his promise to the stone-faced Arapaho riding beside him.

The pinks and golds faded. The sky lightened enough for him to make out a distant figure mounted atop his painted pony, sitting motionless on the crest of a hill. His eagle-feather war bonnet crowned his head and spilled down his back to trail his pony's flanks.

The Sioux didn't move, didn't ride down to meet them halfway. The warriors ranged below him on the hill parted silently to allow the major and the Arapaho scout passage, then just as silently closed ranks behind them. The hair on the back of Andrew's neck prickled with each plop of Jupiter's hooves on the hard prairie dirt.

He reined in a few yards away from the grim-faced chief. Spotted Tail didn't acknowledge the Arapaho by so much as the flicker of an eye.

"Have you come to tell me you will give me the ones who kill my niece, Long-Knife-Who-Walks-With-A-Limp?"

"No."

"Then you will not leave this place alive. Nor will any of the other horse soldiers."

"I came to tell you I will leave the bastard here, on the plains. With Lone Eagle."

Contempt twisted the old man's mouth. "He has not the medicine to avenge a Sioux."

The Arapaho spoke for the first time, his voice as flat and dead as his eyes. "She was my wife. I will avenge her, if I must battle you and every one of your warriors first for that right."

Spotted Tail's gaze flicked to the naked warrior. He sat as still and as immutable as the snow-capped mountains rising far to the west.

"I ask you to think of Walks In Moonlight," Andrew said quietly. "She begged you to give her to Lone Eagle as his wife. She would want him to avenge her, as she would want peace between our peoples. Don't destroy the chance for peace now, with General Sheridan set to board a train the moment you give the word."

Spotted Tail grunted. For a moment his shoulders sagged, as if they carried all the promises made and broken by both sides. Of all the chiefs, he'd spoken the longest and most eloquently for peace with the whites. Signed treaty after treaty. Traveled to Washington to meet with the Great Father.

The battle between his head and his heart was painful to watch.

Spotted Tail sat silent and unmoving for so long his pony snuffled impatiently and thumped the earth with a rear hoof. Tossing his head, he flicked his mane to disperse the prairie mites that swarmed about his eyes and nostrils in a hazy cloud.

Beneath his wool uniform shirt, sweat trickled down Andrew's sides. He was preparing to bargain his life in exchange for safe passage for Suzanne and Julia when the old chief grunted again.

"You will leave the ones who kill my niece," he told Andrew. "Sioux and Arapaho will both avenge her."

27

A brisk afternoon breeze carried the distant sound of bugles down the dun-colored slopes to the fort.

The laundresses bent over the tubs ceased slapping wet uniforms against their washboards. Infantrymen at drill on the parade ground cocked their heads. Troopers in canvas work shirts and pants dropped their sponges and currycombs and rushed out of the stables.

Even Henry Schnell paused. Patting a patient suffering from a severe case of hemorrhoids from too many hours in the saddle on the shoulder, he instructed the hospital steward to administer the normal remedy of a turpentine suppository and left the poor fellow to hop about like a jackrabbit. Stripping off his stained canvas work coat, the surgeon hurried outside to join the crowd streaming to the parade ground. He'd just met his wife enroute when a shout rang out.

"There they are! It's Company C, all right."

The long line of horse soldiers appeared on the low

bluffs above the fort, moving at a slow walk in a column of fours. The company's red-and-white banner fluttered in the breeze.

The bugles sounded again. Tired shoulders straightened. Men sat taller in the saddle. The pace picked up to a trot, then a brisk canter. The column swept down the sloping road, rode past the stables, the sutler's store, the surgeon's quarters. Murmurs of relief rose from the crowd when they spotted no empty saddles.

"Column le-effft, *turn!*"

The waiting crowd cheered as the column wheeled onto the parade ground. Maria Schnell gasped and snatched at her husband's arm.

"Look, Henry! That's Julia riding the horse beside Andrew's. She's got a pair of trousers on under her skirt! And isn't that Suzanne in Andrew's lap?"

"Why the devil aren't they riding in the ambulance wagon?" the surgeon wondered.

He learned the reason shortly after the officer of the day rushed down the steps of Old Bedlam and hurried across the parade ground to stand at attention in front of the flagpole.

The column slowed to a trot, marched past him, halted and wheeled again at Andrew's command. Sitting rigid in the saddle, the major returned the officer's salute.

"Colonel Cavanaugh's compliments," the captain called out. "He asks you to report to his quarters immediately."

"Tell the colonel I'll be with him as soon as Mrs. Bonneaux and her daughter have been attended to, and her husband's body taken to the coffin makers."

Startled gasps rose from the crowd. All eyes turned to the canvas-draped sides of the ambulance wagon, then drifted back to Julia. She stared straight ahead while the officers finished their formalities and the troop dismounted.

Andrew swung down first, then reached up for Suzanne. She tumbled unceremoniously out of the saddle and into his arms, clinging to his neck like a limpet until Mary Mulvaney pushed through the crowd.

"Come with me, poppet. You just come with me."

With a murmur of thanks, Andrew relinquished the girl to Mary's charge. His days in the saddle showed in his limp as he moved to Julia's mount. She lifted a trousered leg over the pommel and slid into his arms. When he would have given her, too, into Mary's care, she shook her head.

"I want to come with you. I think Cavanaugh needs to hear what happened from someone other than you."

George Beauvais elbowed his way through the gawking troopers. "I need to hear it, too."

Henry Schnell joined him. "Dammed if I won't come along as well. Don't argue, Garrett. We might as well all get the story straight out, since we're each of us likely to be testifying before a board of inquiry."

The story, as Julia told it, left the colonel shaking with fury and helpless to do anything about it.

"Kinkaid killed my husband," she related in a hard voice. "The mule driver tried to kidnap my daughter, but Philip wrestled him down. Kinkaid's gun was trapped between them and went off."

"Where in hell did the prisoner get a gun?" the colonel exploded. "Someone was damned derelict in their duties."

"He took it from the trooper whose throat he cut," Julia fired back. "And if we're to speak of dereliction of duty, I'd like you to explain why you sent those murderers out onto the plains with only a twenty-man escort."

"So would I," George Beauvais growled.

"I answer only to my superiors," the colonel sputtered, "but Garrett had demmed well better tell me what he did with Kinkaid and Brewster!"

He swung toward Andrew, the buried resentment and hate spewed from his mouth.

"If you gave them to Spotted Tail against my direct orders, you won't see the outside of a prison cell for the rest of your days! Assuming I don't shoot you where you stand for breaking arrest and taking a troop out without authorization."

"You signed his release," Henry Schnell put in with a lift of his bushy brows.

"After you laced me with opium!"

"Come, come, sir. I left you with your usual dose which, unfortunately, you took too much of."

And no one could prove otherwise, the surgeon's expression shouted.

Beauvais took advantage of Cavanaugh's maddened incoherence to step into the fray. The fur-trapper-turned-peace commissioner had been fuming over the turn of events since Private O'Shea tracked him down.

"If you're chawin' on about the order you gave Garrett not to talk to me, you'd better think twice afore you shoot your mouth off. General Sherman's gonna want to know why you tried to gag him."

Goaded, Cavanaugh swung back to Andrew. "Don't think you're out of this. You still have to answer for Kinkaid and Brewster. Those prisoners were in army hands, under army jurisdiction."

They'd *still* been in army hands the last Andrew had seen of them. More or less. The gut-shot Kinkaid was alive and moaning when Andrew left him staked to the dirt, with Lone Eagle on one side of him, Spotted Tail on the other, their bone-handled hunting knives glinting in the sun. A weeping Brewster writhed and drummed his heels against the dirt beside his friend.

"I'll take my case to any board of inquiry the Army chooses to convene," Andrew answered calmly.

Lieutenant General William T. Sherman headed the peace commission that arrived at Fort Laramie the first week in November. He also served as president of the board chartered by the commander of the Department of the Platte to determine whether the actions of Major Andrew Garrett warranted trial by court-martial.

Andrew was held in house arrest for the three weeks prior to the general's arrival. He hadn't seen or spoken to Julia since their return to Fort Laramie. Nor did he see her during the week-long inquiry, which was considered an Army matter and closed to all outsiders.

When the board finally returned a finding of no inappropriate action, he walked down the front steps of Old Bedlam to a bright, cold afternoon. Crystalline flakes of snow drifted from a leaden sky. It was the first snowfall of the season, feather-soft and powdery white. Clean. Fresh. Covering the scars in the earth left by the summer and fall.

Dennis O'Shea walked Jupiter up and down the path outside the headquarters building. Steam blew from the charger's nostrils and melted the snow on the shoulders of O'Shea's caped overcoat.

"The missus said to tell you she'd be waiting for you, sir. Down by the river, just past Suds Row."

"In this weather?"

"That's what she said to tell you, sir."

Andrew thrust his boot in the stirrup. Moments later, Jupiter cantered past the laundresses' quarters. Smoke curled from the communal kitchens behind Suds Row. With the onset of winter, the washwomen had taken their tubs inside.

He followed the riverbank until he spotted a lone figure. The snow muffled his approach until he was almost upon her. Even then, he wasn't sure it was her. A scarf covered her hair, and she wore a bulky surplus army overcoat that swathed her from nose to toes.

"Julia?"

She spun around. Worry creased her forehead and darkened her eyes to a near purple.

"I heard General Sherman dismissed the board of inquiry," she said anxiously, her breath pearling on the frosty air. "What were the findings?"

"Cleared of all charges." A wry smile curved his lips. "I think the fact that Spotted Tail and Red Cloud have indicated they're ready to talk had more to do with the board's findings than my testimony."

Instead of the exclamation of joy Andrew expected, she stared at him for long moments, then burst into tears. Dismounting, he closed the short distance between them and bundled her into his arms.

"Don't cry, sweetheart. You'll get frostbite on your cheeks and nose. Why the devil did you want to meet me outside in the cold, anyway?"

"It's so beautiful, and—" She lifted her face to his, tear tracks silver on her cheeks "—I didn't want Suzanne to see how frightened I was. I thought you might…might…"

He drew a finger across her cheeks. "Might what?"

"Might have to leave the Army. Or Fort Laramie."

She drew in a shuddering breath. "Or me. Oh, Andrew, I was so afraid they might recommend a court-martial and send you to prison!"

The smile that had started a few moments ago slipped out full and warm. "Haven't I already proved that no prison can keep me away from you?"

He'd held the words in for so long, they now came easily, unshackled, unshadowed. The old ghosts slept peacefully now under their blanket of clean white snow.

"I love you, Julia. I've wanted you since the moment I saw you in that ballroom in New Orleans, and loved you almost as long."

Another long shudder shook her.

"I know it's too soon after Philip's death for this to be right or proper, but I have to know. Did you mean it when you said you'd follow the bugles?"

She nodded, but Andrew needed to hear the words.

"Say it, Julia. Say you'll marry me. Again."

"I'll marry you. Again." She slid her arms around his neck, went up on tiptoe. "And again and again, if necessary."

"Once more should do it," he said roughly, then bent to cover her mouth with his.

Author Note

Have you ever walked into a room or stood on a hill and been transported to another time or place? That's how I felt when my husband and I walked onto the grounds of Fort Laramie National Historic Site. There was Old Bedlam in all its glory, the sutler's store, the surgeon's quarters, the cavalry barracks. I could almost hear the distant sound of bugles on the wind! I knew right then I had to set a book at the fort.

Researching Fort Laramie and its history was a fascinating journey back in time. You might be interested to know the people and key events which provide the backdrop for this story are real. Although the post was never commanded by a Colonel Cavanaugh, and Julia and Andrew exist only within the pages of this book, Chief Spotted Tail did bring his daughter to the fort to be buried. He was among the first of the Sioux chiefs to meet with the peace commission which arrived in November, 1867. Red Cloud held out until April, 1868, when the Army agreed to burn the forts along the Bozeman Trail.

Unfortunately, the peace negotiated at Fort Laramie in 67/68 only lasted until 1874, when Custer led an expedition into the Black Hills and brought back reports of gold. Hoards of eager prospectors invaded the lands promised to the Sioux in the treaty. War broke out once more...a war that would cost the flamboyant Custer and the men of the 7th Cavalry their lives at the Battle of the Little Bighorn two years later.

If you enjoyed learning about the men and women who lived by the bugles, I hope you'll keep a watch for the next book in the Wyoming Winds series. WILD INDIGO is Suzanne's story. All grown up and very much at home in the newly established Wyoming Territory, she's abducted from the Cheyenne-Deadwood Stage by a hard-eyed ruffian who soon discovers she was taught a few surprising tricks by the horse soldier who raised her.

Happy reading!

USA TODAY BESTSELLING AUTHOR

CANDACE CAMP

NO OTHER LOVE

It began with a breathless kiss
from a notorious highwayman,
who believes that Nicola Falcourt
is the wife of the Earl of Exmoor.
He could not be more mistaken,
for Nicola bears no love for the
cruel earl she holds responsible for
the death of the only man she ever loved.
But Fate has brought this masked bandit into
her life to lead a daring plot of greed, deception and murder
full circle. To save those she loves, Nicola must trust a man
who is as dangerous as he is desirable, and risk not only her
life, but her heart.

"Candace Camp is a consummate storyteller."
—*Romantic Times Magazine*

*Available February 2001
wherever paperbacks are sold!*

Visit us at www.mirabooks.com

MIRA®

MCC788

CARLA NEGGERS

Fun and a little hard work was all Tess Haviland had in mind when she purchased the run-down, nineteenth-century carriage house on Boston's North Shore. She never anticipated getting involved with the local residents, and never imagined what it would be like to own a house rumored to be haunted.

Then Tess discovers a skeleton in the dirt cellar—human remains that suddenly go missing. And she begins to ask questions about the history of her house…and the wealthy, charismatic man who planned to renovate it, until he disappeared a year before. Questions a desperate killer will do anything to silence before the truth exposes that someone got away with murder.

THE CARRIAGE HOUSE

"When it comes to romance, adventure and suspense, nobody delivers like Carla Neggers."
—Jayne Ann Krentz

On sale Febraury 2001
wherever paperbacks are sold!

MIRA®

Visit us at www.mirabooks.com

MCN790

International Bestselling Author

DIANA PALMER

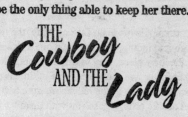

At eighteen, Amanda Carson left
west Texas, family scandal and a man
she was determined to forget. But the Whitehall
empire was vast, and when the powerful family wanted
something, they got it. Now they wanted Amanda—and her
advertising agency. Jace Whitehall, a man Amanda hated and
desired equally, was waiting to finish what began years ago.
Now they must confront searing truths about both their
families. And the very thing that drove Amanda from this
land might be the only thing able to keep her there.

THE Cowboy AND THE Lady

"Nobody tops Diana Palmer."
—Jayne Ann Krentz

Available February 2001 wherever paperbacks are sold!

Visit us at www.mirabooks.com

MDP804

New York Times Bestselling Author

REBECCA
BRANDEWYNE

DESTINY'S
DAUGHTER

Determined to track down her father's killers, Bryony St. Blaze travels to England to find Hamish Neville, the one man who knows about her father's research of a secret order known as the Abbey of the Divine.

But after an attempt is made on Bryony's life, the two are forced to go into hiding, dependent on one another for their very survival. Piece by piece, they assemble the puzzle to locate the lost book her father was murdered for. But time is running out. Can they unlock the secrets of the hidden treasure before the mysterious and deadly order catches up with them?

> "I have been reading and enjoying Rebecca Brandewyne for years. She is a wonderful writer."
> —Jude Deveraux

On sale January 2001 wherever paperbacks are sold!

Visit us at www.mirabooks.com   MRB782

New York Times Bestselling Author

LINDA
HOWARD

Tears of the Renegade

Susan Blackstone married into a powerful Mississippi family; she loved and then lost the Blackstones' favorite son. Even after her husband's death, Susan held her own, running a business empire and winning the support of her in-laws. But those bonds are tested when black sheep Cord Blackstone returns for a long-overdue showdown against the family who robbed him of his birthright. Now, Susan must choose between her husband's memory and Cord, a reckless interloper wreaking havoc with the town, the family and her very soul.

"You can't just read one Linda Howard!"
—Catherine Coulter

Available January 2001 wherever paperbacks are sold!

MIRABooks.com

We've got the lowdown on your favorite author!

☆ Read an excerpt of your favorite author's newest book

☆ Check out her bio and read our famous "20 questions" interview

☆ Talk to her in our Discussion Forums

☆ Get the latest information on her touring schedule

☆ Find her current bestseller, and even her backlist titles

All this and more available at

www.MiraBooks.com
on Women.com Networks

MEAUT1

Should they cross the fine line
between friendship and love?

MIRA®

DALLAS SCHULZE

Loving Jessie

Life has gone out of focus for photojournalist Matt Latimer. He's headed back home to the California town where he grew up, hoping to reconnect with his roots, his purpose and his art.

Growing up, Matt was always around when Jessie Sinclair needed him most. Now she needs him for the most important decision of her life. She wants a baby. Suddenly the lives of Matt and Jessie and others in this small town are about to collide in unexpected ways.

"Schulze delivers a love story that is both
heart-warming and steamy..."
—*Publishers Weekly*

On sale February 2001 wherever paperbacks are sold!

Visit us at www.mirabooks.com

MDS791

A glorious tapestry of love and war,
where the fiercest battleground lies within the heart...

GOLDEN PARADISE

A brilliant scholar, Lisaveta Lazaroff is both beautiful and
outspoken, an independent woman who refuses to play by
the rules that govern men and society. A bold attempt to ride
through the Turkish desert alone nearly ends her life, until she
is rescued by Prince Stefan Bariatinsky, a man whose passions
are as intense as the battles he wages. His only weakness lies
in a woman who challenges him for the one thing
he has never lost—his proud heart.

SUSAN JOHNSON

Available January 2001 wherever paperbacks are sold!

Visit us at www.mirabooks.com

MSJ854